BLACK AUGUST

Timothy Williams was born in Walthamstow in 1946 and educated at St Andrews University. He has taught in Paris, Guadeloupe, Slough, at Jassy in Romania and at the universities of Poitiers, Bari and Pavia. He has now returned to Guadeloupe. Gollancz has published four novels by Timothy Williams: *Converging Parallels*, *The Puppeteer*, *Persona Non Grata* and *Black August*.

BLACK AUGUST

Timothy Williams

GOLLANCZ CRIME

First published in Great Britain 1992
by Victor Gollancz Ltd

First VG Crime edition published 1993
by Victor Gollancz
A Cassell imprint
Villiers House, 41/47 Strand, London WC2N 5JE

A catalogue record for this book
is available from the British Library

ISBN 0-575-05602-9

Printed and bound in Great Britain
by Cox & Wyman Ltd, Reading

questo libro è dedicato a

Wilma
Linda
Annick
Bianca
Julia
Cristina

amiche da sempre

Trotti did not have many pleasures in life.

He told himself that he was an old man and that with the passage of time, he had achieved a certain peace of mind. He had few friends and fewer vices. Peace of the senses.

23.15 hours, Monday, 6 August

Commissario Trotti pushed through the crowd of onlookers and knelt beside the body. The last traces of rigor mortis.

'Been dead for a couple of days.'

The face was badly battered and covered with dried blood. There was blood on the back of the head, forming a dark scab in the long pale hair. The woman had worn her hair in a bun.

Flies hovered in the neon lighting of the small bedroom. The air smelt of death. The onlookers stood around the body, staring down with taut, shadowless faces, relieved by the arrival of Commissario Trotti.

In a hushed but self-important voice, the policeman repeated in Trotti's ear, 'Signorina Belloni's been dead for a couple of days. She lived here.'

The woman lay face down on the floor. Her nightdress had ridden up, revealing pale thighs. She was barefoot. Incongruously, a pair of cloth slippers had been placed neatly beneath the bed.

The sheets had been pulled from the narrow mattress. There were dark stains on the sheets and on the floor. A magazine, published by the Jehovah's Witnesses, lay beside the body. The biblical drawing on the cover was besmirched with blood.

Blood had dribbled from Signorina Belloni's mouth on to the tiled floor.

Trotti was still crouching when Merenda arrived accompanied by the Procuratore della Repubblica, a young woman. Merenda raised an eyebrow on catching sight of Trotti but neither man spoke. Merenda approached the corpse. Without bending over, he looked at the body, his face a mask of professional indifference. The uniformed policeman – Agente Zani – hoarsely briefed him on the gruesome discovery.

Then the doctor arrived.

Dottor Bernardi carried a black leather case and, although it was almost midnight, there were patches of sweat about the short sleeves of his shirt. He looked young and out of place, smelling of disinfectant, eau de cologne and innocence. He ran his hand through his thin hair. A brief glimpse of recognition towards Trotti. He shook hands with Commissario Merenda and smiled disarmingly at the procuratore before kneeling down beside the body.

'Nasty,' the doctor muttered under his breath.

'Where's the photographer, for God's sake?' Merenda asked irritably, turning to Zani.

By now, Trotti was standing. He took a step back and was glad to see Pisanelli leaning in the doorway, his suede jacket undone and his hands in his pockets.

Trotti pushed his way through the crowd towards him. 'Let's get out of here, Tenente Pisanelli,' he whispered impatiently.

'Nasty.' Again the doctor ran his hand through his salt-and-pepper hair. He pulled on a pair of surgical gloves that squeaked unpleasantly. Like an actor on the stage, he was the centre of attraction.

Nobody seemed to notice as Commissario Trotti and Tenente Pisanelli left the small flat.

MONOPOLIO DELLO STATO

'You never did have much time for Commissario Merenda,' Pisanelli smiled as he accompanied Trotti down the stairs, his hands in the pockets of the scuffed jacket.

'I never did have much time for dead bodies.'

'There was nothing to stop you from retiring a couple of years ago, commissario.'

'The first corpses I ever saw were in 1944 – a couple of Partisans who couldn't have been much older than me. The Repubblichini had strung them up and left them to bleed to death.' Trotti repressed a shudder. 'They wore the red scarf – and somebody had amputated their hands.'

The house had been built in the early nineteenth century, but unlike many old buildings in the city centre, it had not yet been modernised and gentrified. The walls needed a fresh coat of ochre paint. The stone stairs were grimy and pitted by the passage of time.

'Part of my nightmares ever since,' Trotti said, taking Pisanelli by the arm. 'Good to see you, Pisa. But I don't see why you called me. I was about to turn the television off and go to bed.' They went down the three flights of stairs into the internal courtyard. In the anaemic yellow glow of an overhead lightbulb, it was apparent that the cobbled yard and the flower beds had been neglected. Cracked flower pots, a rambling rose in need of pruning. By the far wall, there stood a cement mixer; a pile of cement was protected from the elements by a plastic sheet.

'Very attractive procuratore, don't you think, commissario? Signorina Amadeo – from Rome.' From beyond the wooden gate came the dying fall of an ambulance siren in Piazza Teodoro. Pisanelli gave his wolfish smile, 'And nice legs.'

The small door in the wooden gate was thrown open and men scuttled through, carrying a collapsible stretcher. They wore round, white hats, white cotton coats and white shoes. Following them Brambilla, the photographer from Scientifica, saw Trotti and Pisanelli. Brambilla grinned as he took the stairs two at a time. The large camera banged against the side of his leg.

'Who is she, Pisanelli?'

'The procuratore?'

'The dead woman.'

'You knew her, commissario.'

'That's why you called me away from my television?' Trotti looked at Tenente Pisanelli and frowned. 'Hard to recognise anybody who's been battered that way.'

'Used to be headmistress.'

There was no reaction in Trotti's dark eyes. 'Murder's not my responsibility, Pisanelli. Merenda's job – he's head of the Reparto Omicidi.' Thoughtfully Trotti unwrapped a boiled sweet and placed it in his mouth. 'August in the city – I've got better things to do than chase up on corpses. And get under Merenda's feet.'

'In 1978. Anna Ermagni's headmistress.'

'What?'

'The little girl they kidnapped, Anna Ermagni. Remember? You went to see her teachers at the school.'

Trotti clicked the sweet against his teeth.

'The headmistress who wore her hair in a bun.'

'Belloni?' Trotti struck his forehead with the palm of his right hand.

'You're choking on your barley sugar, commissario.'

'Rosanna Belloni? I didn't know she lived here.'

'Been there more than five years, commissario.'

'The corpse is so . . .' Trotti paused. 'When Zani said it was Signorina Belloni, I didn't make the connection. She must have put on weight.'

'Now she's dead.'

'Why?'

'Why?' Pisanelli shrugged the shoulders of his suede jacket. 'I have no crystal ball. A mere flatfoot, commissario.'

'Who'd ever want to murder Rosanna Belloni?'

'Let's hope Merenda will find out.'

Trotti gave Pisanelli another sharp glance. Then he said, 'I met her a few times. I liked her.' He sucked on the sweet, sighed and sat down wearily on a stone bench. 'After a while, we lost sight of each other. She was still at the school?'

'Belloni retired about five years ago.' Pisanelli remained standing. He gestured towards the building. 'The entire palazzo belongs to the Belloni family. Signorina Belloni chose to live in the bedsitter.'

'Rather Spartan.'

'She never married.'

'A shame.' Again Trotti repressed another shudder, 'Thanks for calling me, Pisa.'

'We got the call on 113 about eighty minutes ago. From a journalist who lives upstairs. On the fourth floor,' Pisanelli pointed to a lighted window on the top floor.

'And you contacted me?'

'It's the middle of August. And since you knew the victim . . .'

'I hadn't seen her in years.' Trotti asked, 'The journalist knows Belloni well?'

'Signorina Belloni sometimes spends the weekend in Milan, where she has relatives. He was worried at not seeing her for several days and as he has a key . . .'

'Who is he?'

'Boatti. Giorgio Boatti – a freelancer.'

'The name's familiar.'

'His father was a politician back in the early Fifties – one of the lay parties, Liberal or Republican. Giorgio Boatti comes from a political background.'

'Wasn't there a Boatti we had tabs on?'

'Tabs?'

'In the Seventies, during the Years of Lead.'

'Ten, fifteen years ago Giorgio Boatti was involved in university politics.'

'Lotta Continua?'

'That sort of thing.' Pisanelli grinned. 'We all grow up.'

A sharp glance, 'You surprise me, Pisa.'

'We all grow up sooner or later.'

'Sooner or later?'

'I'm not sure I see what you're getting at, commissario.'

'Still not married, Pisa. Isn't it about time you settled down? Every six months you're engaged to somebody different.'

A wide, self-satisfied grin, 'This time, it's for good.'

'This time? Seventeen different times you've told me the same thing.' Trotti shook his head, 'Tell me about the journalist.'

'She's very beautiful – and you know her.'

Trotti raised an eyebrow, 'The only young woman I know is my daughter – and Pioppi is happily married, expecting her first child any day now. In Bologna.'

'I think you'll approve of my taste,' Pisanelli grinned with ill-concealed pride. 'Eighteen years old.'

Trotti frowned, 'Eighteen?'

'Very mature.'

'At eighteen what does any girl know about life? She'll leave you – just as the others have always left you.'

'Better they should leave me before marriage than after, commissario.'

Trotti turned his head away.

An awkward silence.

'You're probably right, though, commissario.'

'Of course I'm right.'

'At first women seem to like me,' Pisanelli said wistfully. 'Then after a while, that glassy look comes into their eyes. All their passion seems to evaporate.'

Trotti turned to smile at Pisanelli.

'They all say I spend too much time on my job.'

'Tell me about the journalist.'

'This time it's going to be different.' Pisanelli lit an MS cigarette and sat down on the edge of the flower bed beside Trotti. His shoulders slumped forward. Although he allowed his hair to grow down to his collar, Pisanelli was completely bald at the crown of his head. He was now in his early thirties and was beginning to put on weight around the waist. His jaw was losing the sharp lines of youth.

'Tell me about this Boatti journalist, Pisa.'

'Boatti's married. A wife and two children . . . two little girls.'

The air was cool in the small courtyard. The smell of the burning cigarette mingled with the sweeter perfume of wild honeysuckle. It was several hours past sunset.

(Another day without rain.)

The brick wall still gave off the accumulated heat of the day.

('Boatti found the body?')

A banging as the wooden gate was thrown open. Policemen in heavy motorcycle boots hurried towards the stairs, accompanying two carabinieri officers. Despite the late hour, both carabinieri were wearing their black tunics, resplendent with gold braid, and their peaked caps. One of them, catching sight of Trotti sitting in the courtyard, called out, 'Ciao, Rino.'

Trotti didn't answer. He sat with his hands hanging between his thighs. He didn't even raise his head. 'Boatti found the body?'

Pisanelli said, 'Perhaps the murderer thought Belloni kept money under her bed.'

'Rosanna Belloni.' Trotti crunched the boiled sweet between his teeth. He turned and looked at the younger policeman. In Trotti's eyes, Pisanelli could see the damp reflection of the overhead lightbulb. 'Rosanna Belloni was a fine woman.' Trotti turned away.

The bells of San Teodoro chimed midnight.

'Not afraid your teeth'll fall out?'

'Afraid I'll fall asleep without sugar in my blood.'

'Why don't you go home and back to bed, commissario? You're not needed now that Merenda's here. If you're interested in finding out . . .'

Trotti held up his hand to silence Pisanelli. After a brief silence he stood up and started pacing about the courtyard. From time to time he popped another sweet into his mouth, clicking it noisily against his teeth. He was thinking about Rosanna Belloni. He could remember the woman's smile. And her softness.

(May, 1978. The Years of Lead.

Trotti had gone to see Rosanna Belloni at the Scuola Gerolamo Cardano. A wet day. The porter had taken Trotti to her office.

It could have been yesterday.

'A child – Anna Ermagni – has been kidnapped, signorina.'

A sudden movement of her hand and Trotti noticed the absence of a ring. The long, delicate fingers and the clean nails – no varnish – belonged to the hands of a girl. The skin was white. Trotti wondered how old she was; in her mid-forties, he decided. The grey hair made her appear older, but she still had the living softness that disappears as a woman goes through the change. A few years older, perhaps, than Trotti's wife, Agnese.

She thought he had been joking. But when he repeated that Anna Ermagni had been kidnapped, Rosanna Belloni told Trotti about a visit she had received a few months earlier from the girl's father. Ermagni had come to see her, asking for help.

Trotti asked, 'What did you tell him?'

'About his daughter?'

'Yes.'

'Commissario Trotti, I've never had children of my own.' The hint of a sigh as the cardigan lifted slightly, 'I never married, not because I didn't want to.' She looked at the fingers of her left hand. 'There are other reasons that I need not bore you with. However,

I've been in this school for twenty years and I've been teaching for twenty-seven. In twenty-seven years, you learn a lot about children – and adults, too. And one of the most important lessons that I've learnt is that you can't change people. You can help them, you can advise them – but you can't change them if they themselves don't want to change. Change people, force them to be different, to be not what they are but what we want them to be – that's Fascist philosophy. Fascist thinking. And I hope that you and I have had enough of that.'

Rosanna Belloni had smiled, showing brilliant, even teeth. The corners of the hazel eyes had wrinkled.)

Trotti ran a hand over his hot eyes.

At one o'clock Pisanelli went back upstairs into the building to where Rosanna Belloni now – more than a decade later – lay battered to death.

BARLEY SUGAR

At half past one Trotti left the courtyard looking for a bar that was still open. He returned, carrying a couple of plastic cups.

The two men drank the hot coffee.

They waited another hour before seeing Merenda leaving, his head bowed and deep in conversation with the pretty procuratore from Rome. Her heels clicked on the pitted floor, her voice was hoarse in the windless air.

The two carabinieri were behind them, walking ponderously with their hands behind their backs.

The gate was closed and the last siren died in the hot summer night.

'Let's see if we can get something out of this Boatti.'

'How am I going to get married if you keep me up at these impossible hours?'

'You should never've phoned me.' Irritably, Trotti added, 'You should've stuck to medicine, Pisanelli. Or got a job in the town hall.'

Taking the stairs slowly, Pisanelli and Trotti went past Signorina Belloni's door. A police notice had been pinned up, access had been cordoned off. The door was open and inside an NCO sat waiting. The shadow of his feet and a cloud of cigarette smoke were all that was visible. From behind the door came the sound of hushed voices.

'What makes you think my teeth'll fall out?'

'With all that tooth decay, commissario?'

'Been eating these things since the end of the war.' Trotti laughed. 'One of the rare pleasures in my life.'

'Feeling sorry for yourself?'

'Only too glad to be alive.' They went up the last flight. The door to Signor Boatti's flat was ajar. 'Rosanna Belloni was a couple of years younger than me. She was born in '29 or '30. We both grew up during the years of Fascism.'

'You age well, commissario.'

'It's all that barley sugar.' Trotti tapped at the varnished wood, calling out, 'Anybody there?'

Behind the ground-glass window, a light was burning inside the flat. Trotti pushed open the door. The two policemen found themselves in a small hallway. The walls were white and bare except for a couple of Oriental etchings.

There was movement and then the far door opened.

'Signor Boatti?'

The man's glance went from Pisanelli to Trotti, 'Yes?'

'Commissario Trotti of the Polizia di Stato.'

Boatti sighed, 'I thought I had already answered all your questions.'

Trotti held up his hand, 'I realise it's late.'

'Very late.' Boatti had dark eyes, dark hair, fleshy red lips and a pale round face. He was dressed for the street, and despite the late hour, his shirt looked fresh, his blue trousers uncrumpled.

'I saw the light on,' Trotti continued, apologetically. 'If you don't mind our coming in.'

'I've answered enough questions for one evening.' Boatti glanced at his watch.

'I once knew Signorina Belloni. Not very well – but I'd like to think she considered me a friend.'

'Friend of a policeman?' Boatti said flatly.

'May we come in?'

Again the journalist glanced from Pisanelli to Trotti. He stepped back, 'If you think it's absolutely necessary.' The intelligent face was tired. There were circles under his eyes. 'I really don't see what I can tell you that I haven't already told your friend Commissario Merenda.'

EQUATORIAL

The blades of the ceiling fan turned indolently.

There was a beige computer on a mahogany desk. The walls were hidden behind bulging bookcases. An expensive Persian carpet was strewn with magazines – military magazines in several languages. On one of them a kitten had curled up and fallen asleep.

'My wife's gone to bed. I must ask you to speak quietly.' Boatti smiled a boyish smile. In his early thirties, Trotti thought, as he lowered himself on to the leather settee. 'She's working on a translation and she needs her sleep.' He added as an afterthought. 'My daughters are with their grandparents on holiday.'

'I have a daughter, too,' Trotti said, not quite knowing why. 'Married and now expecting her first child.'

Boatti smiled frostily. 'A drink, gentlemen?'

'Not when we're on duty.'

'On duty at three o'clock in the morning?'

Pisanelli remarked innocently, 'This heat builds up a thirst.'

Boatti was standing with his hip against the sill. He glanced through the open window that gave on to Piazza Teodoro and the church, 'When the wind drops and the heat lies motionless over the Po valley, you could be in equatorial Africa.' For a moment he was lost in thought. 'Some mineral water, perhaps, Commisssario?'

Trotti nodded.

Boatti went into the kitchen. Trotti studied the bookcases.

Science fiction and crime novels. There were many titles in foreign languages. Trotti recognised the yellow paperbacks of the Mondadori detective collection. *Il poliziotto è solo.* Trotti winced.

A green light blinked on the computer's screen.

There were more framed Oriental drawings on the wall, tigers and other exotic animals, with Chinese pictograms down one side the image.

'You knew her well, Commissario?' Boatti said, returning with a tray.

'Signorina Belloni? We met a few times – on police business. I didn't know her outside the school – I'd no idea she lived here.'

Boatti's smile hardened, 'You don't consider this part of the city as being the right sort of place for a retired headmistress.'

Trotti took the bottle and poured water into a tinted glass, 'That's not what I meant. Our paths crossed professionally. I liked her and respected her. That's all.'

Boatti raised an eyebrow, 'You feel she could have retired to somewhere better.'

'A bit surprised to see how small her flat is.'

'She didn't require much. In many ways, Rosanna was very ascetic.'

'An intellectual?'

'Not at all. She had worked her way up to being headmistress. The hard way. She didn't have a university education, you know.'

'I left school at seventeen.'

'You surprise me.' Boatti turned to serve Pisanelli with a glass of wine. 'Eighty-seven vintage – Grignolino, guaranteed free of antifreeze,' he said, almost conspiratorially. 'No label – but D.O.C.' Then he sat down in a swivel chair in front of the computer and crossed his legs. He pressed a switch and the light on the monitor disappeared. 'I was very fond of her,' Boatti said, turning back to face Trotti. 'Both my wife and I were very fond of Rosanna Belloni. She was very good with the little girls. Always a hug when they went past her door. But Rosanna knew children too well to be patronising.'

'Who d'you think killed her?'

'No idea.' Boatti shook his head.

'She had enemies?'

'Rosanna was a very retiring person. She must've known a lot of people. She'd taught in various schools in this province and Milan for over thirty-five years. She was originally from Milan, but she felt happier here in our city. She didn't have many friends. Apart from a few old ladies living in this part of the city, I never saw her with anybody.'

'She had men friends?'

'A brother. I met him once. He came up from Foggia for the funeral of a nephew who was killed in a car crash.'

'A nephew?'

'Rosanna has two sisters. One's married and lives in Milan. The other . . .'

'Yes.'

'The other has problems. Some kind of schizophrenia, I don't know what it is . . .'. Rosanna didn't like to talk about it. For a long time the two sisters lived in Via Mantova.'

'And now?'

'About five years ago the sister was found wandering about the city in a nightdress. Rosanna sent her to a special home outside Garlasco.'

'Home for the insane?'

'Rosanna was upset. She wanted to keep her sister here in the city, but it was not possible. She could . . .' Boatti stopped.

'Yes.'

'There were times when her sister could be violent. Otherwise Rosanna would have stayed with her in Via Mantova. But once Maria Cristina took a knife to her . . .'

'You met the sister?'

'Maria Cristina?' Boatti nodded. 'On several occasions, I drove Rosanna to Garlasco.'

Trotti asked, 'Is Maria Cristina ever allowed out of the home?'

'I think she has a part-time job in Garlasco. With Rosanna, she's been down to Foggia. And on another occasion, the two sisters went to Livorno. You know, Rosanna was very good to her.' Boatti shrugged, 'Rosanna was a good person – a genuinely kind person. Yet . . .' The young man paused.

'Yet what?'

Boatti stood up. He held a glass of wine in his hand and he returned to the window. He looked out across the piazza at the dark silhouette of San Teodoro.

Neither Trotti nor Pisanelli spoke.

'Maria Cristina was perhaps the one person that Rosanna was capable of hating.'

GERANIUMS

Tuesday, 7 August

It was nearly five o'clock in the morning by the time Trotti got home. He watched the lights of Pisanelli's car disappear into the night then went up the stairs. The potted geraniums needed watering. He fumbled with his keys and let himself into the empty house.

He kicked off his shoes, threw his jacket over the back of a chair and went into the bathroom. Trotti showered noisily, letting the water splash against the plastic curtains. There were dark marks where the damp had caused fungal growth in the plastic. The walls of the shower needed cleaning, too.

'Too many corpses.'

Trotti turned off the hot tap. The cold water ran through his hair and into his eyes. He then stepped out of the shower and looked at himself in the mirror. 'An old man, Piero Trotti,' he told himself. 'Time you retired.'

Trotti was wrapping a towel around his waist when the telephone rang.

He glanced at his watch before picking up the receiver.

'Piero?' A woman's voice.

His hand trembled slightly, 'Who's speaking?'

'Been trying to get through since before midnight.'

'That you, Pioppi?' Trotti asked, frowning. 'How are you? How's the pregnancy coming along?'

'I'm phoning from the station. I've got nowhere to go.'

There was a long pause. Trotti could feel the water running down his legs on to the floor. 'I told you not to phone me, Eva.'

The South American voice confused the b's and v's, 'I must see you.'

'No.'

'I need your help.'

'I can't help you, Eva. You must help yourself.'

'I swear I've tried.' A hesitation, 'Please, Piero.'

'There's no point.'

There was a long silence. Hissing over the line and the faint sounds of movement in the railway station. 'Please, Piero. I have no one else to turn to. Only you. You've always been kind.' The voice caught, 'Please.'

'Please what? I'm an old man.'

'I want to go home.'

Trotti looked down at the puddles forming at his feet.

'Please, Piero.'

He gave a sigh. 'Oh, for God's sake.'

'Please.' Like a child.

He hesitated.

'You helped me before.'

Another sigh, 'You'd better get a taxi.'

'I spent all my money on the train ticket.'

'I'll pay the driver when you get here.' Trotti put down the receiver, angry at his own weakness.

The first light of day was discernible through the blinds.

QUESTORE

'You seem to have a very flexible timetable, Commissario Trotti.'

With the renovation of the Questura, they had installed a modernistic clock above the desk. 'A bit late, I'm afraid.' It was ten past ten.

'I am not criticising.'

'I didn't get to bed until after five.'

The questore gave Trotti a knowing smile, 'At your age, you certainly know how to enjoy yourself.'

'I was working on a case.'

'You've got bags under your eyes.'

'No worse than usual.'

A pause then the questore asked, 'The San Teodoro murder, Piero?'

Trotti did not reply. He was tired and he could feel ulcers beneath his tongue.

'Merenda's already briefed me about the Belloni woman.' The questore held up his hand, 'The Reparto Omicidi will be in charge of all enquiries.'

'Pleased to hear it.'

'Merenda was at San Teodoro until late. But he was back at work at eight.'

'Commissario Merenda is a young man.'

'Getting too old for your job?' Behind the smile, there was the edge of authority. The questore was from the Friuli. Long years in the Po valley had made no inroads into his accent.

'Too old, Signor Questore?'

'A little joke, Piero.' A short, forced laugh, 'You take everything so seriously.'

The third floor had been devitalised like a decaying tooth; there was a newness that had the meretricious charm of bright, white dentures. Cosmeticised and soulless. Italo-Californian architecture, brass and marble. A real palm tree in a tub, surrounded by plastic ferns. The old desk where Gino and Principessa used to sit had been replaced by a wafer-thin table in black. Gino's seat was now occupied by a peroxide blonde woman. An ample chest beneath the blue uniform shirt and the computerised identity badge. Fingers heavy with nail varnish and gold rings.

(Principessa, Gino's dog, was long since dead.)

'Another two years, Signor Questore, and I will be out of your hair.'

The questore laughed. He approached Trotti and put a friendly arm around his shoulder, 'You really are too sensitive.'

'I'm beginning to feel my age.'

'Nobody wants you to go, Piero – you know that. I need you here – we all need you here.'

'I appreciate your support.'

'You and I have been friends for over six years. We've worked together.'

Trotti nodded.

'You are very cynical, Piero Trotti. There are times when I wonder who you trust.'

'I have learnt that it is always best to count on oneself.'

Again the humourless laugh, 'You can count on me.' The questore started to walk down the corridor towards his office. 'You know that.'

With the questore's arm around his shoulder, Trotti had no choice but to accompany the younger man.

'You know that you can count on me, don't you, Piero?'

Awaiting a reply that did not come, the questore said, 'Care for a coffee? And a chat – it's a long time since we last had a serious conversation.'

'Real coffee?'

'Something to wake you up before lunch.'

They entered the office – functional, large and decorated in the same modern, antiseptic style. The air smelt of synthetic carpet. The questore released his grasp as Trotti lowered himself into a white leather armchair. President Cossiga on the wall.

The questore ordered two coffees over the phone and then sitting behind his desk – bare except for a couple of cordless telephones and an ashtray – he smiled at Trotti. 'I'll be perfectly frank with you, Piero.'

'Please do.'

'I can't have you in on the San Teodoro murder.'

Trotti was silent.

'You were there last night. You arrived before Merenda. I wouldn't be surprised if it was Pisanelli or Toccafondi who contacted you.'

'I got to San Teodoro about five minutes before Merenda and the procuratore woman.'

'It's August and it's hot. Relax, Piero. I don't like it when you're working on murders.'

'So you've already told me.'

'Murders attract attention – precisely because in this city and in this province they're not very common. In Italy there are something like fourteen hundred murders a year, yet here there are never more than eight, often less than two in a year. No Mafia, no Camorra, no 'Ndrangheta, no organised crime – a provincial backwater. Nothing worse than a bit of drug traffic in the university. So understandably when a murder occurs, it attracts a lot of attention – from the local press and sometimes beyond that.' He shook his head. He was still smiling, 'You're a good man, Piero Trotti. One of the best. Honourable in a way' – a vague gesture to beyond the door – 'that very few other people are. Honourable and untainted. But you have never hidden the fact that you don't like Commissario Merenda.'

Trotti took a pineapple sweet from his pocket.

Beyond the window, the national flag hung limp over Strada Nuova.

'This is a small city – and we now have our own Reparto Omicidi. Merenda's in charge, and I won't have you interfering, Piero.' Hearing the vexed tone in his voice, the questore paused. He smiled placatingly, 'Honesty is not enough. Between you and me, I'm not sure it is even necessary. Not in this country. Honesty is not a quality that Italians admire.' The questore sat back in his armchair and folded his arms.

'You don't consider yourself Italian?' Looking at the questore, Trotti realised that he had never really scrutinised the man's face before. The regular features were as they had always been – the thin moustache, the cold grey eyes, the arched eyebrows, the closely shaved skin – but now they seemed to form a different total.

'Honest, Piero, and efficient in an almost Teutonic way – but you tread on too many toes.'

'It's possible.'

'A fact. You know that on several occasions, people – important people in this town – have asked for your transfer.'

'So I'm informed.'

'You are efficient – and that's why I've always followed my own counsel. I want you here, Piero – because you're reliable and efficient. You're a northerner, you understand this place, you grew up in this city. And also, quite frankly, I want you because you're a friend.'

Trotti did not speak.

'But to be honest . . .'

'Yes?'

'I'm not sure you've got over the Ciuffi woman's death.'

'I'd rather not discuss that.'

'You were in no way responsible for Brigadiere Ciuffi's death. Yet you still feel you have a score to settle, Piero.'

Trotti started to get up.

The questore gestured to him to remain seated, 'You and I have one thing in common.'

Trotti lowered himself back into the leather of the armchair.

'One thing in common. We're both outsiders. You're an outsider because your honesty has always ostracised you. I'm an outsider because I come from a different world. I am from the Friuli. You ask me if I consider myself Italian. Sure, with the years, I have learnt to play the Italian game, to be cunning and to know when to compromise. I've read *The Prince* and I've studied my colleagues. I've learnt that it's wise to join a powerful political party and I'm now a card-carrying member. But here,' he tapped the chest of his French jacket, 'here I'm still a little boy from the Friuli. Not Italian, not devious. Innocent. And,' again he tapped his chest, 'still very naïve about my compatriots from south of the Alps.'

'I would very much like to work on the San Teodoro case.'

The questore was about to answer when there was a knock on the door and a woman entered carrying a silver tray with two cups of steaming coffee. The woman's sweet perfume battled with the aroma of the coffee.

'Signorina Belloni was a friend.'

The questore raised an eyebrow.

'Signor Questore, she was a friend. That's why I want to be part of this case.'

The younger man waited until the woman had left. 'Out of the question, Piero. I'm sorry but that must be out of the question.'

'I can ask why?'

'You know you can't work with Merenda – you're not a man to collaborate. Reparto Omicidi functions as a team. You like to do things in your own way – and whatever you say, everybody knows you despise Merenda. With your methods, Piero, you'd be able to work twice as fast as Merenda – I know that. But you alienate people. You brush them up the wrong way. And you give us all a bad reputation. In the normal run of things, that doesn't matter. But murder is different – it attracts attention. You can't work in a team, unless it's your team. You're honest – but that's no help. Your methods are out of the dark ages. And you certainly don't know how to deal with the media.'

'It's not often I ask for a favour.'

'That, I'm afraid, is neither here nor there.' The questore held the porcelain saucer in one hand and raised the cup to his lips with the other. 'We're in modern Italy, Piero. The fifth richest nation in the world. Richer even than England. No longer the Pubblica Sicurezza – we've been demilitarised, because that's what our modern democracy requires of us. We have our union, we can now go on strike – unlike the Carabinieri. Modern, Piero. The Polizia di Stato must show itself to be modern. Your methods – no matter how effective – belong to the past. To a past when there was no press and no television. In those days, you worked alone – and you did wonders. In those days, you could get away with it.' Instead of drinking, the questore lowered his cup, 'I'm sure you understand.'

'Low profile?'

'Precisely, Piero. You take the words from my lips. You have many virtues – but if I let you loose on this Belloni thing, even in the middle of the summer, even when the city is empty, you're not the man to keep a low profile.'

VICES

Trotti did not have many pleasures in life.

He told himself that he was an old man and that, with the passage of time, he had achieved a certain peace of mind. He had few friends and fewer vices. Peace of the senses. He would admit he liked the company of women, but maintained he had learnt to live without them. He did not think about his wife any more, and anyway, she no longer interested him. The woman he had once loved had gone to America, and as far as he was concerned, that was that. She no longer existed, just as the past no longer existed.

Just as Brigadiere Ciuffi no longer existed.

Trotti liked living alone. He enjoyed having the big bed to himself.

Trotti believed that he did not miss his daughter, which did not now stop him from regularly looking at the calendar and counting the days until the arrival of his first grandchild. Somehow he knew it was going to be a boy. He wondered if Pioppi and Nando would call him Piero.

No vices?

There were of course the boiled sweets – rhubarb, barley sugar and aniseed his favourite flavours.

And Trotti liked his coffee. Coffee could be an obsession – creamy with the brown foam of an espresso percolator. Coffee toasted by a local company, Moka Sirs, with two full teaspoons of sugar, in a thick porcelain cup.

The questore was on the phone as Trotti rose and made his exit. A wave of the hand and a brief, 'Leave San Teodoro alone,' before returning his attention to the portable receiver.

Trotti wondered who had boiled down the mud that the questore had served him – served him in the very best French bone china. The gritty taste rasped at the back of his throat.

The blonde woman on the desk – she had been there a year, and still Trotti did not know her name – looked up as he noisily cleared his throat. Her broad smile met with no response.

Instead of going into his office, he brushed past the plastic ferns and took the lift – with the renovation, they had overlooked the hammer and sickle that had been engraved into the aluminium – and went downstairs, accompanied by piped music over the lift's speakers.

He put another sweet in his mouth to take the taste of bitterness away. He stepped out of the lift and was stopped by Toccafondi coming out of the hushed gloom of the Sala Operativa.

'Commissario Trotti.'

'Care for a cup of coffee, Tocca?'

Toccafondi was very young. He was one of the few men in the Questura that Trotti genuinely liked. The Polizia di Stato was full of southerners, and even those policemen who were from somewhere north of Florence had often taken on the manners and mannerisms of the south. Toccafondi was from the other side of the

Po valley, where the Apennines started to rise and where the wine was rich and full of flavour. Toccafondi spoke the same dialect as Trotti, sprinkling his Italian with words that smelt of fresh hay, polenta and woodsmoke. He reminded Trotti of the young men he had known forty years earlier, young men with red scarves and ready, willing smiles. With ageing rifles and an irrepressible optimism. Forty years earlier when everything had been so simple, long before the anguish of the present. In those days, the problem was survival, where the next meal was coming from, and who the Fascists had killed. Not the forty channels on television to choose from. Or which fluorescent knapsack to match your mountain bike.

Toccafondi was a born optimist. He smiled a lot. He was still young enough to have illusions about the purpose of being a policeman. He enjoyed his job and felt that he was being useful. He had an ungainly, lopsided head, large eyes and the large hands of a peasant. His stocky body bulged awkwardly in the summer uniform; the canvas of his gun holster was a grubby white. His beret needed adjusting on the top of his large head.

'You got to San Teodoro last night, commissario?'

Trotti nodded, 'Come and have some coffee – real coffee.'

The young policeman shook his head. 'Going down to the river. Why not come with us?'

'Work can wait.' Trotti slipped into dialect. He held up his hand, 'Everything can wait. I need some coffee.'

A shout.

'Car ready, Tocca?'

Toccafondi turned, raising a thick eyebrow.

Pederiali came running down the stairs, taking them two at a time, one shoulder forward. He nodded towards Trotti. He was buttoning his dark blue shirt. Pearls of sweat had formed on his forehead.

'The Lancia's out there.'

'Let's move, Tocca.'

Toccafondi turned back, grinning, excited. He caught Trotti's arm. 'A suicide in the river. The Vigili del Fuoco have been alerted and they're sending divers.'

'I've seen enough dead bodies.'

'A woman – she left a note.'

'I need my coffee,' Trotti said, but allowed Toccafondi to direct him to the Lancia standing in the morning sunlight.

'Your coffee can wait, commissario.'

With a screech of rubber and a wailing siren, the police car turned into Strada Nuova. Pederiali drove the white and blue car fast towards the Ponte Coperto bridge and towards the sluggish Po.

The excitement of the young men was contagious. Trotti found himself smiling, forgetting about his coffee. Forgetting about the questore.

VIGILI DEL FUOCO

The women of Borgo Genovese wore black dresses and they used to come down to the river to wash the dirty linen. Now everybody had a washing machine and the women had disappeared. For over thirty years, there was just the memory and the photographs in a nearby pâtisserie. Then in the early Eighties, with nostalgia for a past of poverty and drudgery, the city fathers had unveiled a statue in memory of the washerwomen. Standing behind a barrier, a woman in long skirt and a broad brimmed hat, scrubbed away in silence and for eternity at a trestled table.

Trotti could remember seeing the women – large blistered hands and wisps of hair against their tanned and sweaty foreheads – before the war.

A long time ago.

Maiocchi was in charge. He stood on a floating pontoon. With his long hair and baggy trousers, he looked more like a student than a policeman. He acknowledged Trotti's arrival with a grin. There was an unlit pipe between his teeth.

A fireman – vaguely resembling Pope Wojtyla – saluted, 'Ready when you are, Commissario Maiocchi.'

'Go ahead.'

The man turned away and called out to the dinghy.

The dinghy was three metres long and made of red glass fibre. It had been anchored several metres from the shore and now floated downstream, pulling on a nylon cord. 'Vigili del Fuoco' was stencilled in white letters along the sides of the boat, and rope looped from the taffrail. A man in a T-shirt held the wheel while another helped two divers lower themselves into the water. One of the divers laughed, adjusted his mask and then, alongside his companion, slipped from the low gunwale into the river. The two forms disappeared beneath the murky surface.

Toccafondi was standing beside Trotti. 'There was an earlier message.'

'Who alerted the Vigili?'

'Maiocchi, I suppose.'

'They got here fast.'

'There was a first call at four o'clock this morning, Commissario Trotti.'

'To the Squadra Mobile?'

Toccafondi nodded his large head. 'A woman's voice.'

'Saying what?'

'A woman phoned in on 113 saying she'd seen a pile of clothes abandoned at the river's edge – beneath Ponte Coperto, on one of the floating pontoons.' The young man gestured upstream to where the bridge straddled the river. Trotti could hear the rumble of the traffic and could see the rising cloud of exhaust fumes that sullied the misty, morning sky. 'When we got down here, day was just breaking.'

'You were here?'

'Nothing,' Toccafondi said. 'We found nothing.'

'A hoax?'

'That's what we thought.'

'The past was hell.' Trotti leant against the railings surrounding the washerwoman.

'I beg your pardon, commissario.'

Trotti gestured to the bronze statue of the washerwoman. 'In those days, things appeared simpler. But there is no virtue in poverty. If you were poor, you tried to find work. And if you found it, you didn't complain about the long hours and your breaking back.'

Toccafondi said nothing. He ran a hand across his large mouth.

Trotti looked out across the river. The last two summers had been dry, and there had been very little snow in the Alps during the winter. The river lay low in its bed, avoiding recently created islands of gravel and grass. Across the brown-blue surface of the Po, there was the irregular reflection of the city. He raised his eyes to the far bank, to the Lungo Po, to the concrete hangars built for the Duce's sea-planes and to the Cathedral. Its dome glinted, as if it had already grown accustomed to the gaping emptiness where the Torre Civica had stood for nine hundred years.

'Only rich women wore nice clothes in those days. Where I come from, young girls were already wearing their black widow's weeds before they were twenty. No Benetton or Stefanel – no boutiques.' There was bitterness in Trotti's voice. 'Washing other people's dirty linen – or working thigh deep in the rice fields – you were only too glad to find a job.'

Toccafondi was embarrassed, 'There was another call at nine o'clock,' he said. 'The same woman – according to Operativa it was the same voice – claiming there was a bundle of clothes. Maiocchi got here straightaway.' He shrugged, 'Operativa alerted the firemen.'

Trotti's glance returned to the long dinghy and his eyes came into focus. 'I'm getting too old.'

One of the divers had resurfaced and he held up his rubber gloved hand in a gesture that Trotti did not understand.

Toccafondi went off to talk to Pederiali.

'Body's probably floated downstream, Maiocchi,' Trotti said, approaching his colleague.

An unamused grin from behind the pipe, 'If there is a body at all, Piero. There's a farewell letter addressed to a certain Luca.'

'Who's Luca?'

'She signs her letter Snoopy.' Maiocchi took a large box of kitchen matches from his pocket. 'Luca is the poor bastard who she's . . .' he gestured towards the river, 'trying to blackmail into loving her.' He paused, shook his head, 'Women.'

'Women?'

'They're all the same.'

'I can't remember, Maiocchi.'

'All the same. Sweet and light and beautiful – but inside, as hard as nails. Harder and more determined than any man.'

'If that's the way you feel, it's time you got divorced, Lezio.'

'Three lines of attack to get what they want.' He held up three fingers, 'The first and most powerful way is to use their charm, their bodies. A woman's charm is more powerful than a hundred oxen.' Maiocchi folded one of the fingers down on to the palm of his hand.

'Next?'

'If charm doesn't work, it's then they resort to blackmail, moral blackmail.' He folded a second finger.

'And if blackmail doesn't work?'

The index pointed towards the sky, 'The poor bastard of a man is in for one hell of a hard time.'

Maiocchi was smiling but his mirth could not conceal the sadness in the tired eyes. 'One hell of a hard time,' he repeated.

FLYPAPER

'Nobody knew I was in Borgo Genovese.'

Boatti slipped another frogleg into his mouth. He wiped his lips with the stiff, pink napkin.

Trotti asked, 'How did you know I was here?'

'I didn't.' Boatti shook his head, 'Which doesn't stop me from being pleased to see you.'

I Pescatori was a new restaurant in Borgo Genovese – or rather, it was a very old trattoria that for years had stood at the riverside, weathering the fogs of winter, the floods in spring and the mosquitoes throughout summer. Two years earlier, it had been bought up by a consortium from Milan who wanted to exploit the site. The interior had been gutted and renovated. The stuffed fish, the framed paper cuttings, the curling flypapers and the smell of wine and pungent coffee were gone for good. The dark wood was ripped up and replaced with marble, the windows were enlarged to let in the reflected light of the river. The exterior was replastered and repainted. Instead of the traditional ochre, the walls were now a pastel pink, as unreal as a photograph in an architectural review. Potted plants had been set out to prevent cars from parking against the walls and entrance. Where the road was once asphalt, there was now neatly laid pavé in small half circles.

'They don't give you much to eat here,' Trotti said truculently, taking a forkful of risotto.

'A cousin of mine runs the place. He worked for several years in Switzerland.'

The vast terrace – where previously river fishermen used to congregate to down a bottle of wine over a noisy game of briscola or exchange boastful stories – had been transformed into a restaurant welcoming each day wealthy diners who drove down from Milan in order to eat the new cuisine all'italiana.

'In a savings bank?'

Boatti frowned.

'Your cousin worked in a savings bank in Switzerland?'

Boatti appeared surprised, 'I didn't realise you had a sense of humour, commissario.'

'Who told you I was down here?'

'I'm a stringer for several national papers.'

'A stringer?'

'I have contacts and when some interesting story comes up . . .'

'A suicide in the Po?'

Boatti nodded.

'That's why I get a free lunch?'

'Not very gracious, commissario.'

'At my age, I have no time for hypocrisy.'

'Last night, you were a lot less aggressive.'

'Aggressive?'

'I imagine there are people who like you, commissario. I imagine you have friends.'

'Imagine whatever you like.'

'I'm glad to have found you.' Boatti sat back in the armchair – modern, exotic wood, with a high, dark back – and his face was pale, the nostrils pinched. He raised his glass and sipped his wine before speaking. 'I was thinking that perhaps we could collaborate.'

'The service is slow here.'

'That's the whole point. Slow food.' He used the English words.

Trotti frowned.

'Both rice and frogs in the surrounding fields – from here to the Adriatic. But this is the Italian answer to American fast food. You don't like it?'

'I'm glad I'm not paying.'

'Rare for a policeman to pay for a meal, isn't it?'

'Collaborate, Signor Boatti?'

'I thought we could work together – you and me.'

'Nobody can work with a policeman.'

'Collaborate to our mutual advantage.'

Trotti finished the plate of risotto di rane. He wiped his fingers and looked at Boatti, dropping the pink serviette on to the white tablecloth.

'I'm a writer, commissario. I do some journalism, but that's not really what I'm interested in.'

'And all your political stuff?'

'Gave that up years ago. It keeps neither the wolves nor the Politica from the door.' A laugh, 'I see you've checked up on me.'

'Force of habit.'

'I want to write a book, Trotti.'

Remembering the shelves and the rows of Mondadori yellow-backs, Trotti said, 'A detective novel?'

'Faction – something between fact and fiction. Like Truman Capote . . .'

'Who?'

'A book that is about a real murder case.' A boyish grin and Boatti poured more wine into the glasses. Behind him, through the window, the city was silent and motionless, beneath the heavy sky. The wide panorama could have been a photograph. The city was reflected in the slow, muddy water of the Po. 'Didn't get to bed last night. You see, I was very fond of Rosanna. Her death . . . I don't want her to have died in vain.'

'You want to write a book and make money?'

The eyes came into sharp focus, 'Money and kickbacks – if it was that sort of thing I wanted I could have become a politician.'

'Too intelligent, Signor Boatti.'

'Or a cop.' A moment's hesitation before Boatti leant forward, pushing his plate and the thin white frog bones aside. 'A book. I would like to write a book. About Rosanna and her death. And about the police procedures.'

'I'm off the case.'

'What?'

Trotti looked about, 'The service here is very slow.'

A hard edge to his voice, 'You're off the case, Trotti?'

'If you want, Signor Boatti, I can give you the phone number of Commissario Merenda . . . the same policeman you spoke to last night.'

LOYALTY

'What are you going to do?'

Trotti shrugged.

'You're going to let Rosanna's murder drop?'

'Merenda's in charge of the Reparto Omicidi. The questore doesn't want me in Merenda's way.'

'That's going to stop you?'

'Yes.'

'People seem to think you're a good cop, Trotti.'

'Perhaps I used to be,' Trotti shrugged again, turning his head to look for the waiter. 'I'm now sixty-two years old. My career as a policeman is behind me.'

'You could find Rosanna's murderer while Merenda is still cleaning his teeth.'

'His teeth are perfect. They don't need cleaning.'

'Last night you seemed to care about Rosanna. You said she was your friend.'

Trotti turned back to look at Boatti, 'That was last night.'

'Some friend.'

'I knew her – that's all,' Trotti replied.

When Trotti finally managed to catch the waiter's eye, they ordered a dessert of peach melba, coffee and grappa.

'It's all an act, of course,' Boatti said, as the tip of his tongue searched out the lingering drops of grappa along his lips.

'What's an act?'

'Your misanthropy. You could have retired years ago, commissario, but you've stayed on in the Questura because you like your job too much.'

'You know a lot about me.'

'An institution in this city. That's what you thrive on – being wanted, being respected. And last night, you really cared.'

'What does misanthropy mean?'

'The questore can read you like a book.'

Trotti laughed, 'The questore wants me well out of the way.'

'I don't believe you're going to let Rosanna's death go by.'

'You can believe what you want.'

'You're very stubborn.' Boatti clicked his tongue, 'You're also irritable and rather ignorant.'

Trotti smiled without looking at Boatti.

'Commissario, you have one redeeming feature.'

'You flatter me.'

'You're loyal. Loyal to your ideals – and to your friends.' Boatti paused, 'Politically, I should hate you. I suspect that you're still a Fascist.'

'The Fascists killed my brother.'

'At heart, you're not a political animal at all. I don't think you've got much time for ideas. What you care about – despite this surly exterior – is friendship.' Boatti laughed through his nose, 'Fairly obvious the questore can see through you. Divide et impera.'

Trotti's spoon stopped and was held motionless between the plate and his mouth. His glance went from the city beyond the window to Boatti's eyes, 'I beg your pardon.'

'The questore knows you, Trotti. He knows you're loyal. And very stubborn!'

'Which is precisely why he wants me out of Merenda's hair.'

'It wouldn't be the first time you've gone against orders from the top.' Boatti grinned, 'The questore knows you despise Merenda.'

The spoon was placed into his mouth and Trotti ate the ice thoughtfully before answering, 'Merenda is a very competent policeman.'

'You don't like Merenda because he belongs to the new generation of policemen. The kind of man who knows all the answers, top of the class at Pisa, but who's never done the footwork, who's never stayed up all through a winter's night, who's never frozen his balls . . .'

'Yes?'

'Merenda's a university man. Clever and educated. But he doesn't have your experience.'

'I don't have his qualifications.'

'Which is why the questore's quite happy about you going off on your own, personal enquiry. A private vendetta.'

'There'd be no point.'

'It worked with the Ciuffi woman.'

Trotti's face whitened. 'You know a lot about me, Boatti.'

'Like you, commissario, I check up.' A laugh, 'Force of habit. You see, we have a lot in common.'

'I don't think so.'

'You knew Rosanna and . . .'

'So what?'

'The questore's safe.' An amused shake of his head, 'After all these years, you've still not understood the nature of power?'

'An unimaginative policeman.'

'The questore wants results – but above all, he wants to hang on to his position. And the power it confers upon him. There's been a nasty murder and, of course, he wants it solved. If you come up trumps, everybody's happy. You and the questore both get to have your photograph in the *Provincia*. And since you're near retirement, the questore doesn't need to worry about you. You're no threat to him, not at your age.'

'Thanks.'

'Whereas if you screw up, Trotti, he just disowns you. But Merenda is young. He's in charge of the new Reparto Omicidi. Any success of Merenda's can be a threat to the questore. That's why the questore's hoping you'll get there before Merenda and his Reparto Omicidi.'

'Not very likely.'

'Very likely indeed. With me helping you.' Boatti winked an intelligent eye, 'With information that Merenda doesn't have.'

Trotti said nothing. His dark eyes seemed to grow smaller.

'Information that can make all the difference.'

'What information?'

'More grappa?'

'What information, Boatti?'

He seemed to hesitate. 'Merenda doesn't know what you know, Commissario Piero Trotti – that Signorina Belloni had a secret lover.'

SILVER SPOON

Trotti was surprised, 'Signorina Belloni told you that?'

'Rosanna was discreet. She didn't talk very much. And she rarely talked about herself.'

'But she talked to you about her past?'

'I didn't threaten her. As a man, I didn't frighten her.'

'How long had you known her for, Boatti?'

Boatti shrugged, 'She didn't have much experience of men. Rosanna looked after her mother until she was well into her forties. And then she had to deal with her sister.'

'Maria Cristina?'

'Other than professionally, I don't think Rosanna knew many men.' Boatti paused, bit the fleshy upper lip, 'Perhaps she thought of me more like a son.'

'She could have had children of her own.'

'Her pupils were her children – that's what she always said.'

Trotti clicked his tongue impatiently, 'Did she ever tell you why she never married?'

'First her mother, then her sister – what time did she have for her own family?'

'She must've had a lot of free time since her retirement.'

'Rosanna retired at fifty-five – that's a bit old for a woman to be starting a family. And it's only recently Maria Cristina – Rosanna's sister – has been in a special home.'

'And before that?'

Boatti nodded, 'Maria Cristina used to work. She was a secretary with a bank in the city. From time to time she would have a nervous breakdown. It was up to Rosanna to look after her. A full-time job.' Boatti paused, 'She never complained. And she never got married.'

'But she got herself a lover?'

Boatti's eyes narrowed, 'You are judging her, commissario?'

Trotti smiled, 'As a policeman, I gave up judging people a long time ago.'

'You don't judge me?'

'Signor Boatti . . .'

'Call me Giorgio.'

Trotti took a sweet from the almost empty packet, 'I have better things to do with my time than judge you or anybody else.'

'The son of a rich politician – a left-wing journalist from Lotta Continua, born with a silver spoon in his mouth – that's not how you judge me?'

Trotti put the sweet in his mouth, 'Who was Signorina Belloni's lover?'

Boatti shook his head, 'You don't answer my question.'

'A policeman's job is to ask questions.' Trotti held out the packet of Charms, 'Take one. And don't ask questions when you know you're not going to like the answer.'

Boatti took a peppermint Charm, carefully unwrapped the sticky cellophane.

'Who was her lover?'

Boatti lowered his head and gave a small smile, admitting defeat.

'Well?'

He placed the sweet on his tongue, 'One Christmas – it must have been a couple of years ago – I went down to see Rosanna. I'd got her some fresh honey from the Stelvio. And for the first time ever, I had the impression that she was lonely. I think she must have been drinking a bit. Oh, nothing serious – half a glass, at most one glass of wine. She was glad to see me – she had prepared Christmas presents for the girls. She offered me some Barbera and she started talking about her past.'

'Why a lover? She was attractive. There must have been a lot of men who would've been only too happy to marry her.'

'Family commitments. By the time her mother died, it was

already too late . . . or that's what she told me. Over forty and she believed she was past it.'

'The best years of your life.' Trotti smiled, 'If my memory serves me.'

'Sex wasn't something that interested her. She said sex was all that men wanted. And that she wasn't going to give it to them.'

'Yet she had a lover?'

Boatti sat back, folded his arms. 'She had a male friend. Whether she actually went to bed with him I don't know.'

'A minute ago you used the word lover.'

'Too discreet – too shy to talk about that.'

'You believe they went to bed together, don't you, Giorgio? She was an attractive woman – and she looked after her body.'

'You noticed that, commissario?'

'I am a man, Boatti.'

'You found her attractive?'

'Rosanna Belloni was . . . I found her beautiful.'

Boatti put his head to one side while he noisily sucked on the sweet beneath his teeth, 'You two could have made a fine couple.'

Trotti looked away, stared through the window.

'You don't think so, commissario?'

'Signorina Belloni is dead.'

'You don't answer my question.'

'I knew Signorina Belloni in 1978. At that time my wife was still living with me – after a fashion.'

'That was more than ten years ago, commissario. Since then . . .'

'Other times, other preoccupations. Who was her lover?'

'You're going to find her murderer, commissario?'

'Stubborn and ignorant – have you forgotten, Boatti?'

'Stubborn, ignorant and irritable. And also devious, Commissario Trotti.'

'Tell me about her lover.'

Boatti shook his head, 'She never told me who it was.'

'What did she tell you?'

'Rosanna simply said that she had a friend – a false friend. She said that he pretended to be a genuine friend, but that all he wanted was her body. To do his dirty things.'

'So they did go to bed together?'

Boatti shrugged, 'I don't know. She never got to that part of the story – but somehow I doubt it.'

'Where is he now?'

'She told me she broke off with him about five years ago – after having been friends for nearly ten years.'

'He was married?'

'Separated – and was living with his son. Rosanna never mentioned the wife – although she did say she understood why she had left him.'

'Then when Rosanna broke off with him, there was acrimony?'

'One thing at a time.' Boatti held up his hand, 'She was living in Via Mantova. The family has a house there. Rosanna lived on the ground floor with her mother. Her sister lived upstairs and she had a separate entrance.' He paused. 'Rosanna came to live in San Teodoro about five years ago. Before that, she was with her sister. They lived apart but Rosanna could keep an eye on Maria Cristina, in case she had one of her depressions.'

'What did she do during her depressions?'

'I met Maria Cristina a couple of times at the Casa Patrizia.'

'Where?'

'The home she stays in – near Garlasco. Highly strung – you can see that she's Rosanna's sister, but she has none of Rosanna's calm, except when she goes into one of her terrible, black depressions. Although she was a spinster, Rosanna was very feminine. She dressed well, she looked after her body, as you point out. Very coquettish, very human. She loved children, she was always kind. Maria Cristina – she's about ten years younger than Rosanna – appears much harsher, more masculine.'

'Not attractive?'

Boatti shrugged, 'She could have been. Now her body is beginning to sag. She's overweight. Rosanna said it was the hormones that they put her on. And a shiny, bulbous face. No attempt at make up – nothing. And yet . . .'

'Yes?'

'He screwed her.'

'Who?'

'It'd been going on for years. Perhaps it was Rosanna's fault. Perhaps she wasn't giving him what he wanted. A man needs physical companionship just as much as he needs friendship.'

'I wouldn't know,' Trotti said, feeling the ulcers under his tongue.

'Perhaps Rosanna couldn't bring herself to give him that.'

'That?'

'The physical part – her body. One day – not long after the mother's funeral – Rosanna went upstairs on some errand and found her sister and the man – Rosanna's boyfriend – in bed together.' Boatti shrugged, 'That's what brought on Maria Cristina's last depression. She attacked Rosanna with a knife. Once they'd calmed her down, Rosanna finally decided it was time to put her into the home in Garlasco. The Casa Patrizia. And Rosanna came to live here.'

'Poor woman.'

'Who?'

'You know who the man was, Giorgio?'

Boatti shook his head, 'I don't know his name.'

'Thanks for the help.'

'But I know somebody who might know.'

TORRE CIVICA

'A work site.'

They walked up Strada Nuova that was coming alive after the long midday break. There were workmen with pneumatic drills who were digging a narrow trench into the soft ground beneath the street.

'The ENEL are laying electric cables,' Boatti said. He gestured, 'And now our Communist/Conservative coalition are putting down stone slabs where for a hundred years there used to be cobbles.'

Most of the pedestrians were tourists, visitors from elsewhere, who ate large ice creams and, ignoring the noise of the workmen, carefully studied the window displays in the city centre even though most shops had already closed in anticipation of the Ferragosto.

The two men had to step over a rope before turning into Via

Cardano. They came into Piazza del Duomo. It was free of traffic. It no longer seemed the same place – different light, different expectations – since the Torre Civica had gone. The débris had been removed and apart from the remaining, pathetic stump beside the Duomo, the warning flags and the barriers, there was little to remind the casual passer-by of a monument that had weathered more than eight hundred winters of the Po valley.

'Eight hundred years?' Boatti shook his head, 'A lot older than that – it was probably built by a bishop in the eighth century at a time when the City and the Church were the same thing. Then later, at the time of the Comune, it was enlarged and adapted to the demands of the emergent bourgeois democracy. Hence its title of Civic Tower.'

At the foot of what had once been the tower, there was a plaque on a pedestal and several wreaths to the memory of the four people who had died beneath the collapsing rubble.

'I was in Strada Nuova, drinking coffee with a colleague,' Trotti said. 'I never heard a sound. Not until I heard the sirens and saw people running.'

Boatti smiled. He walked with his hands in the pockets of his pleated, large trousers. 'The two girls who heard the tower begin to rumble were trying to phone the fire brigade when the whole edifice fell on top of them.'

'They say that nobody was to blame.' Trotti placed a sweet in his mouth, 'Internal cracks that even x-raying wouldn't have shown up.'

'You believe that, Trotti?'

'The tower must have been weakened by last year's freak tempest. Otherwise why would it have suddenly collapsed after more than eight hundred years?'

'Italians learn their lessons in survival fast.'

Trotti stopped and looked at the younger man, 'What lessons?'

'You forget Giacomo Boni.'

'Who?'

'Boni was the Superintendent of Monuments in Venice in 1902. It was he who pointed out to the Venetian city fathers that St Mark's bell-tower was in danger of falling down.'

'You're writing an article on him?'

'The city fathers had a choice – and they made it. They removed Boni from his post and they thought the problem had gone away.

Trouble was, though, that a few weeks later the tower collapsed in the middle of St Mark's Square.'

Both men laughed, but not with amusement. Trotti resumed his walking.

Piazza del Duomo was almost empty. A solitary prelate in black, beneath a large, broad brimmed hat, was walking briskly towards the Curia buildings. In one hand he held his missal.

The shop was in one of the narrow alleys leading down from Via Cardano to the river. It used to be an art gallery, but after a raid from plain-clothes men from Costume, had been forced to close for over six months. Trotti knew that a hairdresser from Paris had set up a business there, but he had never been inside.

A red mountain bike stood outside the shop; the flat handlebars reminded Trotti of a cow's horns.

Boatti grinned, opened the door and the two men entered, to be met by the hot, pungent smell of chemical lotions. The hairdresser looked up from where he was teasing a woman's hair, raised an eyebrow and gave a prompt, professional smile, 'A little moment, gentlemen.' He had slanting eyes and the yellow skin of an Asian. His spiky hair, however, was almost orange. He wore leather jeans, a white shirt and a thin, black leather tie.

Several women sat in low armchairs, while about them girls in white overalls worked at their scalps. Another couple of women were sitting beneath the dome of their hair-driers, reading.

'My name is Pierre and I am very pleased to meet you.' The hairdresser held out his hand, 'Can I be of help?' He spoke Italian with a lisping French accent. The other hand, which held a long comb remained on his narrow hip. He wore a broad, white belt.

'Polizia di Stato.'

'Police?' He stiffened.

Trotti showed his badge.

'I wasn't warned.' The hairdresser frowned, 'I'm a very busy man.' He gestured towards his clients, 'I've a lot of work to do and many of these ladies will soon be going on holiday. They're most certainly in a hurry. I have no time today to help you look into my finances.'

'We're not the Finanza and this is not a fiscal inspection.'

The hairdresser seemed to relax.

'Signora Isella.' Boatti nodded to where a woman sat beneath the hair-drier. 'Commissario Trotti and I should simply like to speak to the Signora for a few moments.'

The Asian nodded his acceptance. There was the hint of sparse moustache along the sallow upper lip, 'Of course, of course. Please excuse me if I must return to my work.' He smiled, showing regular white teeth and went back to the wet hair that he had been combing. He took short steps, as if unsure of the raised heels of his boots.

'He's wearing make-up,' Trotti whispered.

'Rather suits him,' Boatti moved towards the woman and bent over. She looked up from the newspaper, *Gazzetta della Sicilia*.

'Signora Isella,' Boatti shouted, but she could not hear. She frowned in irritation, disapproval in her old, watery eyes. Her long, white hands held the newspaper against her knees. A walking stick leant against the black imitation leather of the armchair.

'Signora Isella.'

One of the girls stepped away from her client and approaching Signora Isella, turned off the drier. She raised the egg-shaped dome, then, returning to her client, carefully watched Trotti and Boatti in the long, tinted mirror that lined one wall. She had pretty eyes and the thick ankles of a peasant from the rice fields.

'What do you want?' Signora Isella said in an aggrieved tone. Her hair was made of tight, white curls that were firmly held down by a hairnet.

'It's about Signorina Belloni in San Teodoro.'

At the mention of the name Belloni, the face seemed to change, to soften.

'This is my friend, Commissario Trotti.'

'I heard about Rosanna this morning,' Signora Isella said. 'And I who thought she was away on holiday. How very terrible.' The old lady started to cry. 'Very terrible.'

SAN MICHELE

The palace was behind San Michele church; the wafer-thin red bricks low in the walls grew thick as they rose upwards. It was one of those buildings that had been slowly added to over the centuries, subtly changing in architecture as it had neared completion in the eighteenth century. A plaque in the wall announced that the King from Piemonte had slept there during the first war of independence.

'I'm going to visit my son.'

The old lady walked with a stick, yet she wore fashionable high-heeled shoes. The two men accompanied her up the steps to the large wooden door. She rang a well polished brass bell and immediately there were six clicks as the bolt was turned. A maid in uniform appeared.

'Tea for three,' Signora Isella commanded peremptorily. 'With ice.'

The maid carefully bolted the door behind the visitors and hurried away into a kitchen.

Signora Isella led the two men into a large room and gestured for them to sit down on the plump white settee. She lowered herself into a high-backed chair, setting the stick on the marble floor beside her.

The room smelt of polish.

The shutters were drawn, and the only light came from above. Looking up, Trotti saw that the ceiling had been painted with a trompe l'oeil fresco – cherubim and seraphim flitting across a deep blue sky, transporting flowers and fruit to young nymphs whose minds were clearly on other things. The painting was illuminated by hidden lights.

'Early nineteenth century,' Signora Isella said. 'Not particularly beautiful . . . and rather badly damaged by last year's tempest. I'm still waiting for the insurance people to pay. Probably still be waiting on the day of my funeral.' She smiled, revealing teeth that were exceptionally white and symmetrical.

They made small conversation.

'Forgive my not opening the shutters. In the summer, they stay closed because of the heat. It's not good for the ceiling. And because of the mosquitoes.' She added, 'Although with this drought, there aren't quite so many mosquitoes, I believe.'

The maid soon appeared carrying a tray of iced tea and small biscuits. When the girl turned on a desk-top lamp, Trotti saw that the design on the china plates was the same as on the frescoed ceiling.

'I only get to see my son twice a year,' the old lady said, between sips of tea. 'He lives in Sicily – where he was born. In the summer, he likes to get away from the heat and so I spend a couple of weeks with him and the children in the Dolomites.' The word children caused her to smile. 'At Christmas, we all got to Pantelleria.'

'You used to live in Sicily, signora?'

'Forty-five years of my life – but once my husband died, I had to get away. Came back to my native town to live with my brother. But he – God rest his soul – passed on a few years ago and I am left all alone to run this impossible house.' She lowered her cup, 'I sometimes think Signorina Belloni was so right living in a little room. So much more practical – and no need for servants.' Her hand went to the breast of her blouse and the parallel loops of her necklaces in a gesture of sincerity, 'I love Loredana, my maid, as if she were my own daughter – but there are times when I wish I was alone.'

'Of course,' Trotti said sympathetically and nodded.

'Alone – with just my memories for company.' She set the cup down on the guéridon beside her, 'I have had a good life – such a good life.'

'I imagine you were very fond of Rosanna.'

'You knew her, commissario – you know what a lovely person she was. Lovely and so good. So kind.' Signora Isella raised her shoulders, 'Unfortunately, she never married. And for a woman, having a family – a husband and children – is such a great satisfaction.'

'She always said that her schoolchildren were her family.'

Signora Isella gave Boatti a brief glance. 'She loved children, but the poor thing, she was terrified of men – so very terrified.'

'Perhaps because of her religion,' Trotti suggested.

'Religion?'

'She was a Jehovah's Witness, I believe.'

'A Jehovah's Witness, commissario?' A dismissive move of the long, white hand, 'A good Catholic like you and me.'

Trotti nodded, even though the last time he had been inside a church was at the time of Pioppi and Nando's wedding.

(It was also the last time he had seen Agnese.

Agnese, Trotti's wife had sat beside him but had promptly disappeared after the main course at the reception, accompanied by a young American woman.)

'Signorina Belloni was an attractive woman,' Trotti said. 'There could have been no shortage of men interested in sharing their lives with her.'

'Rosanna was a sweet, sweet girl.'

Trotti coughed, 'Without of course wishing to be indelicate . . .'

Signora Isella brought her watery glance on to Trotti's face, 'You are a policeman, commissario. I imagine you must do your duty . . .'

Trotti's face broke into a smile, 'Rosanna was only a couple of years younger than me. We both grew up during the years of Fascism, although we never met until much later. At least I don't think so. But I can imagine her in those days, in the uniform of a "Giovane Italiana". I was a young "Ballila".'

The old woman visibly shuddered, 'Those are years that I'd rather not think about. Unhappy years, very unhappy years for my good husband.'

There was a silence.

'Bad years, undoubtedly – but, like Rosanna, I was young at the time. And we didn't know any better.'

'My dear husband knew Mussolini during the Great War. A liar, a loud mouth and an upstart from Emilia. And a coward.'

Boatti was sitting beyond the yellow circle of light cast by the table lamp. Trotti had the impression he was smiling behind his hand.

'I mention Fascism, signora, because Rosanna once said to me that during those two decades – those two unhappy decades – young people had at least something to believe in. Today, we live in a society without values.'

'Rosanna was a good person. But she could be very naïve.'

'I believe . . .' Trotti hesitated, 'I believe that she almost married.'

'Never.' Signora Isella folded her arms.

Another awkward silence.

'She had a man, of course.'

'A man, signora?'

'I can tell you that, commissario. Now that she's dead, I don't think I'm hurting anybody by telling you that she had a man.'

'A lover?'

'Not what I said.'

'A friend?'

'A podgy little southerner.'

'His name, signora?'

'Not a Sicilian – the Sicilians have Norman and Arab blood, they are a fine breed of people, even the peasants.'

'Who was this man?'

'A little man from Salerno.' Her mouth showed her disapproval, 'I never liked him. Obsequious – you know what they're like. Opening the door for you and bowing and scraping and all that kissing your hand and using the simple past tense instead of the perfect. But their eyes are close together and you know they're wondering what you're worth and what they can hope to get out of you.'

'You met him?'

'A couple of times – when Rosanna was living in Via Mantova. A teacher in her school, that's how she introduced him. It wasn't until later that she told me about him. I was surprised to see a man in her house and, of course, I immediately suspected something.'

'Suspected something?'

'He wasn't the right man for her.'

'What did you suspect?'

'The Belloni family is not poor.'

'And who is this man? Where does he live?'

'He thought he could get his hands on the family fortune through Rosanna. When that didn't work, he tried her sister.' Signora Isella gave a little shudder. 'Like a gigolo, using the poor woman for her money.'

'What's his name?'

'Just like Rosanna's father – or rather her step-father. Another man from the south who married a rich woman to get his hands on the money.'

'Who was Rosanna's lover?'

'I never said Rosanna and this man were lovers.'

'Who was he?'

'He must have left his job not long after Maria Cristina went into a home. Went to live in Liguria somewhere – Ventimiglia or Imperia or San Remo. He went with his son.'

'His name, signora?'

'After all these years, you think I can remember that? An insignificant little man from Salerno?' She laughed briefly, looking at Boatti, and drank her tea.

Her thin, white hair was tinted blue.

BORIS

'A woman's voice, commissario.'

'The cleaning woman – she comes in twice a week.'

Tenente Pisanelli held one hand on the steering wheel. The other hand he ran through the long, lank hair that hung from the side of his head. The crown was now completely bald. 'Very sexy voice for a cleaning woman. Sounds South American.'

'Perhaps you ought to mind your own business.'

'As you wish, commissario. In future, I won't phone you on your home number.'

Trotti sat back in the passenger seat, 'Eva told you where I was?'

'Eva the cleaning lady?' Pisanelli tried to suppress a smile. 'I could do with a cleaning lady like that.'

The late afternoon was still hot. There were no fruit drops left in his pocket and, anyway, Trotti felt slightly sick – Signora Isella's tea had been sweet but very acid. Now he felt tired; he wanted to close his eyes and fall asleep. With Pisanelli driving, he preferred to keep his eyes open. The hoardings, standing like sentinels along the edge of the rice fields, rushed past at regular intervals, advertising the city's furriers and stainless steel saucepans.

The dome of the cathedral and the scaffolded towers of Piazza Leonardo dropped behind them to the west.

Pisanelli had switched the radio on to a classical music station – *Boris Godunov* – that would suddenly fade as the car went under a bridge or ran alongside a high, brick wall of a farm.

They took the minor roads for Garlasco. Occasionally Pisanelli overtook an isolated farm vehicle or a cyclist.

'Thanks.'

'Thanks for what, commissario?'

'For picking me up. I was beginning to get fed up with Boatti.'

'He seems very friendly.'

'Boatti wants to write a book.'

'On what?'

'Police procedure.'

Pisanelli burst out laughing, 'And he came to see you?'

'He would like to write about Rosanna's death.'

'I thought he was a journalist.' Pisanelli glanced at Trotti, 'You don't like him, do you?'

The countryside was flat and a dull haze hung over the fields, between the land and the sky. Already the green crops were turning to brown; Trotti could not help wondering if it would ever rain again. Global warming, hole in the ozone layer.

It was very hot, indeed. Trotti's eyelids were heavy. He opened the passenger window to let in the breeze. There was a strong smell of manure; it was the smell rather than the rush of air that revived Trotti.

'Why don't you like him?'

'He doesn't want Rosanna to have died in vain.'

'No doubt he was very attached to her.'

'You have never noticed, Pisa, that it's the Marxists and devout Christians who have the most liberal and generous ideas – and who're usually extremely self-centred?'

'Like the Italian Communist party, Boatti gave up being a Marxist years ago.'

'He doesn't seem particularly upset by her death.'

'Some people can lose a parent and not cry a single tear – that doesn't mean they don't suffer.'

'Very profound.'

'Thanks for the sarcasm.'

Trotti turned to look at Pisanelli, 'Good of you to pick me up.' He placed his hand on Pisanelli's shoulder, 'I don't think the questore's going to be pleased, though.'

'The questore's got better things to do with his time than to keep tabs on me.' Pisanelli shrugged, 'The city's dead – and like everybody else, I should be on holiday. Cipriani wanted me to accompany him – some "vu comprà" squatters at Malaspina.' Pisanelli took his hand off the wheel to make an obscene, masturbatory gesture. 'Could I give a shit? We tried to colonise Africa and now the Africans are colonising us. Africans and southerners and the Common Market.'

'You sound like a manifesto for the Lega Lombarda.'

'I don't like having to work for Merenda much,' Pisanelli said with bitterness in his voice. 'He wasn't very pleased to see me with you last night at San Teodoro.'

'If you don't like southerners, you shouldn't be in the police.'

'It's a nice day, I suppose. Another rainless day. The city's dead except for Merenda and his friends in Reparto Omicidi.' Pisanelli gestured towards the rice fields, the dry ditches, the row of pylons. 'Let's enjoy the ride – and let's forget about the Questura.'

'And the procuratore from Rome with the nice legs?'

'Tell me about Eva the cleaning lady, commissario. Has she got nice legs? Brazilian?'

'Time you were married.'

Pisanelli was going to say something but his attention was taken by a Lamborghini tractor in a cloud of dust. He reduced speed and overtook, muttering under his breath.

'You need a holiday, Pisa. A wife – not an adolescent, but the real thing. A wife and a holiday and perhaps your hair'll stop falling out.'

'I've tried everything.'

'For your hair or for a wife?'

'Why don't you like Boatti, commissario?'

'I don't like *Boris Godunov*. The Russians never have the tunes of Verdi or Leoncavallo or Puccini.'

'Why don't you like Boatti?'

Trotti turned, 'I never said I didn't like him.'

'What have you got out of him about the Belloni woman?'

'He really does want to write a book about police procedure.'

Pisanelli smiled, 'What does Commissario Trotti know about police procedure? You told him he's pissing against the wind.'

'Apparently Rosanna Belloni used to have a lover – a lover she unwittingly shared with her sister. A southerner who had his eye on the family fortune. At the moment, Boatti is down at the Scuola Elementare Gerolamo Cardano to see if he can find out anything about the man – he used to teach there, apparently.'

'A lover?' Pisanelli's smile slowly died on his face. 'With Rosanna dead, her money reverts to her next of kin – to Maria Cristina and the other siblings.'

At Bereguardo, they turned left and, a few minutes later, the car rumbled over the Po bridge. 'You know,' Pisanelli said, 'if Rosanna Belloni was murdered on Sunday afternoon, as the doctor thinks, the entire building was empty.'

Trotti glanced at Pisanelli, 'You can't be sure of the time of death until the autopsy.'

'The front gate was closed on Sunday. At the time of her death, we can assume Rosanna was alone in the building.'

'When's the autopsy, Pisa?'

Pisanelli lifted his right hand from the steering wheel, his fingers spread, 'No one on the top floor – your friend Boatti and his wife were visiting relatives at Vercelli. On the ground floor, there's a shop. It's owned by Signor Signoroni and his wife – a small stationer's that caters for the various offices and schools in the San Teodoro quarter. The shop was closed and there's no reason to suppose that Signor Signoroni or anybody else was there or in the storerooms behind the shop.'

'Signora Isella told me she thought Rosanna Belloni had gone on holiday.'

'Where to?'

'She normally visits her brother – a step-brother – in Foggia.'

Pisanelli smiled a satisfied smile, 'While you were down at the river, commissario, eating your risotto, I was doing some homework – your homework.'

'Slofu – and very expensive.'

'What?' Pisanelli frowned.

'Slofu – that's what Boatti called it. The opposite of fasfu.'

'Fast food,' Pisanelli said in English, correcting Trotti's pronunciation.

'Whatever you call it, Boatti paid more for a plate of risotto than I earn in a month.'

'Time we all got a rise in salary.' Pisanelli ran a hand through the hair at the side of his head, 'I didn't get to have any lunch at all.'

'You'll make a good policeman one day.'

Pisanelli glanced at Trotti, 'Twelve years you've been saying that.' He sounded slightly aggrieved. His eyes reverted to the road ahead, 'The front gate at San Teodoro is normally left open during the week. But in the evening and on Sundays it's closed. If a visitor rings, you have to go down and open the door – there's no automatic latch.'

'Which means whoever murdered Rosanna had the key to the front door.'

'Or, commissario . . .?'

'Or the murderer was invited in.'

'You'll make a good policeman one day, commissario.'

'One day.'

ROBERTI

Trotti was now feeling a lot less sleepy, 'Who lives on the second floor?'

'Entirely taken up by the Roberti family.'

'Who are the Roberti?'

'They've been living on the second floor for over twenty years, ever since Dottor Roberti was a student in the city. He graduated as a doctor and went to Turin or somewhere.'

'Somewhere?'

'Dr Roberti lived in Turin but he also worked at Varese. Being from a rich family, he could afford to keep up the lease in San Teodoro.'

'Why do that?'

'He was hoping to be offered an internship at the city hospital. In the late Sixties, he married and, from then on, he came down to the city once a month or so. He gave the occasional lecture at the university.'

'Where did you find this out, Pisanelli?'

'Why don't you like Boatti, commissario?'

'Pisanelli, why do you never answer my questions?'

'What questions?'

'All the questions I ask you.'

'I just asked you why you don't like Boatti.' Pisanelli sounded hurt, 'I'm still waiting for the answer.'

Trotti gave a grim smile.

'I don't answer your questions?' Pisanelli asked in an aggrieved voice, 'The autopsy? When's Belloni's autopsy?'

'For example?'

'Tomorrow morning at eleven. Merenda's going to be there.'

'Thank you, Pisa.'

'Why don't you like Boatti, commissario?'

Trotti was silent.

'You're being a bit hard on him just because he doesn't appear upset. He paid for your lunch, didn't he?'

'One day, Pisanelli, I'll make risotto with frog legs and I'll invite you round. Better than any of your slofu. Or fasfu.'

'You'll introduce me to Eva the cleaning lady?'

'How did you find out about Roberti?'

'You never answer my questions, commissario.'

'How did you find out about Roberti?'

A sigh, 'I went down to San Teodoro – and I asked a lot of questions.'

'What's Roberti's speciality?'

'There are always old women who spend their days behind half-closed blinds who are only too happy to share their knowledge with a personable young police officer. And since I'm supposed to have a certain amount of sensitivity and feminine intuition . . .'

'A phallocrat. You and every other male in the Questura.'

Pisanelli frowned as he concentrated on his driving.

'Well, Pisanelli?'

'You never forget a thing, do you, commissario?'

Trotti shrugged.

'You know that Brigadiere Ciuffi liked me. You know that she didn't really think I was a phallocrat.'

'Brigadiere Ciuffi is dead,' Trotti said coldly. 'Roberti's specialisation, Pisa?'

Pisanelli's voice was cold, 'Dermatology and STD.'

'What?'

'Sexually transmitted diseases.' A slow, boyish smile as Pisanelli's face brightened up, 'About two years ago, Roberti's daughter moved into the apartment.'

'Why?'

'She's at the university. Studying the Science of Communication.'

'Why not go to Turin?'

Pisanelli shook his head. Pulled by the centrifugal force, the long hair rose from his collar, 'For over twenty years, Roberti's been paying a Sixties' rent for a big, centrally situated apartment in one of the most expensive cities in the Peninsula. Expensive because it is supposed to have one of the best universities.'

'Supposed?'

'We're Italians – the easy victims of our own rhetoric. If you say something often enough, you begin to believe it. Perhaps it is the best university in Italy.'

'Italian universities aren't up to their foreign counterparts?'

'Being the best doesn't mean it's a good university.'

'Is that why you gave up your medical studies?'

Pisanelli didn't answer. He paused before saying, 'Italy is the only country in the European community that has no qualification after the degree. If you want a PhD you have to emigrate.'

'The Lega Lombarda would like a university for every province in Lombardy?'

'You seem to think, Commissario Trotti, that I vote Lega Lombarda.'

'Over twenty per cent of the population does – and if you assume transplanted "terron" from the south don't, that means nearly forty per cent of the native population in Lombardy votes Lega Lombarda.'

'Most provinces in Lombardy have got their own university, anyway. And people don't vote Lega Lombarda just to have a university on their doorstep.' Pisanelli again ran a hand through his hair, 'If Rosanna Belloni had renovated and then rented out to students, she could've made ten times the money she was getting from Roberti.'

'Who told you all this, Pisa?'

'A little old lady in San Teodoro church. I bribed her with a candle for the altar. And I bought her a tattered old copy of *Nigrizia*. Trouble is with all these "vu compràs" hawking their wares in our cities, nobody cares any more about Christian missions in black Africa.'

'Why didn't Rosanna let the flat out to students?'

'Not interested in money.'

'People who aren't interested in money are normally people who already have enough money.'

'The Belloni family isn't poor. They have land and property. But they also have the expense of keeping this sister at Garlasco.'

'People who have enough money don't put their money under a mattress.'

'Was it ever said that Signorina Belloni put her money under the mattress?'

'You suggested that the motive behind the murder was robbery.'

'Her mother was from an old bourgeois family – and she was connected with one of the local banks, the Banco San Giovanni. There's an uncle who's a director there. Belloni wasn't the sort of person to keep money about the house – just enough for her to survive the week on.'

'Tell me about the Roberti girl.'

'What about her?'

Trotti said, 'Is she the only person to stay in the apartment at the moment?'

Pisanelli shook his head, 'It's possible she's staying in the city over the summer to prepare her exams. There are always students around, whatever the time of the year. But in August, most leave to be with their family.'

'A nice girl?'

For a moment Pisanelli appeared to hesitate.

'Well?'

'My informant sitting by the Holy Water is all *Famiglia Cristiana* and counting her beads. The old generation who still believe that Catholics shouldn't vote and that the mass should be sung in Latin.'

A blue signpost announced another five kilometres to Garlasco.

'She wears black and anybody in Benetton is the devil incarnate. The sort of pious Christian who loved the poor Africans until the "vu compràs" started invading our city. The sort of person who still thinks nice girls ride side-saddle.'

'Well?'

'A whore – the good Christian lady says the Roberti girl is a whore who sleeps with a different man every evening.'

WORLD CUP

Two old men sat in the sun on a painted bench at the roadside. They wore loose coats over their striped pyjamas and they both smoked, sharing the same stub of cigarette. A thin trail of blue cloud hovered over their heads.

It was late afternoon and the air still hot. Trotti shivered.

The building stood at the top of a small hill that ran down to the Po, to the upriver waters, alpine and relatively unpolluted before the confluent with its industrial discharge from Milan. A discreet house, built by a discreet nobleman at the beginning of the nineteenth century, in an amalgam of Austrian and Italianate styles. A broad, red brick façade that dominated the surrounding flat countryside.

A couple of hundred metres past the old men Pisanelli turned left and entered a long drive. There was an unlit neon sign announcing the Casa Patrizia. On the other side of the drive, a white statue of Mary holding her dead Son in her arms. Mother and Son had been stained by the frequent fogs and the polluted rain of the Po valley.

The drive was lined with chestnut trees. There were several benches and old people sat or stood in the shade, taking no notice of the passing car. It was past five o'clock and the afternoon was beginning to lose its heat.

The windscreen of the car had developed a yellowish patina of dead insects.

Pisanelli parked in front of the building, behind an ageing white Fiat van. Trotti no longer felt tired. With Pisanelli, he went up the flight of stairs and through the modernised glass doorway that opened automatically.

The cool interior smelt of floor polish, medication and old men's urine.

'I should like to see the director, please.'

The girl behind the desk had a small, pretty, unsophisticated face. There was too much make-up under the eyes and the fuchsia lipstick was smudged. She wore a white spencer over an orange T-shirt – the words, Best Company, printed above her small breasts. She put down the *Visto* magazine she was reading and smiled, revealing uneven teeth and dark gums.

'I am Commissario Trotti.'

She picked up the telephone, 'If you could . . .'

Trotti pushed her hand and the receiver back into the receiver's cradle, 'Commissario Trotti of the Polizia di Stato. The director, please. Now.'

The girl closed the magazine – she had been reading an article on 'Cacao Meravigliao' – stood up, said, 'This way,' and without another word, her lips pressed resolutely together, led the two policemen down a long corridor. Her shoes were too big for her at the heel, and to stop them slipping, she walked with an unnatural stoop. Pisanelli kept his eyes on the white skirt and the hips which were large for her narrow body. The two men followed her up a flight of carpeted steps to a darkly varnished door. She tapped on the door, entered and after a few mumbled words spoken to the person inside, beckoned Trotti and Pisanelli to enter.

Pisanelli grinned. 'Arrivederci, signorina,' he said, running a hand through his long, loose hair.

The girl disappeared, keeping her dark, disapproving eyes on her outsize shoes.

'Polizia di Stato?'

The director of the Casa Patrizia was a small, wiry man who looked like a retired army sergeant. He wore a shirt with epaulettes and his grey hair was very short. He had been sitting in a stuffed leather armchair. He now stood up, a forced smile on the narrow face, and held out his hand. 'Emmanuele Carnecine,' he announced, pointing to where his name had been placed in sculpted wooden letters on the desktop. 'How can I be of help?' Next to the name was a small vase filled with yellowed bullrushes. A folded copy of *La Repubblica*. And hidden beneath it, the pink pages of the *Gazzetta dello Sport*.

Trotti shook hands without enthusiasm.

'You would like something to drink, perhaps?' As an afterthought, he added, nodding his head briskly, 'The Finanza was here several months ago. We reached a very satisfactory agreement.' More nodding, 'A very satisfactory agreement. I am sure that along the corridors of power there can no longer be dissatisfaction with my humble establishment.'

'It's about one of your patients,' Trotti said.

Carnecine looked down, then up again, his face blank. 'One of our guests?' The eyes were intelligent and dark.

'A purely personal enquiry.'

Carnecine nodded. 'Gentlemen, please be seated. You're most welcome. Please be seated.' He nodded the small head repeatedly, like a plastic puppy at the rear window of a car, while the deep-set eyes remained on Trotti, assessing him. 'A vermouth perhaps? I know that the officers from the Finanza have no longer any cause to be unhappy about the Casa Patrizia.'

Trotti took the second armchair. Pisanelli remained standing.

'Not always very easy to run a home for . . .'

'For what, Signor Direttore?'

'A personal enquiry, you say?' Carnecine went to a cupboard and took out a sticky, half-empty bottle of Cynar. Like a bottle in a bar, it had a doser fixed within the cork. Even with his back towards Trotti, Carnecine continued to nod his head. He placed three glasses on a tray, took ice cubes from a refrigerator that was recessed into a bookcase, and served the drinks.

Pisanelli drank fast, the ice cubes rattling against his teeth.

'This is a home for old people?'

'You know, commissario . . .' A perplexed smile.

'Commissario Trotti.'

'You know, commissario, that here in Italy, there is no such thing as a mental asylum.' He raised his narrow shoulders, and Trotti noticed that the white shirt was grubby at the collar and sleeves. The fingernails were bitten and the knuckles were not very clean. 'We live in a backward country. A backward country which nonetheless has all the pretensions of the West and of advanced western thinking. Italy.' He clicked his tongue, 'Here in the north, we don't have enough beds in our hospitals for the sick and the lame. So you can just imagine what things are like in Naples or Reggio Calabria. And yet knowing that, our legislators – whom we have voted into power, commissario – our legislators think they can abolish the very concept of the mental asylum.' He shrugged, 'You can't abolish the weak and the feeble. Absurd. You can leave them to fend for themselves, you can turn them out into the street. You can say there is no problem. But they won't disappear. There is no magic wand, the problem isn't going to go away.'

Pisanelli asked, 'You vote Lega Lombarda?'

The man raised his eyebrows before continuing, 'We're richer than the English, we export more than the French – and we are totally incapable of looking after our own people.' He drank, 'To compare Italy with the third world is merely to insult the third world.' He hastily finished his drink. 'We are in Colombia or Uruguay. A banana republic that doesn't grow bananas and isn't a republic. And all we can worry about is the World Cup. We don't need new football stadiums – we need hospitals.'

'And private clinics,' Pisanelli said.

'Our city is special,' Carnecine gestured vaguely towards the west. 'Everybody tells us so. We are the Austrians of the north – low unemployment, schools and competent teachers for our children. We like to compare our ancient university with Cambridge in England.' He snorted, 'Yet in our proud, hard-working and wonderful city, the Torre Civica was standing for a millennium. And it fell over. Bang. It fell over, just like that, killing four people including two young girls.'

'Nobody could know it was going to fall.'

'Commissario.' Carnecine held up a hand, 'We let it collapse. Believe me. You think the new stadiums are going to collapse?' He shook his head, 'Too much Mafia money has been invested in them. But a historic monument, a priceless, irreplaceable element of our patrimony. What sort of investment is that for the politicians and the developers? We just don't care. Will Inter win the Scudo? Why didn't Italy win the Mondiali? We don't care about the past, about our history. There is no money in history, there is no profit. The Torre Civica – who cares about the Torre Civica? Perhaps they're going to build a shopping mall in its place. After all, in our city, the priests and the Communists are now in charge together. Strange bedfellows.' He slapped his thigh. 'At first sight, you wouldn't think the Communists and the Christian Democrats had anything in common. But the reason of profit, of patronage, of power-brokering is more powerful than morals, than human values.' He glanced at Pisanelli, 'Your young friend asks me if I vote Lega Lombarda. The answer is yes. I am not a racist. I have nothing against the southerners. But I have a lot against the south. The southern way of doing things – the Mafia way, the Camorra way. The way that all the other parties, the Christian Democrats, the Socialists, even the Communists have learnt to adopt – to their advantage. They have brought Calabria and Sicily to Lombardy, they have turned Milan into Palermo.'

Trotti nodded absentmindedly, 'This is a private establishment, Signor Carnecine?'

Carnecine raised his shoulders, 'Unfortunately we don't get any help, either from the Ministry or from the Region.'

'Unfortunately,' Trotti repeated.

Carnecine's pink tongue licked the edge of his glass. With his eyes on Trotti he then placed the glass back on the tray, 'But that doesn't stop people from growing old. It is no crime when age begins to play tricks with the mind. We're all fragile in one way or another. Some people are unfortunately more fragile than others. They need attention, they need care, they need help. Above all, they need love.'

'Of course,' Pisanelli said.

Carnecine gave Pisanelli a smile. The eyes remained lucid and questioning. 'Somebody must look after them. Ours has fast become an urban society. The family no longer exists as it used to, twenty, thirty years ago. Children leave their parents and go to work in the cities – and there's no room for the unproductive in modern society. The old, the feeble. We're like the Eskimos, we put our old and weak out to die.' He paused, 'A personal enquiry?'

'This isn't a religious foundation?'

'Some of the aides are nuns.' Carnecine shook his head sadly, 'But the Church – once the backbone of our society – can no longer find young men and women willing to sacrifice themselves in the service of a greater good.' He placed his hands on the desk – short fingers and irregular, bitten nails. He continued to nod his head. 'We live in a society where there's no alternative to Mammon. Money, commissario – money is the only sure form of intercourse at this end of the twentieth century.'

There were two photographs on the wall, one of the Pope, the other of Mother Teresa of Calcutta.

'Understaffed and overworked.' He nodded, his eyes on his ungainly hands, 'You come, however, at a time when many of our guests are away; in a few days it will be Ferragosto – August is a time of the year when families can break out of the infernal routine of work and for a few precious weeks, look after their dear ones. Be with them, cherish them, give them the love that they need.'

(The man's tone and manner reminded Trotti of Buonarese's uncle, a priest at the Cremona oratory in the early years of the war. For reasons that were never made clear, the priest was later defrocked and went on to make a fortune in the years of reconstruction, running a fleet of lorries between Cremona and Bologna. As for Buonarese, he went into politics and married a Swedish cover girl half his age.)

'Signorina Belloni,' Trotti said.

'I beg your pardon?'

'Maria Cristina Belloni. I'd like to have a few words with her.'

The director sat back in his armchair. He looked at Trotti for a few moments. Then he lifted the receiver from its cradle and spoke in a soft, but imperative voice.

Through the windows, evening was coming to the countryside. Somewhere a train hooted, one of the slow commuter trains along a rural branch line. The type of brown, ageless commuter train from Milan that was stuffy and rancid with tobacco smoke in winter, hot and almost empty in August. On the horizon, in a sea of rice fields, a distant church pointed its spire towards the unchanging Lombardy sky.

Swallows darted low and fast beyond the window; perhaps it was at last going to rain.

A long row of plane trees, like immobile soldiers, stood on the banks of the Po.

Carnecine put down the phone and looked at Trotti. 'If you can wait a few moments.' He smiled, nodding his head, 'I believe Signorina Belloni is one of our guests who goes out to work during the week. Little jobs in Garlasco – it gives them a sense of responsibility – and it gives them some pocket money. But we have to be careful, of course. Many – indeed too many – of the residents here are taking treatment.'

'You don't like the drugs?' It was Pisanelli who spoke.

Carnecine shrugged, 'Most of our guests are on some form of medication – and, of course, it often blunts the sharpness of their minds. But . . .'

'Yes?'

'If a partial sedation can give to some of our residents a semblance of a normal existence, who am I to complain? The problem is' – Carnecine smiled – 'that you can never be sure of the long-term effects of the medication.'

'You are a doctor?' Pisanelli asked.

A slight hesitation before Carnecine shook his head, 'There's always a doctor on the premises during the day. I have two doctors on a rota basis. It's they who prescribe the medicines to be given.'

'And at night?'

'At night, we use the local emergency number.'

Pisanelli took a second glass of Cynar which Carnecine served him, the obsequious smile on his nodding head.

A knock on the door.

The girl with the smudged lipstick entered, her shoulders hunched. She held a green register in her hand, a finger between the pages. She opened the register on the desk in front of the director. She whispered in his ear while her dark eyes peeped up surreptitiously at Pisanelli.

Pisanelli, holding the glass to his chest, grinned back.

Carnecine stood up. 'I see.'

Trotti said, 'We will be able to speak to Signorina Belloni?'

The small man nodded his head rapidly. 'I don't think I can help you, Signor Commissario. Signorina Belloni left here on 19 July for a month's holiday. She'll be with her sister in the city until the second week in September. With her sister, Signorina Belloni, Rosanna.'

LEONARDO DA VINCI

Trotti, unlike Pisanelli, was wearing his seat belt.

'We could go for a pizza.'

Trotti replied, 'I had a big lunch.'

'I was intending to go to the cinema.'

'Do as you please, Pisanelli.'

'To go to the cinema with my girlfriend.'

'Whatever happened to the psychiatrist you were engaged to, Pisanelli?'

By the time they got back to the city, it was late evening. The street lamps had come on and the car ran softly along the broad avenues.

'Psychiatrist? I don't remember any psychiatrist.'

In Viale Alessandro Brambilla Trotti told Pisanelli to stop. He unbuckled the belt and got out of the car.

A tobacconist's was open, throwing its white neon light on to the dusty pavement. Trotti entered, nodded to the buxom woman behind the counter and asked for four packets of boiled sweets. The woman sat beside a fan whose grill was clogged with filaments of dust. She had small, bright eyes; a deep line separated the two freckled breasts that were only partly hidden behind the plunging neck of a cardigan.

Trotti took two packets of aniseed-flavoured sweets and another two packets of cherry flavour from the plastic stand beside the rack of old postcards – Piazza Duomo with the civic tower still intact.

The woman tried to refuse the five thousand lire note, pushing the money away with a pale, pudgy hand – Trotti had helped her husband get a job after a hunting accident in 1979 – but Trotti insisted, allowing a harshness into his voice. 'You're very kind, Signora Belcredi, but I must pay.'

'Ah, Commissario Trotti, you are too proud.'

'You'd better give me a receipt – just in case the Finanza is outside, waiting to pounce.'

She laughed and rang up three thousand lire on the cash register. She gave him his change and the receipt.

'Buona sera, signora,' Trotti said, stepping out into the street. He unwrapped a cherry sweet and popped it into his mouth. Like an addict getting a fix, Trotti seemed to relax. He smiled at Pisanelli as he climbed back into the car. 'You can drop me off in Via Mantova. And then you can take your psychiatrist to the cinema. Or to her couch.'

'Number six, Via Mantova, commissario?'

The centre of the city had been closed to through traffic for over ten years. At the time of its inauguration, people had talked proudly about the biggest pedestrian zone in Europe. Now they were more realistic; they knew that there were times of the day when the Vigili Urbani turned a blind eye to cars in the restricted zone. And since most people had a friend in the city hall, there were more parking permits issued for the city centre than there were inhabitants.

In a recent referendum, people had voted for an extension to the pedestrian zone. As yet the Christian Democrat and Communist city fathers had done nothing.

Theoretically there were no restrictions of movement for a police vehicle. However, Pisanelli had to take a detour.

'Nice to be back in the pedestrian zone,' Pisanelli said.

Since the destruction of the Torre Civica, both the City and the Ministry of the Environment had rushed to protect the remaining medieval towers. The three towers behind the university in Piazza Leonardo da Vinci had been hurriedly inspected and even more hurriedly bolstered with scaffolding. Similar intervention had occurred elsewhere. Many citizens, much to their surprise, discovered that humdrum houses and even some shops were in fact part of other, unnoticed towers that had been transformed over the centuries into something more practical.

'When Mariani introduced pedestrianisation,' Trotti said, almost to himself, 'I thought that I would be getting fit, cycling everywhere on my Ganna.'

'We Italians are victims of our own rhetoric.'

'You've already said that. Like an old man, Pisa, you're beginning to repeat everything.'

'Fortunately, it doesn't take us too long to see through the myths of our own creation.'

Trotti crunched the sweet between his teeth, 'I liked Rosanna – I liked her a lot.'

Pisanelli glanced at him, 'And now you're going to find her murderer?'

'That's what Boatti wants.'

'You're going to look for her murderer tonight and I'm going to have to go without supper, miss my date and spend another exciting evening having to put up with the synthetic smell of your cherry cough sweets.'

'There'll always be another psychiatrist, Pisanelli.'

Pisanelli turned into Via Mantova – a small, cobbled street with high walls on either side, closed shutters in the tall, narrow buildings and dark bats fluttering about the rooftops.

'Another psychiatrist. But there won't always be another Commissario Trotti.' Pisanelli laughed to himself, as he peered through the car window, looking at the house numbers.

'You enjoy being a cop, tenente. And what better excuse than to say you're working late with your obsessive boss, the infamous Commissario Trotti?'

Pisanelli braked and cut the motor. 'Number six, Via Mantova.'

They got out of the car; the evening air smelt of lime trees and petrol fumes. The mosquitoes had returned to the city after a long, hot day in the rice fields. Pisanelli said, 'Commissario, there never was any psychiatrist – she was a psychiatric nurse and she was from Mortara. A happily married woman for the last three years. Her husband sells shoes in Vigevano.'

There were no lights on in number six.

'She got fed up with waiting for me.'

The small switch in the wall was grubby with the passage of dirty fingers.

'A wise girl, Pisanelli.' Trotti pressed the bell. They could hear a distant ringing. Nobody came to the brown, wooden door.

Putting another cherry sweet in his mouth, Trotti glanced at Pisanelli.

Pisanelli nodded sadly, 'I think I'm going to miss my date.'

BUGS

There were steps leading up to the narrow door and the key had been slipped over the coarse concrete, behind a row of neglected potted plants. The lock turned noisily and Trotti let himself into the corridor. There was a light. He turned the rotary switch. Overhead, a single bulb glowed dully beneath its enamel shade.

Out of the street, the air was cool. The thick-walled houses of Lombardy had been built to resist both the cold winter and the oppressive, windless heat of summer of the Po valley.

Pisanelli and Trotti found themselves at the foot of the stairs. There was a brown wooden door to their right, with a small iron handle and long, rusted hinges. 'Rosanna's place. She used to live here with her mother. Maria Cristina lives upstairs.' Trotti whispered. The handle did not move. The door had not been opened in a long time.

They went up the stairs.

Half way up, the stairs curved to the right and the two men came to a small, dusty landing and another brown door. The same handle, the same hinges; everything had been painted over in a muddy, brown paint.

From beyond the door came the soft mumble of men's voices.

Trotti rapped against the wood with his knuckles.

No answer. The mumbling continued.

Trotti turned the handle. The door was not locked. He looked at Pisanelli, knocked again. The two men waited.

Pisanelli smiled. In the feeble light his face seemed to have lost its youthfulness. He stood close beside Trotti. Trotti pushed at the creaking door.

'Don't even have a warrant, commissario?' Pisanelli's breath was warm on Trotti's cheek.

The door moved slowly, ponderously. The two men entered a kitchen. Pisanelli switched on the ceiling light.

A fly paper, almost black with dead flies, hung from the single bulb.

A stone sink with a few dirty plates beneath the accusatory finger of a rubber pipe. Dried tomato sauce and pasta on the plates. An espresso coffee machine on an electric stove; coffee had run from the side of the machine on to the round, rusting electric plate. A box of matches had fallen to the floor and plastic matches lay scattered across the red stone.

A car went past in Via Mantova.

The sound of voices continued its low mumbling.

Pisanelli ran a finger along the top of the kitchen table and then looked at the dust on his finger. 'A week, five days,' he said. He was no longer smiling.

Trotti nodded, sucking noisily, while his eyes searched the kitchen. He, too, seemed pale in the poor light.

Beyond the kitchen was a bedroom.

The two men advanced together.

The television was on, the reflected grey light flickering against the low ceiling and the grubby, plastered walls. The nasal voice of a cartoon rabbit.

'Bugs Bunny,' said Pisanelli. He even laughed, but the laughter caught in his throat as he approached the television set.

Insects danced blindly and insistently against the black and white screen.

SPAGHETTATA

Neither Pisanelli nor Trotti had eaten.

'The light is on.'

There were a few parked cars in Piazza Teodoro and a police motorcycle stood beside the large wooden doorway.

An officer in uniform – one of the recent recruits whom Trotti did not recognise – saluted briskly, despite the windless heat.

'I wish to speak to Signor Boatti. He lives on the top floor.'

'At your orders,' the man said and saluted again. He wrote

something down in a small notebook, checked with his watch and then held the door open as Pisanelli and Trotti brushed past him. 'Another hot evening, commissario. And still no sign of rain.'

They found themselves in the rundown courtyard.

Pisanelli laughed, 'A feeling of déjà vu.' He took a cigarette from his jacket pocket and lit it.

'Perhaps Maria Cristina's gone back to Garlasco,' Trotti said.

'She left in a hurry – didn't even turn the television off.'

'Or perhaps she's just very untidy – the opposite of Rosanna.'

The air was cool in the small courtyard. The smell of the burning match mingled with the sweeter perfume of wild honeysuckle. It was several hours past sunset. Still the brick wall gave off the accumulated heat of the day.

'What's déjà vu, Pisanelli?'

'The feeling you've seen the same thing already.'

'You saw the same thing at four o'clock this morning.' Trotti shrugged. 'Déjà "vu comprà"? At my age, you've seen everything before.'

'Commissario, you talk as if you were getting ready to leave this world.'

'This world, perhaps not. Not yet, at least.' With two fingers, Trotti made the horned gesture to ward off bad luck.

'You sound very jaded.'

'Ready to leave the Questura.'

'You've been saying that for at least ten years.'

'You think I'd miss you?' Trotti allowed himself a thin smile. Taking Pisanelli by the arm, he went up one flight of stairs.

They came to a door. There was an oval name-plate in burnished brass, 'Dott. Roberti.' Pisanelli rang the bell and after a couple of minutes, a light came on behind the opaque glass. The door was opened.

'Gentlemen?'

She looked very young. Signorina Roberti was slim, dressed in jeans and a Lacoste shirt. She had black hair that caught the light. She did not wear make-up. On her feet she wore blue espadrilles.

'Commissario Trotti, Polizia di Stato.' Trotti's tired face broke into a smile. 'I wonder if we could come in for a while.' He shrugged, still smiling, 'A few questions that I need to ask you.'

'I suppose it's about the poor . . .' She did not finish her sentence.

The girl gestured with her hand to the floor above. Her eyes went from Trotti to Pisanelli. She stepped back, her hand still on the door knob, 'Please come in.'

She closed the door behind them.

They followed her into a big apartment. The floor was of polished wood and the walls were covered in crimson silk that had begun to wear thin in places. Various crucifixes and stoops, dark furnishings and the sound of their footfalls as they went towards a well lit room at the end of a windowless corridor.

The girl walked gracefully. She scarcely moved the upper part of her body, stepping silently on her rope-soled shoes. She said, over her shoulder, 'Only just got back from the Langhe this afternoon.' She spoke with a slight, lisping Turin accent that Trotti found pleasant. 'My father has a little vineyard there.'

Within the large apartment, she had her own flat. It was bright and inviting. The air was cooled artificially; the discreet hum of air conditioning.

There was a small television in one corner, emitting the dubbed dialogue of an American soap opera. The shuttered window gave on to Piazza San Teodoro, while along the opposite wall there was a kitchenette, with dishwasher, refrigerator, cooker and an overhead air aspirator. A couple of posters, 'Fiera del Levante' and Marilyn Monroe, on the wall above a low, unmade bed. Clothes and shoes were scattered across the floor. There were several matching suitcases – the same Vuitton suitcases that Agnese had bought before she left Italy for the last time – from which clothes tumbled on to the wooden floor and the beige carpet.

'When did you find out about the death of Signorina Belloni?' It was Pisanelli who spoke.

Her black hair glistened. It had been cut in a straight line. Despite the boyish style, her face was gentle. She pushed several strands away from her eyes and looked at Trotti. 'Please excuse the mess.' There was eucalyptus on her breath.

'About Signorina Belloni?'

'The poor, poor woman. She was so very kind.'

Pisanelli said flatly, 'Now she's dead.'

A mixture of hurt and disapproval in her glance at Pisanelli. 'So I discover.' The girl sighed, looked down at her shoes, 'So I discover.'

'Would you mind, signorina, if we sat down?'

An apologetic smile that reminded Trotti of other women he had known. 'I can give you gentlemen something to drink?' The young face seemed to brighten.

He lowered himself on to the soft cushions of the sofa, feeling the weight of his years. Trotti shook his head.

'I was about to make myself a spaghettata.' She tapped at the flat belly beneath the pink cotton shirt, 'Famished after the drive back from Piemonte. So hot, so very hot. If you gentlemen would care to eat . . .' she gestured to where a saucepan gave off steam.

Trotti was about to shake his head in refusal. Something – the weight of years, perhaps – stopped him. Smiling he said, 'You're very kind. Neither of us has eaten all evening.'

She stood in the middle of the room, her hands behind her back, her small feet revealing the neat demarking lines of a summery tan.

Agnese, Pioppi, Ciuffi.

Tanned skins, bright, frank eyes and wide, generous mouths. Their need to be loved. Their need to give.

Rosanna.

Trotti let his head fall back on the settee and closed his eyes.

He was living a lie, of course.

There never was, there would never be peace of the senses for him. He could never get by on just coffee and sweets. Women – Trotti needed them too much.

'You mustn't put yourself out for us – but some spaghetti would be most welcome, Signorina Roberti.'

He needed women – and Trotti knew he liked them too much.

PETRARCA

Pisanelli had reverted to an uncharacteristic sullenness. Even sitting at the girl's table, eating the spaghetti that she had hurriedly prepared, he seemed aggressive. He had not taken off his jacket, but sat with his arms propped against the pretty check tablecloth, one hand holding a glass of dark wine. His lips were still greasy from the food. The long hair at the side of his head needed combing. He had removed his tie; beads of sweat had formed along his forehead.

'Some more, commissario?'

Trotti shook his head. The bolognese sauce had been retrieved from the refrigerator and heated, yet was surprisingly tasty. The wine, too – Grignolino from an unlabelled bottle – was good. The girl sat opposite, her eyes scrutinising him.

'You are very kind, signorina.'

'Call me Laura.'

He could not repress the spontaneous smile, 'A pretty name.'

'The girl Petrarch fell in love with in Avignon in 1327.' She stood up and made coffee. 'She was only twelve years old.'

'Laura died in the plague,' Pisanelli said.

Later, Laura Roberti piled the dishes in the sink and they returned to the settee. The television – RAIDUE in electronic letters at the corner of the screen – continued to show its soundless, flickering image.

'You have a boyfriend, signorina?'

The girl nodded.

'Where is he?'

'Gian Maria? He's in Ferrara.'

'He's a student at this university?'

She smiled, lowering her head, 'He was. But now he's working for Signor Rognoni – for his father in Ferrara where they have a small printing company.'

'And when did you last see him?' Pisanelli asked. He held an open notebook on his knee and a pen in his left hand.

Laura turned to look at him, 'Why d'you need to know that?'

'We are indiscreet,' Trotti touched the knee of her faded jeans. 'Asking indiscreet questions is part of our job.' He lowered his head, 'Please try to forgive us – and try to understand.'

'Gian Maria and I are engaged.'

'Congratulations,' Pisanelli said.

'We intend to get married just as soon as I've finished my degree – I've got another seven exams to sit.' A tone of weariness had entered her voice, 'It should be over by the spring.'

'Your degree or the marriage?'

She ignored Pisanelli. 'Gian Maria and I've been engaged for nearly two years.'

'And you're very much in love?' Pisanelli asked.

She looked at him coolly.

Pisanelli wrote something down.

Despite the air conditioning, the room was hot. Trotti ran a hand along his forehead. 'When did you leave this city for the Langhe?'

'My parents have a little estate and father produces wine there. It's a hobby – even though he manages to sell some of the wine. The Grignolino – you liked it?'

'Excellent.'

'Santo Stefano's a nice place to get away to.'

'Then why are you here?'

Laura sat back, folding her arms against a boyish chest, 'I had to return to the city to get on with my work.'

'You can't study there?'

'At Santo Stefano?' She shrugged, 'I haven't got all my books there.' She made a vague movement of her hands towards the bookshelves beneath the blinds. 'And there's no university library in the Langhe.'

'So you came back to the city?'

'This is the best time to work – in the middle of August. There are no students around, no distractions. You can find what you want in the departmental library – and you can find a place to sit down. In the afternoon, I can go down to the Lido on the river for a swim – and in the morning, I can sleep. There's no traffic in the piazza. Sometimes I go for a round of golf at the Country Club.' She gestured over her shoulder to the Piazza San Teodoro, beyond the closed blinds. 'September seems to be when I get my best results.' She propped her small feet on the edge of the coffee table. She had kicked off the French espadrilles.

'And Gian Maria?' Pisanelli asked.

'What about him?'

'When are you next going to see him?'

'He rings in the evening – and perhaps next week he'll drive up. He knows I'm busy. He wants me to get on with my exams.'

'When did you go to the Langhe? When did you last see Rosanna Belloni, Laura?' Again Trotti allowed his hand to touch her knee. Sitting beside her, his head against the settee, he could smell her hair, warm and muskily sweet.

'You really think she was murdered?'

Beneath his hand, Trotti could feel her whole body tremble. He folded his arms, 'Tenente Pisanelli and I saw the body. Somebody had hit her from behind, breaking the skull. Her nose and jaw were broken, her face badly battered.'

'I find that so hard to believe. Signorina Belloni was a very kind and gentle person. I can't imagine anybody wanting to be violent with her.'

'Behind every violent death, there's normally one of two motives.'

'Money or sex?'

Trotti raised an eyebrow, 'You sound well informed for a young lady.'

A girlish laugh, 'I did a course in popular fiction – including detective novels.'

'Money or sex,' Trotti said, nodding his head. 'And sometimes both.'

The smile died on her face.

A silence fell on the room. Nobody spoke. The television image jumped and flickered, unheeded.

'Perhaps if I had been here, none of this would have happened.' Laura had closed her eyes, her head tilted back.

'You can't hold yourself responsible for her death, Laura.'

'Sometimes she'd come down here and we'd chat. Rosanna was a retiring person and I always felt flattered and pleased when she came to see me. Generally speaking, though, it was more often me who'd go up to her place.'

'Why?'

'Why what?'

'What did you do with Rosanna Belloni?'

'She liked to talk.'

'What about?'

'Children.'

'What?'

'She regretted never having had children. And she missed the children from the school.' A pause, 'Rosanna liked to tell me how lucky I was to have a nice boyfriend . . .'

'She knew Gian Maria?'

'They met.' The girl raised one shoulder, 'She liked him and I think she wanted me to be happy with him. "Have lots of children – lots and lots of children" – that's what she used to say.' She added softly, 'She absolutely adored Signor Boatti's two little girls.'

'You're going to have lots of children?' Pisanelli asked.

'A career – before I have any children, I want to have a job and a salary.' She turned her head slightly to look at him.

Pisanelli pretended to jot in his notebook.

'Please tell me when you last saw her, Laura.'

'I've been away for eight days. It must have been the Thursday or the Friday. We met on the stairs. I was going off to the university, she was coming back with coffee from the grocer store in Via Lanfranco. And fresh bread.'

'What did she say?'

'She said "buongiorno" and smiled.'

'Anything else?'

The girl shook her head.

'Why was she interested in the Jehovah's Witnesses?'

'Jehovah's Witnesses? I know nothing about that. Rosanna was a good Catholic – or, at least, I think so. She often went to mass on Sundays – and sometimes during the week.'

'Were you aware of her having enemies?'

The dark eyes opened wide, 'Enemies?'

'Was there anybody she didn't like? Or anybody who didn't like her?'

'Since her retirement, Rosanna didn't go out very much.'

'But she had visitors?'

The young girl sat beside Trotti, the smell of her hair like a forgotten, forbidden pleasure in his nostrils. 'Visitors?' she repeated, without looking at him.

'Did you ever see Rosanna with anybody?'

A slight shrug, 'Sometimes she was with her sister – Maria Cristina, a younger sister who stays somewhere in Garlasco. She occasionally comes down at weekends. Or once or twice with some woman friend.'

'Who?'

'I don't know their names.' She shook her head, 'Old ladies – older than her, that always smell of lavender water when they go past my door.'

'You never saw her with a man, Laura?'

A pause.

'Did you ever see Rosanna with a man?'

'I don't think so.'

'Yes or no, Laura.'

'Signorina Belloni – I really didn't see her all that much.'

'You saw her with a man?'

'Other than Signor Boatti?'

'Did you ever see Rosanna Belloni with a man other than Signor Boatti?'

She shook her head. 'No.'

'But you saw her with Signor Boatti?'

'He lives on the top floor. Signorina Belloni was fond of his two daughters.'

'Signor Boatti visited her a lot?' Pisanelli looked up, awaiting her reply with a raised eyebrow.

'The only man I ever saw her with was Signor Boatti, commissario.'

'That struck you as quite normal?'

She caught her breath. 'Quite normal.'

Soon after, Trotti and Pisanelli took their leave. 'I have to drop in on Signor Boatti,' Trotti said. 'If you meet him, I'd rather you didn't go into any details about our conversation, signorina.'

Laura nodded thoughtfully and slipped her narrow feet back into the espadrilles. She accompanied the two policemen to the door.

As they went up the stairs, Pisanelli said softly, 'You're not telling me, commissario, that you can leave a bolognese sauce as good as that in the refrigerator for eight days.'

'Tema Sturbo.'

The three men sat in the car. Pisanelli held one hand on the steering wheel. Trotti seemed to have fallen asleep yet from time to time he would click the sweet in his mouth against his teeth.

The inside of the car smelt of sweat, garlic and Trotti's cherry sweet.

'Tema Sturbo,' Pisanelli repeated, worrying at his teeth with a worn toothpick, disappointed that nobody laughed at his joke. 'Cicciolina's car – a Tema Sturbo.'

Boatti was in the back seat. In his soft, educated voice he dictated something into a hand-held recorder. From time to time he belched softly.

It was hot and there was very little draught through the car, even though the windows were wide open. What breeze there was brought the petrol fumes from Via Matteotti. It was nearly midnight and Pisanelli had parked the blue Lancia Delta on the edge of the forecourt of the railway station. The car was just beyond the circles of light cast by the overhead lamps.

'Thanks for fetching me, commissario,' Boatti said after switching off his machine.

Trotti did not open his eyes, 'I have an interest in your book – if you ever write it.'

The occasional rumble of a train shunting on the far side of the long wall.

'I'll write it.'

'You got the address?'

Boatti said, 'The school's closed, but I managed to talk with the porter. There used to be a teacher at Rosanna's school who left about three years ago. Now lives in Ventimiglia. The porter believes there was something between him and Rosanna. Man called Taleri – Achille Taleri. Has a grown-up son.'

Trotti nodded, without opening his eyes.

There were very few people about; some railway workers coming off duty, their blue uniforms crumpled and creased after the day's summer heat. A tramp who had gravitated towards the station, having nowhere else to go. At this time of night, there were no travellers. It was late and before dawn, only a couple of international trains, heading for Genoa or Venice, France or Yugoslavia, full of tourists, full of light, would thunder through the provincial city without ever slowing down.

In their sidings, the brown, local trains for Vercelli or Codogno or Alessandria humbly awaited the early dawn.

The end of another rainless day. Another seven days to the Ferragosto.

'Tema Sturbo.' Pisanelli yawned noisily without putting a hand in front of his mouth. The smell of garlic grew stronger. He tapped his teeth with the toothpick.

Nobody seemed to be paying any attention to the car. It had ordinary plates and only the whiplash aerial indicated that it was in any way different from the other half dozen or so cars beside which it was parked. Trotti would have appreciated the air conditioning, but by running the motor, they would have attracted unnecessary attention.

'What exactly are we doing now?' Boatti asked.

'Waiting.'

'I can make a note of that?'

The rear of the car was opposite the station wall and a series of identical posters, some advertising a football match that had been won and lost many months earlier, others announcing a Spanish circus.

'Deposito bagagli'. The overhead sign burned in neon isolation, above a doorless entrance and a sulphurous water pump.

The front of the Lancia faced the square, ready for departure.

'Tema Sturbo . . . Te masturbo.'

Nobody laughed.

Pisanelli shrugged, 'I thought you might like a joke or two in your book, Boatti.'

No reply.

Offended, Pisanelli picked up the night vision binoculars. 'Nice little body, the Roberti girl. Very lithe.' He made several broad sweeps along Via Trieste. 'I think she was interested in me – in my animal magnetism.' The view was partially hindered by the intervening fir trees and the film hoardings in the small square that stood between the station and Via Trieste. Southwards, towards the Po, rose three illuminated towers, three pieces of post-modern architecture, replicating the medieval towers that had once populated the city. Three tubular structures, white except where the concrete had been chipped away to reveal the reinforced steel frame.

(The columns had been built when three lime trees had died, probably from the petrol fumes in Via Trieste.)

Pisanelli whistled. 'More whores,' he said without removing the binoculars from his eyes.

'What have you got against whores?' Trotti opened his eyes and turned towards Pisanelli.

'How can anybody want to fornicate in this heat?'

'Husbands whose wives have gone off to the coast.'

Boatti whispered, 'My wife's going off to the coast tomorrow.'

'The Nigerian girls are doing a special summer offer, Boatti, if that's what you want. You see that black girl over there . . .'

Trotti said, 'You think that prostitutes are a special race, Pisanelli?'

'There's no need to get angry, commissario. I just don't understand anybody wanting to screw in this weather.'

'What were you going to do with your psychiatrist after the cinema, Pisanelli?'

'She's not a psychiatrist.'

'Worse crimes than being a prostitute.'

For a moment, Pisanelli sulked. 'I like women, commissario. That doesn't mean I need to make love to all of them. And what they give me, they give me because they want to. I don't pay.'

'Why were you so aggressive with Laura Roberti?'

Pisanelli ignored the question.

Trotti took another cherry sweet from the packet.

'You can't buy women,' Pisanelli said with hurt dignity.

'You were gratuitously unpleasant towards Laura Roberti.'

'Of course you can buy women, Tenente Pisanelli. We buy women all the time. With money and with everything else. Women buy us with their looks – and with their bodies.' It was Boatti who spoke. 'There's no such thing as a free gift in nature. If you want something, you have to pay for it, one way or another.'

'A philosopher, Boatti?'

'No one gets the free screw.'

'You don't believe in love?'

'A woman knows if you desire her body. She will always want something in return. She opens her legs, you open your cheque-book. Or worst still, you open your front door, your soul and your life.'

'The last romantic, Boatti,' Trotti said. He had closed his eyes again.

'Women are the same as men, no better, no worse.'

'Women find me sensitive,' Pisanelli said.

Via Trieste was about ninety metres away. Much of the zone was well lit and they could see the scantily clad women – coffee-coloured Brazilians and dark Nigerian women in high heels and strangely outdated mini-skirts – except when a car coming off the ring road slowed down and the driver or his passenger haggled with the girl over her price.

'Angela.' Pisanelli handed the binoculars to Trotti.

'Poor bastard.'

It was Pisanelli who laughed, 'Poor bastard? Angela is richer than you or me, commissario. And now with all this AIDS, he refuses anything more risky than a hand job. Angela's nearly forty years old and he doesn't want to jeopardise his retirement.'

The transvestite stood in a doorway and was talking to one of the prostitutes. He wore a mini-skirt and held his yellow handbag behind his back.

'He's got a son doing athletics at CONI in Rome.'

In the back seat, Boatti laughed. 'Angela's lucky.'

'Lucky to be homosexual?'

'Most male prostitutes are old at twenty. Maybe he's got something that the others haven't got.'

'A sphincter and years of practice,' Pisanelli said.

'Or perhaps he hasn't got something the others have got – like a viral infection.'

Boatti was interrupted by Trotti holding up his hand. 'Here comes Beltoni.' Trotti raised the binoculars.

The atmosphere within the Lancia suddenly grew tense, expectant. Trotti ceased to click the sweet in his mouth. He put the large binoculars to his eyes, resting the front edge on the windscreen.

Behind him, Boatti leaned forward, forearms propped against the driver's backrest.

'In the T-shirt.'

The figure walking along Via Trieste must have been between thirty and thirty-five years old. He had his hair in plaits, like the footballer Gullit. He walked with a light, skipping gait, as if about to break into a run. Basketball shoes.

He nodded towards the whores as he went past. His greetings were not returned. Angela turned his back on him. The man went towards the lights of the Bar Il Re, where viale Vittorio Emmanuele came out on to the railway square. A few late drinkers – mainly railway workers – sat at the small tables set out on the pavement, almost on the road's edge, to catch the slight breeze along the viale.

Beltoni approached a table.

'Should have something,' Trotti said.

'There hasn't been much stuff in the city for a couple of months.'

'Who says?'

'Narcotici.' Pisanelli bit his lip, 'They're not going to be very pleased with your elbowing in on their terrain.'

'They won't even know. If . . .'

'You really think Rosanna Belloni's sister's on drugs?'

'How else do you think they keep them quiet at that place in Garlasco?'

'Tranquillisers, commissario – not the hard stuff.'

'Maria Cristina's been away from the home for several weeks. Probably they gave her a supply of tranquillisers, but that doesn't mean she's been taking them. She needs something – and perhaps she's been needing money.'

'So she attacked her sister?'

Trotti was silent.

'Maria Cristina was capable of killing her sister?'

'I wonder if there's a connection between the river suicide and Maria Cristina's disappearance.'

'Why should there be?'

'Where is Maria Cristina?'

'Because she's disappeared . . .'

Trotti held up his hand; the man in plaits had suddenly stopped – an animal that had scented an enemy lying in wait. He was two metres from the first table. He took a small, hesitant step and then turned away. He went back in the direction he had just come, now walking faster. The skip had disappeared from his gait.

Boatti asked, 'He suspects something?'

'No reason to.' Trotti took his eyes from the binoculars. 'Beltoni pays his dues.' He glanced at Pisanelli who was now sweating profusely even though he had at last removed his suede jacket.

'He's meeting somebody,' Pisanelli said simply.

An African – a 'vu comprà' with shining white teeth who had been standing near the entrance of the Il Re, an empty glass in his hand – came out on to the pavement and taking the same direction, walked towards the whores. He carried a leather satchel on one shoulder.

A Volkswagen coupé with four young men pulled up alongside the kerb. One of the men said something and a whore replied with an obscene gesture. The prostitute had light brown skin.

(Most of the Brazilians were male transvestites.)

In the back seat, Boatti was fanning himself.

The man in plaits had gone into a doorway. Only a part of him was visible through the binoculars. He was soon joined by the African.

'Turn on the engine.'

It was not possible to see the transaction from the car.

'Let's get going,' Trotti whispered harshly.

Pisanelli had switched on the ignition. Behind him, Boatti gripped the seat.

'It's Beltoni I want,' Trotti said. 'OK, Pisa, but slowly.'

Almost silently the car slid across the empty piazza. Half way towards the Via Trieste, Trotti said 'Now.'

Pisanelli accelerated, the wheels screeched. He flipped on the headbeams and the two men were caught in the circle of light. The African's eyes were as white as his teeth. Beltoni instinctively raised a protective arm to his eyes.

The African turned and ran.

The Lancia took the kerb at a right angle. The car bounced and for a moment, Pisanelli could have lost control.

Above the roar of the engine, a whore was screaming in Portuguese.

Pisanelli slammed on the brakes before reaching the wall. A controlled skid.

Boatti whispered hoarsely, 'My God!' He still held the recorder in his white hand.

The dealer was trapped in the door entrance by the snarling Lancia. The exhaust pipe sent grey, swirling fumes into windless air.

The prostitute in need of a shave continued to scream.

CALIBER 7.65

'Cuffs, Pisanelli.'

'You, shit.'

Trotti held the gun against the nape of his neck.

'Hands against the wall, legs apart.'

Beltoni smelt of old sweat and unwashed clothes. Pisanelli frisked him.

'What's your name?'

'I'm clean.'

'Clean? You have to be joking.'

A hesitant crowd had gathered, prostitutes and passers-by; they stood at a respectful distance from the car. The Lancia blocked the pavement; the motor was still on and, like actors on an empty stage, the three men were caught in the bright light of the headbeams. Trotti could feel the silent hostility of the onlookers. One of the transvestites was still screaming Brazilian insults.

'What's your name?'

'You know my name, Trotti – you and all the pricks of the Questura.'

Pisanelli thumped him with his left hand as he took a caliber 7.65 from the man's pocket and whistled. 'Some heavy artillery, commissario.'

'Where did you get this?' Trotti asked.

'It's not mine.'

'Where's it from?'

'A friend gave it to me – ten minutes ago a friend gave it to me. It's not mine – you know me, commissario, you know I don't carry guns.'

'I don't know you – and the way you smell, I don't want to know you.'

'Bastards.'

'Pisanelli, put the cuffs on him. We're taking him. A year – six months if he's lucky. Keep him off the streets for six months, we'll be doing a lot of people a favour.'

'For God's sake, that gun's not mine.'

'Check his pockets for illegal substances.'

'I'm clean.' He shook his head and the plaited hair danced on the grubby forehead.

'Nothing that a fumigation can't solve.' Trotti was out of breath, 'Look in his shoes.'

'Why don't you take the nigger?'

'Shut up.'

'Take the nigger, he's got the stuff.' The whining voice was marked by a strong Milanese accent. The eyes appeared unnaturally large and bloodshot, 'I haven't got anything – it's the niggers who deal. Why don't you take the vu comprà?'

Boatti was still sitting inside the car, the rear door open and one leg on the ground. His round face was pale.

'Hurry up, Pisanelli. Look in his shoes.'

The dealer's breath was fetid, an unpleasant mixture of hunger, alcohol and cigarettes. Beltoni did not wear socks. From the inside of the left basketball shoe Pisanelli removed a flick knife. Pisanelli was still frisking the pockets of the jeans when the man kicked backwards, trying to turn his thin body.

'Bastards!'

The kick was not very powerful, it merely grazed the side of Pisanelli's head. 'Leave me alone, you bastards.'

Trotti, without losing hold of the gun – the Beretta that Pisanelli carried in a holster – punched the man in the small of the back. Then as Beltoni turned, Trotti kneed him in the groin.

Beltoni grunted, slumped forward and Pisanelli snapped the cuffs round the white, narrow wrists.

'Scum of the earth.'

Pisanelli finished frisking the man. 'Ah.'

'What?'

Pisanelli looked up at Trotti. His face was damp with sweat and still taut with emotion. He grinned without conviction, 'Jackpot!' In his left hand, he held a thick wad of one-hundred-thousand-lire notes.

CAMOMILLE

The stubs of the Muratti cigarettes stood to attention, like black-headed soldiers in a long line across the kitchen table. A couple of saucepans were in the sink and the ceramic was splattered with the remains of food. Under the sink, tomato sauce had trickled down the side of the plastic bin and on to the floor.

Eva was in the bedroom, asleep, lying diagonally across the bed. The side lamp was on. A couple of magazines lay open on the carpet. The shutters were closed and the room was stuffy with the smell of musky perfume, nail varnish and cigarette smoke.

Trotti went back into the kitchen and put hot water in a saucepan. While waiting for the water to boil, he tidied up. He removed the cigarette filters and started washing the dishes.

He was pouring the boiling water on to the camomile when Eva appeared in the doorway. She was fumbling with a cigarette. She had found one of Agnese's dressing gowns – a present from Trotti when they were in Bari – and had put it on without tying the cord. The gown hid Eva's breasts but not the dark triangle of her pubic hair.

'You're late.'

'This place is a pigsty.'

'I made food for you, Piero Trotti.'

'That's very kind but it wasn't necessary.' The saucepan slipped between his fingers and the metal handle burnt his fingers. He threw the saucepan into the sink where it fizzled angrily. A brief cloud of steam rose towards the ceiling.

'Don't lose your temper.'

Trotti said, 'I never lose my temper.' He turned away, poured more cold water into the sink.

'I've been waiting here all day. You could have phoned, Piero.'

Trotti did not answer.

'I was worried about you.'

'I told you not to answer the phone. My colleague rang and you answered – you shouldn't have done. If the phone rings, I don't want you to answer it. Nobody must know you're here.' He noisily washed the remaining plates, banking them on to the draining board. 'For your sake, nobody must know you're here.'

'There's spaghetti in the refrigerator.'

He threw the dishtowel over his shoulder and turned to face her. 'Eva, you will have to leave.'

She had managed to light the cigarette and she now sat down on one of the kitchen chairs. The folds of silk fell between her smooth black legs. 'You're going to throw me out?' The scars of the cigarette burns on her chest were just visible, above the lapel of red silk.

'You can't live here, Eva.' Trotti spoke without taking his eyes from hers.

'You're throwing me out?'

'I never invited you, Eva.'

'Where can I go?'

'You can go back to Uruguay. Back to your son.'

'I've got no money. I need somewhere to stay.'

'You can't stay with me. I am an old man, Eva. I can't help you.'

She sat with her elbows propped on the plastic top of the table. She had dyed her short, woolly hair blond. The roots were black. She mumbled something inaudibly in Spanish. She smoked the cigarette down to the filter.

(Boatti had said, 'No such thing as a free screw. A woman knows if you desire her body. She will always want something in return. She opens her legs, you open your cheque-book. Or worst still, you open your front door, your soul and your life.')

Sitting down at the table opposite her, Trotti placed his hands on the plastic surface.

The parish news sheet – at least eight months old and left there by Pioppi – had been tucked behind the alarm clock on top of the refrigerator. The clock ticked softly.

'Give me a cigarette – I've used all mine.'

'I don't smoke.'

'Christ.'

Trotti fumbled in the knife drawer. There was an old packet of Benson that Nando had forgotten there last Christmas. The packet contained three filter cigarettes, 'You can't stay here, Eva.' Trotti handed her a stale cigarette.

'What am I going to do?'

'I can't help you any more.'

'If I go back to Uruguay, they'll find me.'

'You think they won't find you here?'

She nodded, 'I need you.' She sniffed. Self-pity and Trotti knew she was going to cry. 'They'll come looking for me. They're looking for me now. They'll want their money.'

He shook his head, 'I tried to help you before. You didn't have to come here, Eva.'

'What else was I supposed to do?'

'I got you a passport. And a ticket. You could've returned to your son. You said you'd get a job.'

'In Uruguay?' Eva shook her head.

'You could've gone back. You could've got a job to be with your little boy.'

'He's happy with his grandmother.' She shook her head. She seemed to have forgotten about the unlit cigarette in her mouth. 'Nobody's ever cared for me in Italy the way you cared for me, Piero Trotti.'

Trotti felt angry. 'Why didn't you take the plane back?'

'Don't abandon me now.'

Angry because he was trapped.

'The only person who has ever given without asking for something in return.' Her eyes were red when she looked up. The unlit cigarette trembled between her thick lips. Her face was puffy, the pillow had left creases on her skin.

'I can't help you.'

Eva Beatrix Camargo Mendez, twenty-eight years old from Cerro Largo state, Uruguay, mother and prostitute, started to cry. Without another word, she stood up and pulled Agnese's dressing gown close to her body. To her young, lithe dark body.

She was wiping at a tear with the back of her hand as she went out of the kitchen.

Commissario Trotti, soon to be a grandfather, resented his desires.

Peace of the senses?

NEUROLEPTICS

Wednesday 8 August

The Questura seemed almost empty.

Maserati, now plump from marriage, gave Trotti a hurried, perfunctory wave and disappeared into the newly refurbished bureau of Scientifica, a plastic cup of instant coffee in his hand.

Trotti took the lift.

Inside the lift – with its permanent smell of old cigarette smoke and the hammer and sickle scraped into the aluminium paint – he pressed the button for the third floor. The lift moved slowly. Since the renovation, there had been piped music, muffled and indistinct, from a speaker in the ceiling of the lift.

On the third floor a blonde woman – he could not be sure if it was the same woman as the previous day – gave Trotti a bright, 'Buongiorno' and a smile of glossy red lipstick. Trotti mumbled a reply without looking at the woman and went down the corridor to his office.

It was a new office, smaller than the old one, with a view on to the courtyard and the facing wall of grey pebble-dash. With the renovation of the Questura, Trotti had been shunted here, to the end of the corridor, out of harm's way. Since his was the last door, people rarely dropped by, and when they did, it was because they wanted something.

Persona non grata.

Nobody had thought of renovating the telephone – or even cleaning it.

'Put me through to the director of the Casa Patrizia home in Garlasco.'

He had been given a new desk. There were no cigarette stains or carved graffiti. The surface was bare except for the telephone, a photograph of Pioppi when she was a child and a couple of sweet wrappers that had stuck to the artificial teak for over a week.

(The cleaning women rarely ventured into Trotti's office.)

Trotti sat down, holding the telephone to his ear – the same telephone he had always had, with a ponderous dial that hid most of the grubby green plastic and an ancient sticker advertising Columbus cycle frames.

(Status in the Questura was revealed in the allocation of the telephones. Those in the odour of sanctity had cellular phones and fax. Lesser beings had digital phones and answering machines.

Trotti had to go through the operator.

The chair on the other hand was new. Tubular black metal that had already begun to chip and which had never been either comfortable or aesthetic. Trotti could still remember with nostalgia the greasy canvas armchairs. Like everything else he had grown fond of, the armchairs were to disappear with the renovation. Like Gino and his dog, Principessa.)

Another hot day.

It was not yet half past nine. The pigeons were already cooing among themselves.

'Putting you through, commissario.'

'Pronto.'

'Pronto.'

'Signor Carnecine?'

The voice was doubtful, 'This is Dottor Carnecine.'

'Commissario Trotti speaking.'

'Ah.' Hesitation and the muffling sound as a hand was placed over the mouthpiece. 'I hope you're well, commissario.'

'No worse than yesterday. Tell me, Carnecine, she's on medication, isn't she?'

'Who?'

Trotti did not try to hide his irritation. 'What is Maria Cristina Belloni on? You said that she was allowed out to work in Garlasco. In the town.'

'That is correct.'

'I imagine you put her on some sort of tranquillisers.'

'Tranquillisers?' Carnecine pronounced the word as if meeting it for the first time.

'What is she on?'

A long pause. Trotti stared out of the window, without even focusing his glance on the pebble-dash opposite. 'Carnecine, is the Belloni woman on neuroleptics?'

'We have our doctor here, commissario. I don't have much direct contact with the pa . . . with our guests. I must check with Dr Rivista.'

'Check now.'

'I'm afraid that's not possible.'

'Check now, Carnecine, and phone me back immediately . . . within the half hour.'

'Commissario Trotti . . .'

'Within the half hour – if you want to hang on to your licence. If you don't want the Finanza and the Anti Sofisticazione on your doorstep and the place closed down before lunch time.' Trotti banged the receiver back into its cradle.

Almost immediately, the red light started to blink. Trotti – in the process of unwrapping a sweet – reached out again for the telephone.

'You get around for an old man, Trotti.'

Trotti laughed, 'Maybe I'm not as old as you think, Maiocchi.'

'Do you want to come over?'

'What have you got to offer me?'

'You still believe there may be a connection between the drowned Snoopy woman and the Belloni affair?'

'I haven't yet located the younger sister. She's out of the home and she's probably not been taking her tranquillisers.'

'So you're still working on the Belloni affair, Trotti?'

'The questore has taken me off. I told you that yesterday.'

Maiocchi laughed his casual, youthful laughter. Trotti could imagine him on the other end of the line looking more like a student than a commissario of the Polizia di Stato, an unlit pipe between his teeth, a hand in his long hair. A shame that Maiocchi's marriage was coming apart.

'I've got somebody, Trotti, you ought to see.'

'Who?'

'Luca.'

'Who's Luca?'

'The Luca in question. The boy our drowned Snoopy lover was so in love with. He says he's just got some photos.'

'Photos of the woman?'

'Trotti, I'm driving down with him to Broni in half an hour.'

Trotti clicked his tongue, 'Good of you, Maiocchi – and I appreciate it. I appreciate the collaboration. But this morning I have to be at the autopsy. I think . . .' He looked up.

Without knocking, the questore had entered the small dingy office.

'I'll ring you back, Maiocchi.'

Slowly Trotti replaced the grubby receiver back in its cradle. He stood up and smiled with the sincerity of a Pavlovian reflex, 'Buongiorno, Signor Questore.'

Despite the heat of another hot, dry August day, despite the fact that the city was almost empty and that the Questura was on tick-over, the questore was wearing a linen jacket, a club tie and a soft cotton shirt. His face was closely shaven and he was accompanied by the strong smell of his eau de cologne.

'What is all this shit, Trotti?'

'Shit?' Trotti repeated, taken aback.

His face taut with anger, the questore threw the morning's paper on to Trotti's desk. One of the cellophane sweet wrappings, after a week stuck to the desk, at last floated to the floor.

'Low profile, Trotti?' An angry snort.

PROVINCIA PADANA, 8 AUGUST

Has the mysterious 'Snoopy' really committed suicide by throwing herself into the Po? The Vigili del Fuoco of our city will probably renew their search today. There are many strange aspects to the disappearance of the young woman from Milan, and the possibility of a well-mounted hoax cannot as yet be excluded.

Let us try to reconstruct the story from its beginning.

An anonymous phone call to 113 is made yesterday at dawn. A woman's voice says that she has seen clothes left at the river's edge, in Borgo Genovese, near the statue of the Washerwomen.

A 113 patrol car, immediately despatched to the area, finds nothing.

A few hours later, at about seven-thirty a.m., there is a second anonymous call. At the other end of the line, the same female voice says, 'On a floating pontoon, near the Ponte Coperto, you will find a packet.' The officers of Pronto Soccorso, following the instructions of the mysterious caller, will this time find a corduroy bracelet, a black plastic bag and two small furry Snoopies. There is also a note, 'Luca, I love you'. In the bag is a letter that talks of suicide, contemplated because of an unreciprocated love affair. The letter commences, 'Feelings are not to be thrown away, like a discarded toy . . .'

The letter is not signed.

From the address scribbled on the envelope, the investigators, under the leadership of one of our city's finest detectives, Commissario Gustavo Maiocchi, have been able to identify the young man for whom the tragic letter was intended. The Luca in question is a twenty-five-year-old man resident in Broni (Pv), who was truly stunned to learn that the woman he had met in a Redavalle nightclub and with whom he had a brief adventure, could have made an attempt upon her own life by throwing herself into the waters of our river.

The events recounted by Luca to the officers of the Polizia di Stato are strangely reminiscent of the Hollywood film, *Fatal Attraction*, that not so long ago was being shown on the screens of our cinemas.

'One evening late in July, along with a friend, I met a woman who said her name was Beatrice. She claimed she was from Milan and at first said that she was thirty-one years old. Later, she admitted she was older. She said she was separated from her husband, who was impotent and had been unable to give her any children.'

A story of true love – or simply a midsummer adventure?

After an evening spent dancing, Luca drives Beatrice back to his parents' villa in Broni, and makes the most of his parents' absence.

The following morning he accompanies the young woman to Garlasco, where she intends to catch the train for Milan. A brief kiss on either cheek, a little present of twenty thousand lire – and the adventure seems to be over. Luca leave Broni to join his parents on the Adriatic coast. And in his absence, Beatrice sends him a long letter every day, stating how much she is in love with him. Understandably, Luca, who is engaged to be married, never replies to Beatrice's letters.

'Ten days ago, I had to return to the villa for personal reasons. Beatrice appeared on my doorstep in Broni. She had been weeping, and between her sobs, she told me that she had poisoned herself. Of course I did not believe her. I brought her into the house and I managed to calm her. Later I called a taxi and I paid for her return journey to Milan.'

The following day, Beatrice contacts Luca again, this time by telephone. She tells him that she has to see him because she has something to give him. The rendezvous is at the railway station of our city. Beatrice turns up, carrying a large shoulder bag. She is very pale and appears nervous. Luca explains to her in no uncertain terms that he cannot go on meeting her, and that she must leave him alone. Beatrice, before turning away, mutters under her breath, 'You'll soon be hearing from me, Luca.'

The frogmen of the Vigili del Fuoco will continue their underwater search today.

Commissario Maiocchi will no doubt be aided by Commissario Trotti – the same Commissario Trotti who won national and international fame several years ago in solving the Anna Ermagni kidnapping case and more recently in the discovery of a masonic lodge in our city. Commissario Trotti is also coordinating the enquiry into the tragic murder of Sig.na Rosanna Belloni, the ex-headmistress of the Gerolamo Cardano elementary school (see page 3).

Neither Commissario Maiocchi nor Commissario Trotti was available yesterday for comment.

'Cult of the personality.'

Trotti frowned. He lowered himself back into the chair.

'Low profile – that's what I asked for. And instead you get yourself into the newspaper, you get journalists to write about you, you get . . .'

'What journalists, Signor Questore?'

'How should I know?' The questore was standing by the desk and with the back of his fingers he angrily tapped against the newspaper spread out before Trotti. 'I don't know who wrote this stuff.'

'Neither do I.'

'Cult of the personality, Trotti, cult of the personality – and I won't have it. Not here, not among my men.'

'I know nothing about it.'

'You allowed yourself to be interviewed. You seek the limelight.'

Trotti replied hotly, 'The article says I wasn't available. Nobody interviewed me.'

For several seconds the two men looked at each other. There was the hint of perspiration along the questore's brow. His eyes held Trotti's as he made his, quick, silent calculations. 'You don't seem to understand,' he said, his voice now soft, sounding more aggrieved than angry. He adjusted the silk tie.

'Understand what?'

The questore shook his head in exaggerated disbelief, 'You're not a stupid man.'

Trotti gave a shrug, 'You never know.'

'The older you get, Trotti, the more determined you seem to put your private spanner in the works. A good policeman – I've always said that.' Again the shake of the head, 'Can't you see?'

'See what?'

A glance towards the window and the shadowless wall on the far side of the courtyard, as if the questore were seeking external support. 'This cult of the personality, that's what. Commissario Piero Trotti, the best policeman this city has ever known.'

'Because I'm in the *Provincia padana*?'

The questore allowed himself to relax slightly.

'You don't think you're overreacting, Signor Questore?'

The questore lifted his thigh and sat edgeways on the side of the desk. The linen of his trousers touched the photograph of Pioppi. 'We're a team here, Piero – and we must work as a team.' A second time he tapped the newspaper with his knuckles, 'Perhaps you didn't give an interview. As I understand it, Maiocchi is in charge of the enquiry.'

'I spoke to Maiocchi. That's all. I went down to the river yesterday – but I didn't stay more than ten minutes.'

'You were on the phone to him a moment ago.' The questore gestured towards the telephone.

'We're colleagues. We collaborate.'

'Of course, of course.'

'You don't want me to collaborate?'

'I suspect this silly woman's disappearance is no more than a hoax.'

Trotti was silent.

'I like and respect you, Piero Trotti.' Absentmindedly, the questore started to play with the photograph of Pioppi, running his fingers along the perspex edges. 'But I can't have this.'

'I know nothing about the article, Signor Questore.'

'No stars, no prima donnas. You're not Ceaucescu. We work together as a team. You understand?'

'I've never tried to be a star.'

'You've never tried to be part of the team, either.' He gave a preemptive smile, 'Teamwork doesn't interest you because you despise your colleagues.'

'You've no right to say that.'

'You despise Commissario Merenda – and I genuinely believe you despise me.'

Trotti was silent.

'You don't know how to work in a team – do you, Piero? You don't know and you don't care.'

'You've just told me off for collaborating with Maiocchi.'

'You need Maiocchi's help – you seem to think there may be a connection between the missing woman and the Belloni killing.'

For a long moment, Trotti did not speak. There was silence in the small office except for the cooing of the pigeons and the faint noises of the somnolent city beyond the Questura.

'I hope you're letting Merenda get on with the Belloni affair.'

'I've never interfered with Merenda.'

'I've already told you to drop the Belloni killing. And leave Tenente Pisanelli alone.'

'Rosanna Belloni was a friend.'

'You let friendship cloud your judgement.'

'I liked Rosanna Belloni – she once helped me in an enquiry.'

'That is irrelevant. You're a policeman, a public servant.'

'I'd like to know who killed her.' Trotti paused, his eyes on the photograph of his daughter at her first communion. 'You have chosen to call me off the case.'

'And I want you staying off. It's best for everybody that way.'

'Best for the killer?'

'Sometimes, Trotti, your arrogance astounds me.'

Trotti held up his hand. 'As you wish.' He kept his eyes on the photograph – it had been taken outside the Duomo at the foot of the Torre Civica. He shrugged his acquiescence. 'I'm a policeman. I obey orders.'

'Orders?' A dry laugh.

'I obey orders – even if it means sitting here doing nothing.'

'Doing nothing, Piero? You think I was born yesterday?'

'I don't think anything.' Somewhere there was the sound of tyres screeching. 'A public servant – I'm not paid to think.'

'What were you doing last night at the railway station?'

Trotti was silent.

'At the station, Trotti?'

'Who told you I was there?'

'In front of hostile witnesses, fooling around with informers? What have you got to say about that, Piero Trotti? Informers that Narcotici have taken years to build up. What do you think you were doing?' The questore shook his head, 'No, Trotti – perhaps there's no cult of the personality. Maybe it's just the pleasure of stirring shit.'

'As you wish.'

'Whatever your motives, you clearly have no time and no consideration for your colleagues.'

'Signorina Belloni was a friend. I was hoping . . .'

'You merely care for what you want. With your eyes on your goal, you fail to see the obstacles. And you fail to see all the people whose feet you trample on.'

A pigeon cooed noisily.

'A holiday, Trotti. You've got a villa on Como.'

'On Lake Garda, Signor Questore.'

'I want you to take a holiday. It's nearly Ferragosto. Take a holiday – go up to the lake. At Gardesana, isn't it? Go with your wife and your daughter.'

'I don't feel the need for a rest.'

'I want you out of the Questura for a couple of weeks. A rest. Go to Gardesana, Trotti, and perhaps you can get things into perspective.'

'My wife is in America, Signor Questore. You know that Pioppi is in Bologna and expecting a child any day.' Trotti could hear the rising anger in his voice and there was little he could do to control it. 'Just say you want me out of your hair, out of your Questura. You don't want me on the Belloni case.'

'You take time to understand.'

'I'm a policeman, I've got to be doing something.' Trotti banged the table with the flat of his hand, 'Do you really just want me to sit around, collecting my salary?'

The questore raised an eyebrow. 'Ah.' He slid his thigh from the table.

Trotti ran his tongue along the edge of his dry lip, 'Twiddle my thumbs and wait for my retirement?'

'A rest, Piero Trotti, and then in September we can have a long chat about your future.'

NAZIONALI

'Where are you going, Trotti?'

'The hospital.'

'I'll give you a lift.' Gabbiani leaned across the front seat towards the handle of the passenger door of the grey Innocenti. 'I can see you're in a foul mood.' Gabbiani took a carton of Nazionali cigarettes and threw it casually on to the back seat. 'Try smiling.'

Trotti climbed into the car beside him.

Trotti had a mathematical turn of mind, neat and rigorous when possible. He liked order and he liked to group things into categories. In particular, he liked to be able to categorise people. For Piero Trotti there was family, there were those people he liked, those towards whom he was indifferent and there were those people he disliked.

(With age, when he should have been growing more tolerant, Trotti found that the category of people he disliked increased daily.)

'I didn't know you were in the city, Gabbiani.'

Gabbiani was one of those rare people that Trotti could not place. Trotti's fifth category.

Trotti repeated, 'I thought you were on holiday.'

'I am on holiday, Trotti.'

Physically, he was handsome. Dark hair that had kept the lustre of youth, a regular face and a generous mouth. Grey, intelligent eyes, with long, dark eyelashes. Gabbiani dressed more like a big city journalist – corduroys and a checked shirt, good quality casual shoes – than a provincial policeman.

There were frequent rumours about Gabbiani, head of the Questura's Narcotici.

Personable, intelligent and efficient, he had been with Narcotici for two years after several years spent in Geneva, apparently with Interpol. Gabbiani was generally believed to be doing good work. It had been his idea to liaise with the university health service – on the assumption that prevention is better than cure – to inform the student population of the dangers of drugs and drug addiction. And for those addicts wanting to throw the habit, he had introduced a blue (toll-free) telephone line.

For a university city, the drug-related AIDS and hepatitis rates were impressively low. On several occasions, Gabbiani's photograph had appeared in the local paper.

'Cult of the personality.'

'I beg your pardon, Trotti.'

'The questore has just accused me of indulging in a cult of the personality.'

'The questore prefers us to work as a team. That way we share the workload. And he gets all the kudos – and his photograph in the paper.'

Trotti shook his head and settled into the low bucketseat of the car as Gabbiani took the Innocenti over the cobbles, heading out of the city centre, away from the white signs of the pedestrian zone. 'He wants me out of the way – and it's still too early for him to pension me off.'

'He wants everybody who's not a Socialist out of the way.'

'What?'

'The questore got where he is because he's a good Craxi man. But now that the Socialists are out of government, he's very sensitive. We live in a partitocrazia, Trotti – you seem to forget that. Rule by political party. And at the present moment, the poor questore finds that he's not on the winning team. The Socialists are out of power in Rome – and here, the city's being run by the Christian Democrats and the Communists. He's scared. And he doesn't like to see potential rivals jockeying for his place.'

'I'm not a rival.'

'You're not anything, Piero.' Gabbiani laughed, 'You've never understood power politics – too honest. Too honest for the Polizia di Stato.'

The air was windless and already very hot.

'Why the hospital, Piero?'

'Autopsy.'

The rumours about Gabbiani – Trotti had heard them from various sources. He did not pay them much attention. Like most policemen, Trotti was cynical, believing very little until he had been able to check for himself. 'You're like St Thomas,' Magagna used to say, 'You'd insist on seeing Christ's scars – and then you would demand a report from Scientifica.' Trotti knew about professional jealousies within the Questura.

Gabbiani drove well, one hand on the wheel, two fingers on the gear lever. 'The Belloni affair?'

Trotti turned to look at Gabbiani, 'I suppose you're pissed off with me.'

Gabbiani braked, keeping his eyes on the traffic lights. The city was virtually empty for the mid-August holidays, but the lights changed with a maddening slowness. 'Too professional, Trotti, to be pissed off.' A slow, indulgent smile.

'Glad to hear it.'

'I'm not sure I can get excited about my work any more. This isn't Milan or Rome or Naples. Marking time, Trotti. I'm marking time.'

'I wish I still had your youth.'

'You really believe that, Trotti? Being the grand old man of the Questura gives you a lot of advantages.' Gabbiani turned the grey eyes towards him.

'Perhaps that's why the questore wants me out of his hair.'

'I'd like to know why you're getting into mine. Last night you were on my turf. Perhaps you'd like to tell me why.'

'You were waiting for me outside the Questura?'

'We need to talk,' Gabbiani nodded.

'Nice of you to give me a lift.'

'What exactly did you think you were doing last night, Piero Trotti?'

'I thought you were on holiday, Gabbiani.'

Gabbiani raised an eyebrow, 'And so you move in on my informers?'

'I need any information I can get.'

'Why?'

'Merenda is on the Belloni case – and the questore wants me to go on holiday.'

'Then go on holiday, Trotti.' A dry laugh, 'You've got bags under your eyes, you haven't been sleeping and your shirt is crumpled.'

Trotti lowered the anti-glare screen and glanced at his reflection in the small mirror. His face looked back at him – a thin face, a narrow nose and closely set eyes. His dark hair oiled and no longer as thick as it once was. White hair at the temples, thin creases running down his cheeks.

'Why do you care so much, Trotti?'

'Care?'

'About everything. You carry this city on your shoulders.'

'What else have I got?' Trotti laughed.

'What do you care about the Belloni killing?'

'Rosanna Belloni was a friend.'

'You still believe in friendship?' Gabbiani gave a tight smile, 'And so you piss in my garden? You elbow in on my informers?' The lights turned to green and with an unwarranted surge, the car moved forward, a squeak of tyres and a sharp wrenching at Trotti's neck. Despite Gabbiani's relaxed manner, the knuckles on the wheel were white.

'I was told you were in Switzerland.'

(In town, Gabbiani ran around in his little Innocenti.

The rumours claimed that he had a big, German car that he kept up in the hills, along with a luxurious villa at Pietragavina. The rumours claimed that once out of the Questura, Gabbiani had a standard of living that could not come out of a policeman's salary.)

'You could have spoken with di Bono or Fattori.'

'Gabbiani – I'm sorry.'

'You're not sorry, Trotti. You're never sorry.'

'Why d'you say that?'

'You're not impulsive. Before doing anything, you carefully weigh up all the pros and cons.'

'I didn't know you were in town, Gabbiani.' A pause, 'I need help.'

'You need a rest.' A brief, mocking glance at Trotti that was not devoid of genuine affection, 'You're obsessive, Trotti – obsessive about something that's really not important. The Belloni woman's dead – you're not going to bring her back to life. You can forget about friendship, think about yourself. Let Merenda get on with it, let him sweat out the Ferragosto. Think about your own life – enjoy life, while you've still got your health. Forget Rosanna Belloni.'

'By putting a bit of pressure on a dealer . . .'

'Carpe diem.'

'The African?'

'Seize the day – enjoy yourself. We're all getting old.'

'The dealer, Beltoni . . .'

Gabbiani banged the steering wheel in a sudden outburst of exasperation, 'For God's sake, Trotti, leave the poor bastard alone. You know what Beltoni is like? You cause a commotion, you get the whores screaming at you. Beltoni is a poor shit – an eternal student who's never been able to move on. And who hasn't got the balls to give himself the final overdose.'

'He has his contacts in the city.'

'Beltoni?' Gabbiani had regained his calm. He said softly, 'Beltoni is a poor shit, Trotti. But you can cause him trouble. Leave him alone.'

'It's possible that Rosanna Belloni was murdered by her sister. I haven't been able to locate Maria Cristina Belloni, but it's likely that she's schizophrenic. She's been out of her home for nearly three weeks.'

'What home?'

'In Garlasco – Casa Patrizia.'

Gabbiani raised an eyebrow.

'It's possible that Maria Cristina wanted uppers – and that she needed money.'

They went along viale dell'Indipendenza, following the old branch railway line that had been cut into the ground behind the Sforzesco castle. With his left hand resting on the steering wheel, Gabbiani changed gear smoothly.

Trotti asked, 'What did you tell the questore, Gabbiani?'

'Tell the questore?'

'It's not every day we see you hanging around the Questura.'

'It was you, Trotti, that I was looking for.'

'What did you tell the questore?'

'You think I'd tell that pompous card-carrying Socialist bastard from Friuli that you were shitting on my informers?'

'How else did he know?'

'He knew that you'd been pestering Beltoni?'

Trotti nodded and Gabbiani laughed.

Trotti said, 'Somebody must have told him – and it wouldn't have been the whores.'

The smile on Gabbiani's face disappeared. 'What the hell did you want with Beltoni?'

'Somebody wanting money fast, somebody in need of ready cash.

It's possible that money was the motive behind Belloni's death and . . .'

'You believe that?'

'People who need money fast are the sort of people who have an expensive habit to pay for.'

Gabbiani brought the car to a standstill outside the hospital. 'Terminus.' He leaned backwards to the back seat, 'You'd care for a packet of Nazionali's, Trotti? A present from Customs.'

Trotti shook his head, 'I've smoked three cigarettes in the last twelve years.'

'Doubt if you've been laid much more, either.'

Trotti fumbled with the door handle. He had to pull himself out of the low seat. 'Think what you like.'

'Leave Beltoni alone. If you need information, come to me.' Gabbiani took his hand from the steering wheel and held up a finger, 'It's just possible that I may know what you need.'

'Meaning?'

Gabbiani laughed and the Innocenti pulled out into the traffic.

MARYLAND

'Bottone makes my flesh creep.'

The sensation of heaviness in his belly had been getting worse. Trotti felt angry and unhappy. Gabbiani – and the questore – were right: he needed a holiday.

Right now he needed a coffee.

'Been waiting long?'

Boatti had parked his car at the back of the hospital, in the small piazza between the psychiatry ward and the morgue. Folly and death.

The journalist's pale face was pinched. He held the small dictating machine in his hand; he stood in the shade of a plane tree.

Already browning leaves had started to fall to the ground. Trotti ran a hand along his forehead and wished for the coolness of autumn – rain along the Po.

'A quarter of an hour.'

'Where's Pisanelli?'

Boatti shrugged. He wore a white shirt, unbuttoned to reveal hair on a fleshy, pale chest, and a pair of jeans that had been ironed with a crease. Saxone loafers.

Trotti clicked his tongue in irritation.

Boatti grinned, 'My first autopsy.'

'Hope you enjoy it.'

'You don't sound excited, Trotti.'

'Dr Bottone is a zombie.'

'He's supposed to do a good job.'

'That's how he's become a zombie.'

Boatti reassured himself with forced laughter.

They stepped through the sliding doors of the main entrance, where they were met by the cold, antiseptic smell of the building. Trotti glanced at Boatti and silently wished that Pisanelli was with him. 'The article in the *Provincia* – did you write it, Boatti?'

'What article?'

'Beatrice, the missing woman – and the enquiry being made by Maiocchi and Trotti.'

Boatti shook his head, 'I never got to talk to Commissario Maiocchi – I was having lunch with you.' He buttoned his shirt. 'Remember? Slow food?'

The two men went down the three flights of stairs into the basement. Their shoes were almost silent on the rubber floor. Boatti walked briskly, slightly in front of Trotti, as if to convince himself that standing in on an autopsy was just another journalistic task.

'I'd never seen somebody who'd been murdered,' Boatti said, trying to keep a lightness in his voice. 'Before Rosanna.'

'I've seen too many.'

'It'll soon be over, commissario, won't it?' Boatti grinned, 'How long does an autopsy last?'

Trotti brushed past him. 'Depends on how sharp the blades are.' Not bothering to knock, he pushed open the doors of the morgue, letting the rubber barriers swish against the floor.

'Ah, commissario.'

Dr Bottone stood up as Trotti entered the room. Light twinkled in the steel frames of his round glasses. He held out his hand which Trotti shook without enthusiasm. The hand was cold and dry. Dr Bottone smelt of formaldehyde and coffee.

Trotti looked at the row of empty chairs, 'Commissario Merenda's not here?'

It was a small, windowless laboratory. Most of the floor space was taken up by two tables, made of dull, glinting steel, each with a perforated surface. At the end of each table was a sink. Above each table hung a stainless basin attached to a weighing scale.

Trotti could feel his belly lurching, almost out of control. Despite the cool air, sweat continued to trickle down his back.

Overhead, the banks of neon lights gave off a shadowless whiteness. Dr Bottone had not yet switched on the long-armed directional lamp that was set directly above the steel tables.

Dr Bottone smiled his thin smile. 'How is the little girl?'

'Little girl?'

'Your daughter, Signor Commissario.'

'Little girl? Pioppi's nearly thirty years old and she's expecting a child any day. Perhaps even today.'

'You see?'

Trotti shook his head, 'See what?'

'You were always too worried about her. Your daughter's a healthy girl – a healthy woman. I told you, commissario, that there's a limit to what a parent can do for his child.' He turned his narrow head towards Boatti.

Trotti gestured, 'Signor Boatti is a journalist – and a friend. He's working on a book about police work.'

'How exciting,' Dr Bottone remarked. 'Glad to have you along.' Behind the round glasses, the eyes carefully scrutinised the journalist. 'Very glad,' Dr Bottone showed a thin smile.

Trotti released a repressed sigh, 'Ready when you are, Dr Bottone.'

The doctor nudged at the rim of his glasses, 'We'll be needing a formal recognition of the body.'

Trotti shook his head, 'I'm just standing in – Merenda's in charge.'

'Then that leaves just Commissario Merenda and whoever he's found to identify the body.' The doctor picked up his mug – ever since a year spent at a university in Maryland, Dr Bottone drank his coffee American style, diluted and tasteless – from where he had placed it on the table. He glanced at his watch. 'I'd like to start in ten minutes.'

'Ten minutes?'

'I hope Merenda can get here by then.'

'Have I got time to make a phone call, doctor?'

The coffee mug carried the word Orioles in blue letters.

'Ten minutes,' Dr Bottone opened and closed the fingers of his left hand twice, 'I don't want to start any later than eleven o'clock. I hope to leave by one o'clock.' He raised his shoulders in humility, 'Even doctors need to get away for the Ferragosto.'

'Ten minutes.'

Leaving Boatti in the chill of the morgue, Trotti hurried through the door and took the stairs two at a time, breathing deeply. Despite the August heat he ran all the way to the hospital entrance.

OLD MORTALITY

The hospital porter was whistling the aria, 'A te, o cara', from *I puritani*. He had his hands in his pockets and stared out at the sparse morning traffic. He had taken off his serge jacket but still wore the peaked cap.

The city was almost empty.

There were a couple of telephones at the main entrance to the hospital but they were both out of order. Trotti ran across the road, relieved to see that the Bar Goliardico had not closed for Ferragosto. He entered the familiar bar. The smell of roasted coffee and lemons reminded him of his colleague Ciuffi. He had never been back since her death.

'A te, o cara.'

Two men, both in the navy blue uniform of the ENEL, were playing on the pintable. One of them wore the company cap on the back of his head and a cigarette hung from his lips. They had placed their toolboxes on the top of the pintable. Electronic beeping and the slightly forced laughter of the men.

Trotti went to the telephone. It was one of the new type, requiring a phone card. He bought a card from a boy behind the counter and pressed it into the slit. Trotti swore under his breath; he had to insert the card three times before the machine recognised the validity of the magnetic strip.

Trotti dialled and waited impatiently.

'Pronto?'

'Signor Beltoni?'

'Who?'

'Signor Beltoni, please.'

'I'm not sure . . .'

'Please. It's urgent.' Trotti ran his hand across his forehead. He was sweating.

There was the sound of footsteps and then muffled movement as the receiver was picked up on the far end of the line. 'Pronto?'

'This is Trotti.'

'Christ, you had no call to beat the shit out of me. I'm bruised, Trotti – covered in bruises.'

'Beltoni, ring me back on this number. Use an outside line – ring me back straight away on 34 38 25. I'm in a hurry.'

'I'm not dressed yet.'

'Ring me back immediately, Beltoni.'

Trotti hung up and went to the bar. Outside, in the almost deserted streets, the yellow buses rumbled past the Policlinico. The teenage barman prepared an espresso coffee; Trotti put three spoonfuls of sugar into the cup, and then drank, feeling the scalding liquid course down his throat.

He was spooning the brown, part dissolved sugar into his mouth when the phone rang. Leaving the cup on the zinc bar, he picked up the receiver.

'Beltoni, I'm sorry about last night.'

'There was no need to beat me up.'

'It was your idea to kick out at Pisanelli.'

'That's what you wanted.'

'Overreacting, Beltoni.' Trotti paused, 'Are you hurt?'

'Who was the other man in the car?'

'A journalist – he's writing a book. Pisanelli and I wanted to give him a bit of excitement. Bit of local colour.'

'There was no call to thump me in the back. If he wants colour, I can show him the bruises.'

'Where the hell d'you get that money from, Beltoni?'

'It's not my money.'

'Then what were you doing with it – a million lire?'

'Why does it matter?'

'You're a free man just as long as you're useful to me.'

'Commissario, you once did me a favour. I'm grateful. But I don't work for you.'

'Be careful, Beltoni, or you go inside.' Trotti laughed humourlessly. 'You told Commissario Gabbiani?'

'I don't work for you, Trotti, and there's nothing you can do to me. I've paid my way. I'm protected.'

'Protected just so long as it suits me, Beltoni.' Trotti did not hide his impatience. 'Did you tell Gabbiani that Pisanelli and I asked you a few questions?'

'That's what you told me to do, isn't it?'

'When?'

'I left a message on his answering machine.'

'What time, Beltoni?'

'What's wrong with you, Trotti, for Christ's sake? You're getting old.'

'When did you phone Commissario Gabbiani?'

A slight hesitation, 'Before crawling into bed. That's what you told me to do.'

'You told no one else?'

'After the way your friend Pisanelli knocked me about, I wanted to lie down in peace. I just want to be left alone. I just hope that my balls are going to grow back into place.'

'The questore knows.'

'You can tell Pisanelli to start wearing steel Y-fronts, Trotti.'

'How did the questore know that I was at the Bar Vittorio Emmanuele?'

'Sooner or later, I'm going to rip Pisanelli's balls off.'

'You didn't inform the questore?'

'I was in bed until five minutes ago.'

'How did the questore know?'

'Perhaps you ought to be a bit more discreet, commissario, when you beat law-abiding citizens up in the middle of the street.'

Trotti glanced at his watch, 'I want to see you.'

'I'm busy.'

'At twelve-thirty. In the small bar opposite your place. The dopolavoro.'

'Leave me alone, Trotti.'

'Twelve-thirty – that gives you over an hour to get washed and cleaned. You smell like a goat.' Trotti hung up. He was still sweating.

POISON

'Thank God,' Trotti said under his breath, catching sight of Pisanelli, huddled in his suede jacket and sitting beside Boatti.

Merenda, too, had arrived, accompanied by Signorina Amadeo, the young procuratore from Rome. Both nodded as Trotti entered the chill air of the morgue. The woman wore a silk scarf in red, white and green. Her pretty face was pale. Pearl earrings.

'Please sit down.' Dr Bottone gestured to a spare seat in the row of hard chairs placed against the walls of glazed tiling. 'You'd like some coffee, Commissario Trotti? Or perhaps something a bit stronger? You look as if you've got a cold coming on.'

'Just had a coffee, thanks.' Trotti glanced at his watch, 'It is nearly five minutes past eleven . . .'

'I've some cognac in my drawer. For medicinal purposes, you understand.' Bottone glanced at Merenda and winked awkwardly.

There was another man. He was wearing a grey suit, a blue shirt and a bow tie.

'You know Signor Belloni?'

Trotti frowned. The man stood up and holding out his hand, shook Trotti's. He gave a small, sad smile. 'Rosanna's uncle,' he said quietly and sat down again. He was well groomed, with thick white hair and long, thin fingers. The skin of his face was wrinkled from too much exposure to the sun. Signor Belloni was about sixty-five years old and looked healthy. He had pale eyelashes.

Trotti turned back to Bottone, 'What have you been able to find out about Signorina Belloni?' He crossed his arms against his chest.

Bottone opened the bottom drawer of a filing cabinet and took out an opaque medicine bottle. It was half-full. The label bore the legend, 'Poison'. Crossbones and skull. 'You're sure you wouldn't . . .?'

'Neither Pisanelli nor I is thirsty,' Trotti said.

'Not for your thirst, commissario.' He held up a finger.

Boatti gave Dr Bottone a crooked smile.

'Tell me what you've found out about the body.'

'Signorina Belloni?' Bottone poured the cognac into a plastic cup which he held out for Boatti. He then turned around, and pulled a wooden stool towards him. He was wearing loose cotton trousers and white leather and wood clogs. Because of the chill air, he also wore a cardigan. His white lab coat and cap hung from a hook on the back of the corridor door. Dr Bottone had a thin, intelligent face. His skin was waxy, and was pulled tight across the bones of his skull.

Boatti drank in one gulp, throwing his head back. He smiled; tears appeared at the corners of his eyes.

Trotti could feel the sweat beneath his shirt drying in the cold air, 'You now have established time of death?'

'You will recall that I was not called to the scene of the crime.' Bottone sounded slightly aggrieved, 'I have Anselmi's report to go on.'

'And?'

'As usual, Dr Anselmi has done a professional job.' Bottone spoke in the direction of the young procuratore, 'Anal or vaginal reading of body temperature is subtracted from the normal body heat of 37 degrees centigrade. You then divide that by one point five and you get a rough idea of the number of hours the person's been dead. Obviously, it's rough and ready – and once the body's reached the environmental heat, there's not much you can learn.'

'Meaning?'

'Meaning that you have to work with other parameters.'

'Rigor mortis?'

'Anselmi put the time of death at somewhere between eleven

o'clock on Saturday night and late Sunday afternoon. This would be reasonable. I didn't get to see the woman until several hours after Anselmi, when she was brought in here.' He gestured with his thumb towards the grey metal door in the far wall, and beyond it to the mortuary lockers. 'There were still slight signs of rigor mortis. As you know, when the weather is warm – as it has been for the last few days – the process of rigor mortis is speeded up.'

Trotti nodded his head.

'Anselmi seems to have taken the heat factor into consideration. All things considered, I'd go along with Anselmi's theory.'

'Sometime during the day of Sunday?'

Dr Bottone said, 'Saturday or Sunday up to about nine o'clock.'

'And lividity?'

An irritated smile, 'Always in a hurry, commissario.'

'I imagine you've had time to look at the body.'

Dr Bottone stood up and went to the wall-phone. 'Bring me Number 2, Leopoldi. I'll be starting the autopsy in five minutes.' As he placed the receiver back in its cradle, he said over his shoulder, 'Post-mortem lividity would appear to coincide with the photos I have.'

'Indicating?'

'The body, once it fell face down to the ground, was not moved.'

Trotti glanced at Merenda who had got up and who now stood with his hip against a wall table, near a camera. The camera had elongated bellows and was attached to a vertical steel rod. Merenda stood with his arms crossed, a notebook in one hand, a ballpoint pen in the other. Like Trotti, he was not dressed for the chill air of the laboratory. His face had acquired a yellowish tinge in the bright neon light.

Merenda caught Trotti's glance. The glint of his teeth, 'Don't quite see why you're sitting in on this, Piero.' His voice was flat. 'You or Tenente Pisanelli. Since when has Pisanelli been working for you?'

'Signorina Belloni was a friend of the family.'

Merenda nodded thoughtfully.

Dr Bottone raised his shoulders, 'I have no more than glanced at the cadaver. In a few minutes, while taking a much closer look, it'll . . .'

'In your opinion, once the body fell to the ground, it remained there until it was discovered by Signor Boatti?'

The woman procuratore, who until now had not moved, turned her head and looked at Boatti.

'Any opinion I may have, Commissario Trotti, is based on little more than a superficial glance. However, I can say . . .'

Dr Bottone was interrupted by the arrival of a young assistant. He wore a white lab coat that set off the dark skin and regular features of the boyish face. The assistant walked with a spring in his step. He shook hands with Trotti, Pisanelli, Commissario Merenda, Signor Belloni and Boatti. He nodded cheerfully towards the woman, a twinkle in his eye. He then crossed the room and opened the door to the morgue.

Dr Bottone went to the sink and scrubbed his hands before putting on his white coat and the round cap.

Trotti glanced through the open door of the morgue, down the long walls of stainless steel lockers. He bit his lip. He could feel the sweet coffee lying on his belly.

'Sure you don't care for some medicine? This isn't the first autopsy you've sat in on . . . a little cognac can go a long way in soothing the nerves.'

'I'll stick to my aniseed sweets.'

Each locker was large enough to contain a wheeled stretcher.

In a matter-of-fact voice, Bottone said, 'Shouldn't take more than forty minutes. I don't envisage any real difficulties. Perhaps you'd all like to put on a mask now.'

Pisanelli, without taking his eyes off the doctor, whispered, 'Smug bastard', and Trotti winced at the smell of cognac on his breath.

'I could do with one of your cigarettes, Pisanelli.'

Merenda looked up from his notebook, 'You already have an idea of how she was killed, dottore?'

'Cause of death?' Dr Bottone raised an eyebrow, and Trotti was reminded of the day when Bottone had come down to the beach at the Lido to identify a piece of corpse that had washed ashore. Nearly twelve years ago.

Bottone laughed a dry little laugh and then turned as Leopoldi, the assistant, sprightly and grinning, wheeled the stretcher into the laboratory.

Dr Bottone rolled a fresh pair of plastic gloves over his long, dry fingers. He stretched his arms like a pianist before a concert.

'I regret not having been able to get down to San Teodoro. The amount of blood spilt can tell you a lot about the nature and the timing of a wound.' He turned back to face Trotti. He took the coffee percolator in a gloved hand. 'But I've got the photos from Scientifica. Surprised, perhaps, that there wasn't more blood, given the nature of the wounds. Are you sure you wouldn't like something to drink?'

Trotti shook his head.

The laboratory assistant shifted the body – still covered with a sheet – on to the autopsy table. Bottone switched on the overhead light. With the other hand, he filled his Orioles mug with coffee. He drank, his eyes hidden by the glint of his glasses. 'Poor thing.'

Leopoldi opened the evidence case and placed the seven polaroid photographs of the body as it lay on the floor in the flat at San Teodoro. He ordered them in two neat rows on the table top where Dr Bottone could refer to them.

Trotti noted that Boatti's nose appeared pinched. The laboratory seemed to get even more chill.

Trotti sneezed.

Leopoldi set out a series of wooden spatulas, plastic jars, glass slides.

'Poor thing,' Dr Bottone repeated flatly. He looked down at the grey feet while testing the microphone of his recorder.

The body was no longer human, Trotti told himself; it was dead and the inert limbs that poked from beneath the thin sheet had nothing to do with the woman who had once been alive and well.

Coffee flavoured bile caught at the back of his throat.

Dr Bottone finished his cup of coffee with a purposeful click of his tongue. He checked the label attached to the big toe of the cadaver. Then he turned on the cassette-recorder, 'Dr Davide Bottone, forensic doctor at the Policlinico of this city, medical examiner under oath for the Polizia di Stato, in the presence of Signorina Amadeo, procuratore della Repubblica, the Commissarii Merenda and Trotti and the officer . . .'

'Tenente Pisanelli,' Pisanelli said.

Leopoldi was carrying a circular saw. The teeth of the blade were sharp and spotless. He smiled brightly as he plugged the lead into the heavy duty socket.

Bottone pulled back the sheet.

'A woman, believed to be Signorina Belloni, Rosanna, approximately forty to forty-five years of age, height one metre sixty, weight sixty-three kilos.'

Trotti had got to his feet.

Dr Bottone switched off the recorder and turned to Signor Belloni. A thin smile. 'Signor Belloni, in the presence of the procuratore, I must ask you to step forward. As Signorina Belloni's closest relative in this city, I must ask you to identify the corpse.' He held out his hand and gestured to Signor Belloni to approach. 'Can you identify this corpse as that of Signorina Rosanna Belloni of Piazza San Teodoro in this city?'

The blood had been carefully washed from the bruised and battered face. The hair had been pulled back with an elastic band.

The old man, leaning on Bottone's arm, peered forward. The patrician features were pale and taut. The blond eyelashes batted nervously in the harsh white light.

'Signor Belloni, is this your niece?'

The man did not move. He stared down unhappily at the inert, swollen jaw.

'Is this the body of your niece, Signorina Rosanna Belloni?'

He turned and glanced at the young procuratore. Then at Merenda.

'Please identify the corpse.'

He mumbled something.

'I beg your pardon.'

'It is my niece,' the old man said, a hand going to his bow tie. 'This corpse was once my niece – but it was never Rosanna. My niece, but no, not Rosanna.'

GERANIUMS

'Then where the hell is Rosanna Belloni?'

They hurriedly got into the Lancia and Pisanelli drove. The heat was almost pleasant after the chill of the morgue.

'We should've waited,' Pisanelli said.

'No need,' Trotti shook his head. He was smiling – a rictus that revealed neither pain nor pleasure. 'I'll get a synopsis from Bottone later.'

'Bottone's going on holiday.'

Although the city was almost empty, there was a jam where Strada Nuova crossed Corso Mazzini. Pisanelli cursed. 'Why don't they go on holiday, instead of cluttering up the city?' He angrily placed the revolving beacon on the roof and switched on the siren.

'The vigili are rounding up the "vu comprà",' Boatti remarked. 'The mayor wants to send them back to Africa while there's nobody in the city. Our Christian Democrat mayor.'

'The sooner the better.' Pisanelli put the car into reverse. 'Damned Africans.' He pulled hard on the steering wheel and turned down one of the side streets beside the university. A couple of oncoming cars drew to one side, stopping in the shade of the ochre buildings, beneath the geranium boxes.

'You must know where she went, Boatti.'

'I thought Rosanna was in Milan, commissario.'

'She can't just vanish.'

'Rosanna never told me she was going away.'

Trotti unwrapped a sweet, 'You'd better give me the Milan phone number.'

'I've already told you I phoned her sister in Milan the night of the murder.'

'Night of the murder?'

'The night I found the corpse. Monday night – the first thing I did after alerting the police.'

'Why?' Trotti turned in his seat.

Boatti shrugged, 'I phoned the sister in Milan and the brother in Foggia – don't ask me why. Because it was the right thing to do.'

'Why isn't the sister at the autopsy?'

'Step-sister – she's not a blood relation.' Boatti paused, 'Listen, Trotti, if Rosanna had been in Milan staying with her step-sister, you don't think the woman would've told me? And you don't think she'd've told me if she thought Rosanna had gone on holiday?'

'Then where the hell is Rosanna Belloni?'

Boatti shrugged.

'Where the hell has she gone?'

Instead of answering, Boatti spoke softly into the hand-held recorder.

Pisanelli at the wheel of the Lancia Delta cut across Piazza Vittoria and along Via Lanfranco. Vanizza's, the furriers, was open, hoping no doubt for out-of-town customers attracted by an advertising campaign on television – elegant women, the covered bridge and Alain Delon.

Many of the bars were closed for the Ferragosto.

'The brother in Foggia,' Pisanelli said, glancing over his shoulder. 'What did he say?'

Boatti switched the machine off. 'What?'

'When you phoned the brother in Foggia, what did he say?'

Boatti shook his head, 'No reply – I imagine he's on holiday.'

'And Rosanna never told you she was going away?'

'It's rare for me to stay in the city during August.'

'It wasn't the first time she'd gone on holiday?'

'Normally when Rosanna goes away, she lets her post pile up – not that she has much post. *Famiglia Cristiana* . . . That sort of thing. Letters from the bank. And she had some shares, too.'

Trotti asked, 'You know where she got the Jehovah's Witness stuff from?'

'I always thought she was a practising Catholic.' Boatti shrugged, then spoke to Pisanelli, 'Rosanna didn't say anything about going away – other than that she was thinking of taking Maria Cristina somewhere. But not for Ferragosto.' He shook his head, 'I assumed Rosanna was in Milan for a long weekend.'

'In mid-August?'

Again Boatti shrugged.

'In the past where'd she go in August?'

'Last year she spent ten days in Foggia – she took her brother's children somewhere in the Gargano.'

'Then I think we'd better phone her brother again,' Pisanelli said. 'Don't you, commissario?'

Trotti was staring through the car window. He did not speak.

'A few years ago she went to Ravenna. But that was before. She stayed with a colleague who had a small pensione there.'

'In Ravenna?'

'About two or three years ago.' Boatti paused to sigh, 'I remember Rosanna sending me a postcard from Emilia. I don't know if she's ever been back.'

The siren echoed emptily off the high walls of the city.

'You know where Rosanna stayed?' Trotti turned to look at him.

'In Ravenna?' A shrug, 'I never paid much attention.'

'Why not, Boatti?'

'We – my wife and the children – don't normally stay here in August. Rosanna was always back before us.'

'She went to the same place? A hotel?'

Boatti shrugged. 'Chiesa or Chiesi – a name like that. A spinster like Rosanna, who had once taught in the same school.' He shook his head unhappily, 'I really don't remember.'

They reached San Michele and Trotti got out of the car before Pisanelli has stopped. He half walked, half ran into the courtyard and up the marble steps, two at a time, to the large wooden door. He rang insistently on the polished brass bell.

It was midday.

The maid in uniform took her time before opening.

'Signora Isella?' Trotti said, pushing past the woman.

The maid held her hand to her chest, 'The signora has left.'

'What?'

'For the Dolomites – she left early this morning. She's going to stay with her son and the grandchildren.'

Outside, the police siren on the car roof died a mournful death.

Trotti was sweating, 'Damn it.' He turned, rubbing the side of his head. 'Damn it.'

'You are the policeman gentleman who was here yesterday?'

He nodded, his attention elsewhere. 'Damn.' Through the open front door, Trotti could see Boatti coming ponderously up the marble stairs. He turned back to the maid, 'You've got the phone number, signorina?'

'Phone number?'

'Where Signora Isella is staying.'

The woman – she had a simple, plain face beneath the white maid's hat – shook her head. 'I'm leaving for home tonight.' She added with a certain pride, 'I live at Mirandolo Po.'

'I want to contact Signora Isella. How can I phone her?'

The maid shrugged.

'She has an address book?' Trotti looked at the woman for an instant and then brushing unceremoniously past her headed towards the room where he and Boatti had taken tea the previous day.

'The signora takes everything with her.'

'How was she going to the Dolomites?'

A frown.

Trotti repeated the question, 'How's Signora Isella getting to the Dolomites?'

'She's driving up with her son.'

Trotti turned on the flat Ticino switch. The concealed lighting flickered before coming on, revealing the cherubim and seraphim caught on the ceiling in their silent, eternal quest for carnal satisfaction. 'Where's her writing stuff?'

The maid made an unhappy gesture towards a Venetian desk, then stepping towards it, turned on the shaded lamp.

Standing on the desk was a burnished iron frame, containing several photographs. Some were old, and even beneath the glass it was possible to see that the yellowed images had cracked with age. One of the photographs, slightly larger than the others, more recent, and in colour, showed three women. One was Signorina Isella. Rosanna was in the middle. Trotti did not recognise the third, younger woman.

'Signorina,' Trotti tapped the photograph, without glancing at Boatti, who had now entered the room, 'would you happen to know where Signorina Rosanna Belloni spends her holidays?'

'Signorina Belloni who is dead?'

Trotti touched the back of the woman's hand. It was very cold, 'Perhaps Rosanna Belloni is not dead after all.'

'Not dead?' She put her hand to her throat, 'Oh.'

'Try to remember, signorina.'

'I didn't know her very well – but she was a very nice person. When I heard that she had been murdered . . .'

'Commissario!'

Trotti turned. The maid turned, now both her hands at her throat.

'Commissario!' Pisanelli stood in the doorway, grinning sheepishly. 'A postcard in Signora Isella's letterbox downstairs.' He held out his hand, pleased with himself. 'It would appear to be from your friend Rosanna Belloni.'

DELTA

('The line between land and water is normally a clear line, drawn by sea coasts, by river banks and by the edges of lakes – the same line that defines the limits of man's existence. The Po Delta is, however, quite different. Here the meeting place of land and water is mobile, unstable. The river, carrying the detritus of North Italy, robs the sea, extending the land, while at the same time, allowing the tea-coloured waters to penetrate inland. Neither land nor sea, a no-man's-land of the two competing elements.'

Rosanna Belloni had written the postcard on 4 August, in her neat, schoolmistress handwriting and sent it to Signora Isella. There was a picture of a man fishing in a delta boat, and on the other side, the postmark was Comacchio, dated 4 August.

There was also a postscript, 'I am very happy – very happy.'

'She's alive,' Pisanelli had said triumphantly, holding the postcard delicately on the palm of his hand, like a holy relic.

There was a careful signature, but no written address.

'At least, she was in the Delta on 4 August.')

Pisanelli had taken a Ferrara telephone directory from the battered, jumbled ranks of Italian directories that lined the far wall and was now working his way through the hotels in alphabetical order.

He stood in the number six cabin, the door open and his head bent forward as he consulted the yellow pages or spoke into the phone.

From time to time he called out to the woman behind the counter, 'Another line, signora.'

Boatti was calling the smaller towns – Lido di Nazioni, Porto Garibaldi.

Trotti had taken the Rovigo and Ravenna directories, but after making several brief calls, had given up. The small print tired his eyes. He needed his glasses.

Rosanna was alive.

Trotti had managed to speak to the Questura in Chioggia, Rovigo, Ferrara and Ravenna. It was now time to get back to the office and hope for a phone call.

Not that it really mattered. It would not take a very long time for Rosanna to turn up. Mistaken identity, thank God. Rosanna was alive and a sense of warmth had worked its way into the pit of Trotti's belly.

(Trotti had almost forgotten about the dead body, the identification attached to the big toe and the whine of the electric saw in the morgue.)

No further need to worry.

Piero Trotti had done his duty. His duty by an old friend, by a woman whom, in his begrudging, surly way, he had admired. Perhaps even loved.

Piero Trotti could now take a holiday, he could drive down to Bologna. Await the arrival of his grandson.

Although tired, Trotti felt light-headed and very hungry.

It was lunchtime and the telephone office of the SIP was nearly empty. It had been entirely refurbished, in the ubiquitous Italo-Californian style – plastic, brass and marble, much like the Questura. There was even a computer that answered enquiries, provided that you knew how to make them.

A couple of women sat at the counter. One knitted in preparation for the winter while the other stared at the three men. From time to time, in response to Pisanelli or Boatti, she pressed a button hidden beneath the thick wooden slab of the counter.

The only other customer was an unshaven student, most probably waiting for an overseas call. He read a back-to-front magazine in Arabic script.

Again Trotti looked at the postcard, turning it over, looking first at the picture, then at Rosanna's neat handwriting, and the impersonal message.

'Like something copied from a travel brochure,' Pisanelli had remarked, 'Except for the postscript.'

Alive.

It was Rosanna's younger sister, Maria Cristina, who was now lying in the morgue. Trotti glanced at his watch and wondered if Bottone had finished his autopsy. He repressed a shudder.

Maria Cristina – not Rosanna – had been murdered.

'Lido di Scacchi!'

Possible, of course, the card was an alibi.

Perhaps Rosanna had beaten to death her younger, troubled sister – the only way to put an end to an intolerable situation. Perhaps the younger sister had tried to blackmail Rosanna. Blackmail to get money for drugs.

'Lido di Scacchi.' Pisanelli was calling from the telephone booth, one foot in the stuffy cabin, one foot on the marble floor. 'We're in luck, commissario.' He held a hand over the mouthpiece of the telephone, 'Lido di Scacchi, at the Pensione Belvedere.' He was grinning from ear to ear. Pisanelli was having a good day.

Trotti got up from the red plastic chair and took the receiver. 'Whatever made you shave off your moustache, Pisa?'

'It's now you notice?' Pisanelli ran a hand across his mouth. 'Six months and now you notice?'

'I prefer the moustache.'

'Commissario, I can go now and have lunch with my friend?'

'Pronto?'

'What do you want us to do with the luggage?'

Trotti frowned, spoke into the telephone, 'I beg your pardon.'

'What do you want us to do with the luggage?' The man on the end of the line talked in the hard Emilian accent, 'She said she was going away for three days in the Delta, your Signorina Belloni, and she left her luggage. She has not been back. Nearly five days. Of course, she's paid for the room, but, if she's not coming back, I'd like to have the use of it. It's the Ferragosto and . . .'

Trotti asked, 'You haven't seen her for five days?' He glanced at his watch.

'Signorina Belloni is a very good client. I've never had cause for complaint. She's paid for the room until the sixteenth but . . .'

'She hasn't been back to the hotel in five days?'

'In Lombardy you are all deaf? Or just daft?' A muffled, derisory laugh, 'I've just been telling you and . . .'

'She went off by herself?'

'Did I say that?'

'When did you last see Signorina Belloni? Was she by herself?'

The unpleasant laughter.

'A murder enquiry – it is possible that Signorina Belloni has been murdered.'

A brief hesitation, 'Your Signorina Belloni went with a man in a Fiat – one of those four-wheel-drive things. None of my business, of course. They seemed very friendly. He picked her up early one morning. None of my business – free country, this is a Republic and people can do as they please. None of my business. She's a nice lady, your Signorina Belloni, very good customer. I wouldn't like anything to have happened to her. Very nice lady. Always been a good client. None of my business.'

'Registration? Did you notice the registration on the vehicle?'

'I've got work to do.'

'You didn't notice the number plate?'

A sigh, 'Ferrara registration.' The man hung up.

'Ferrara registration,' Trotti repeated absentmindedly, handing the dead phone back to Pisanelli.

'Ferrara – isn't that where the Roberti girl's boyfriend lives?' Pisanelli asked. 'Gian Maria.'

CHINOTTO

'What are you going to do?'

Trotti shrugged.

Boatti invited them home for lunch.

'Other than putting out a general alert, there's not much we can do . . . short of going down to Scacchi.'

Pisanelli grinned, running his hand through his hair, 'I'm having lunch with Anna.'

'Anna?'

'My fiancée.'

Trotti shrugged again, 'Rosanna will turn up. We can assume she doesn't know what's happened to her sister.'

'Unless she killed her sister.' Pisanelli looked at his watch.

'Stop looking at your watch, Pisanelli.'

'I'm looking at the date.'

'I've got to pick up my car at the hospital,' Boatti said.

Pisanelli counted on his fingers. 'Five days, commissario – that means Rosanna could well have been here in the city at the time of the murder.'

'Well done,' Trotti said drily.

'It would also explain why the flat was so tidy. If it was Rosanna who killed her sister, she'd have had time to clean the place up.'

Trotti nodded, 'And, unexpectedly, Boatti comes barging into the flat.'

'Commissario,' Boatti said, leaning forward in the back seat, his round face glinting with sweat, 'you don't really think that Rosanna killed her sister, do you?'

Trotti glanced at the journalist, 'Rosanna wasn't expecting you. She knew you had the key to her place – but she thought you were in Vercelli.'

Pisanelli nodded. 'Commissario, I've got to go. I've got a date.'

'Stay with me. I need you with me, Pisanelli.'

'I'm meeting my fiancée for lunch.'

'You'll have time enough to meet her.'

'You said that about all my other girlfriends.'

'You'll have time enough.'

'When?'

'When I've retired.'

Boatti looked unhappy. He wiped his forehead with a paper handkerchief. He said, 'Pisanelli, you can run me back to the hospital?'

'You don't want me to get married, do you, commissario?'

'I don't want you to make a mistake.'

Pisanelli drove to San Teodoro. He had removed the revolving lamp from the roof. Occasionally he gave a sideways glance at Trotti who appeared strangely relaxed and who whistled under his breath.

I puritani: 'A te, o cara.'

'You honestly believe Rosanna is capable of killing her sister, commissario?' Boatti asked.

'We're all capable of killing – if the conditions are right.'

At San Teodoro Pisanelli parked in front of the church; a dog sleeping in the shadow of the high portals opened one eye and watched the three men get out of the Lancia before returning to its midday slumbers.

The policeman on the front door had disappeared, no doubt for the Ferragosto.

Boatti rang the downstairs bell and preceded the two policemen up the stairs. His wife met them at the top of the last flight.

'I'd run you to the hospital, Boatti, but Commissario Trotti seems to think he's lost without me.'

They entered the flat, to be met by the warm smell of Mediterranean cooking, olive oil, tomatoes, basil and thyme.

Boatti hurriedly presented the two men to his wife.

'Of course there's enough food for everybody, Giorgio,' his wife said happily.

Signora Boatti appeared older than her husband and already had white streaks in her short, black hair. The face was thin and, despite the smile, rather hard. She shook hands with Trotti and Pisanelli and, leading them into the apartment, invited them to sit down. The blinds of the study were closed. An air conditioner on wheels wheezed asthmatically in the middle of the room. 'If you gentlemen would care for a drink . . .' She spoke with a Tuscan accent, transforming her c's into h's. 'Or a Hoca Hola? A Hinotto?' Between the fingers of her right hand she held a smouldering cigarette.

Several books, open and face down, were scattered across the settee. The cat appeared to be sleeping, his black fur rippled by the breeze of the conditioner. The computer screen had been turned off.

Boatti phoned for a taxi and then left the flat quietly, a nod towards his wife and the visitors. The intelligent, pale face was taut, anxious.

The echo of his shoes as he went down the stairs.

'An apéritif, perhaps?' Signora Boatti asked.

Rather than accept her invitation, Trotti said that he would like to go downstairs for a few moments. He added that he had not been into Rosanna Belloni's apartment since the night that Signor Boatti had discovered the body.

'My husband was very fond of Rosanna Belloni,' she said and Trotti wondered whether he detected a note of reproach. Signora Boatti accompanied them to the door. 'Back in fifteen minutes, please,' she said and it was difficult to say whether the slightly hectoring tone was humorous or not. 'I've made a focaccia with sfrizzoli.'

'Sfrizzoli?'

'Nothing very fancy, mind. What you people in Lombardy call ciccioli – fried pork scraps.' A tight smile as she stood with her hand on the iron balustrade. The two policemen went down the flight of stairs to Rosanna's apartment and the scene of the crime. Signora Boatti's dark eyes followed them, while a thin, blue wisp of smoke danced from the cigarette to the stained ceiling of the stairwell.

ZANI

The police tape was still up and when Trotti tapped at the open door – the brass nameplate announced in engraved script, Sig.na Belloni – it was Zani who answered. 'Ah,' he said.

'I see your colleague on the front door downstairs has left for the coast.'

'Can I help you, Commissario Trotti?'

'Come to have a look around.'

Zani frowned. He had the red, sly face and small eyes of a peasant and he seemed ill at ease in a uniform that was too small for his chunky body. A taciturn man in his late forties, he had joined the police on leaving the army, and had returned to his native city after nearly a decade spent in the Marche. He had the reputation of being uncommunicative. He did not have many friends, and when he took his morning coffee laced with grappa in the bar opposite the Questura, he normally stood by himself at the counter. He had the reputation of being a drinker, a solitary drinker.

'Commissario Merenda is in charge of Reparto Omicidi. I take orders from him,' Zani said, more an accusation than a statement. He had been reading a local newspaper. Beside the chair was a bottle of wine.

Trotti placed a hand on Zani's bulky shoulder, 'Rosanna was a personal friend of mine.'

Agente Zani bit his lip hesitantly. The round face was more flushed than usual, 'The questore said – and he insisted . . .'

'Zani, you know me.'

'Of course, commissario.'

'You have nothing to worry about.' Trotti glanced around the small room. 'You and I have been friends for a very long time.'

(Zani had a son who worked in a bookshop in the city centre. On various occasions the twenty-four-year-old Alberto Zani had been arrested with other young men for disorderly or threatening behaviour. It was no secret in the Questura that Alberto, despite his aggressive behaviour, his air of virility and the many girls who accompanied him at different times on his Ducati motorcycle, had several homosexual lovers.)

The apartment window gave on to a panorama of terra cotta roofs that ran down to the AGIP hotel and the river. The hot breeze pulled at a curtain. Scientifica had been thorough in its search for contact traces. Several surfaces were hidden beneath sheets of plastic. The bed sheets removed. The blood stains, now black, remained on the floor, staked out by a barrier of small flags.

Rosanna Belloni's flat was both a living room and bedroom. The kitchen sink had served also as a bathroom. A mirror was attached to the cream-painted wall and various toiletries stood on the glass shelf – shampoo and skin lotions. On the wall above, Rosanna had pinned a linen dishcloth, with the word 'Bewley's'.

'A shop in Dublin,' Pisanelli said, translating the English. He held an unlit cigarette between his lips.

'Dublin?' Trotti repeated.

'A town in Ireland.'

'I know that,' Trotti snapped, 'I wonder who gave her that.'

'As a school teacher she must've built up a lot of friendships over the years – children who had grown up.'

Trotti glanced at Pisanelli, 'I didn't know you could speak English, Pisa.'

'Once went out with a Canadian girl – French Canadian from Montreal. She spoke English.'

'She taught you English?'

Pisanelli folded his arms against the chest of his suede jacket, 'She wanted to marry me. Couldn't resist the animal magnetism.'

Zani said, 'Commissario Trotti, the questore was quite categorical . . .'

'Don't worry about the questore . . .' Trotti gestured to where Zani had slid the bottle of wine into the small gap between the bed and a tall bookcase that also served as a desk, 'He won't know of anything.'

Zani nodded unhappily.

'What do you think, Zani?' It was Pisanelli who spoke, glancing again at his watch.

Zani was in the process of lighting a cigarette. Like Gabbiani, he was able to get hold of filterless Nazionali. The smell of the black tobacco filled the small room. 'What do I think?' Zani held out the light to Pisanelli and then closed the gold lighter.

'Who killed the Belloni woman?'

He folded his arms against the rumpled uniform shirt, 'Sexual, wasn't it?' The lips turned downwards in disapproval, 'Sexual crime.'

'What makes you say that?'

'Why else kill a woman?'

'Money.'

Zani snorted two brief clouds of tobacco smoke, 'If Belloni had any money, she didn't keep it here. And her will all goes to her nephews and nieces.'

Pisanelli smiled behind his unlit cigarette, 'How do you know that, Zani?'

He looked glumly at Trotti and Pisanelli. 'I'm merely repeating what I've heard.'

'Heard?'

'Even a flatfoot on door duty gets to hear things.' Zani brushed ash from his shirt, 'No – not money. There are easier ways of getting money.' The corner of his lip turned downwards, 'Sex, commissario.'

'Sex,' Trotti repeated glumly and went to the tall bookcase.

There was a frame, glass with rusting clips. Trotti picked it up. It contained three photographs. 'Seen this, Pisa?'

The largest photograph was of a young woman sitting on a scooter – one of the old Vespas with the handlebars separate from the rounded faring. The laughing head of a cowboy – the long forgotten advertisement for Alemagni ice creams – had been stuck on to the paintwork of the faring. A fannion was attached to the chrome headlamp. The girl leant forward, her dark head to one side, smiling into the camera. Long, thin, tanned arms held the handlebars. The girl – Maria Cristina, Trotti decided, with the same features as Rosanna, but slightly coarser, despite the long eyelashes – was wearing a lightweight summer dress, with a neckline that dropped to where the full, youthful breasts began to swell.

The second photograph was of a young adolescent girl, her gloved hands together as if in prayer. She wore the white dress of a communicant or a maid of honour at a wedding. Forget-me-nots in the gossamer veil of her headdress. She was smiling, showing irregular teeth and irrepressible optimism.

The third photograph was of Rosanna.

Rosanna held a young baby in her arms. Rosanna appeared to be in her late twenties, and on inspecting the photo from close up, Trotti thought he recognised a wall portrait of President Gronchi in the background. The photograph had probably been taken in a town hall. Rosanna, wearing a tight-fitting black sweater over a rigid brassière à la Gina Lollobrigida, smiled cheerfully at the camera, while the baby, dressed in frilly bib, a bonnet and bootees seemed to be fascinated by something on the ceiling, out of the picture.

'What do you make of this?' Trotti turned to show the photographs to Pisanelli.

Pisanelli had disappeared.

Zani sat by the door, his hands clasped between his knees, pensively smoking his cigarette.

'Where's Pisanelli?'

'Sex – or revenge. Mark my words, commissario.'

'Where the hell do you get your Nazionali from, Zani?'

SPINSTER

'Sex and revenge,' Trotti said under his breath, ringing the bell and opening the ground-glass door.

'Ah, hommissario. Where is your young friend?'

Signora Boatti was in the dining room, setting a white cloth on to a walnut table. The window was open but the wooden blinds were closed to the blaze of the street below. It was cool and dark, cooler and darker than in the adjoining study. The asthmatic conditioner had been wheeled into the dining room and now hummed beside the sideboard.

The cat had migrated to the low settee.

Trotti asked for the bathroom and Signora Boatti, a cigarette in her mouth, accompanied him to a cupboard-like room that had been transformed with bright tiles. 'Bit small, I know, hommissario, but these houses were never built for the bodily functions.'

He smiled, 'Like me.'

She pointed to a neat pile of towels. 'If you'd like to shower, there's hot water.'

'Cold water's what I need.'

She left him and, stripping to the waist, Trotti washed his face, hands and body, finally dipping his hair into the chill, sulphurous water. Refreshed, he opened the glass cabinet, searching for a comb. Looking at his reflection, he combed the thin, black hair. Pulled backwards against his skull, it made Trotti look older. The hollow eyes stared back at him humourlessly. 'You need a holiday, Piero. Forget about Rosanna. Time now to go and see Pioppi and the baby.' He removed the hairs from the plastic teeth and replaced the comb in the cupboard. On the other shelves there were toiletries – children's toothpaste, Atkinson's talc but, Trotti noticed, no eau de cologne or perfume – and a couple of jars of pills. The cupboard smelt of sweet, dry chalk.

Sleeping pills.

'Hommissario, you'd care for the aperitif now?' Signora Boatti asked from the kitchen.

Her Tuscan accent made him smile. 'Mineral water, signora.' He returned to the dining room and lowered himself on to one of the chairs. Trotti propped his arms against the walnut table. There was a bowl of fruit, a square wicker basket of fresh bread and several packets of grissini. Two bottles of mineral water. Signora Boatti had set out two plates of sliced salami and a bowl of olives. 'Your husband isn't back?'

She came from the kitchen, wiping her hands on a cloth. She was considerably older than Boatti, Trotti realised, in her early forties. Her body was thin and her frame angular. 'Gassy?' she asked, and, without waiting for a reply, opened a bottle of mineral water.

'From Tuscany?' He smiled as she poured the water into his glass.

'From France – they were selling it cheap in the supermarket. The wonders of the EEC.' She placed a plastic cap on the bottle of mineral water and then served herself two fingers of William

Lawson which she drank without water or ice. 'Good whiskey is one of my lesser vices.'

'You knew Rosanna well, signora?'

The woman sat down on the settee, a few feet from Trotti. In the penumbra, it was hard to see her face. Sunlight from the kitchen fell across her knees and the hand which held the glass of amber liquid. With the other hand, she caressed the cat. She was wearing a polo shirt.

'I do translation work,' she said. She lit a cigarette. 'For the publishing houses in Milan, I translate books from Chinese – and now a bit of Japanese, too.'

'You don't answer my question.'

She laughed. 'I used to teach Oriental languages at the university, but my job was cut. They probably needed the money for something useful like nuclear physics. Or international relations. And so I work at home. I was offered a job at Trento at the university there, but it would've meant spending three days a week away from the children . . .'

'The children are on holiday?'

'I'm driving down tonight to join them. My family has a little place in Viareggio.'

'Viareggio?'

'I'm from Volterra.' The shadows on her face moved as she smiled, 'My father has a business in alabaster.'

'And that's how you got interested in Chinese?'

'You'd've preferred I worked in the quarries?'

The gassy water jumped at his lips, tickling his nostrils.

'Giorgio said that Rosanna's alive, hommissario.'

Trotti said, 'And so, rather than go to Trento, you prefer to stay in the city?'

'Rosanna is alive?'

'I certainly hope so.'

She looked at him – he saw the glint of the dark eyes. 'Hommissario, I married late – at a time when I never thought I was going to marry. When a woman has her first child at thirty-five, motherhood for her is something very special.' She paused, 'I have two very lovely children. The joy of my life. There is nothing that I won't do for them.' She shrugged, placed the cigarette in her mouth. 'When I met Giorgio, I never suspected that I could feel this way about children. Product of the Sixties, I was very much a revolutionary. A Maoist, a structuralist. And a feminist. I never burnt my brassière but I wore bell bottoms, tight sweaters and platform shoes. And in my time I've made my share of Molotov cocktails.' She laughed, 'My present way of life – at that time I'd never've dreamt I could be happy. But I am. Happy and terribly bourgeois. Happy because I have a family of my own. Giorgio is a good father and although he doesn't have a regular salary, we have never gone hungry.' She inhaled deeply and then sent the smoke from her mouth to the ceiling. 'Rosanna is really alive?'

'Your father isn't poor?'

'We prefer to get along by ourselves. Papa has promised to pay for the girls' education.'

'I have a daughter,' Trotti said and smiled.

'Why won't you give me a straight answer when I ask whether Rosanna is alive?'

'I think she is.'

'You think?'

'I have good reason to believe that Rosanna Belloni is alive.'

Signora Boatti gave a sigh, 'Thank goodness for that.'

'You don't sound particularly relieved.'

'Relieved for myself.'

'Meaning?'

'If you want more water, hommissario, serve yourself.'

'You don't like Rosanna?'

'Whose body was it that my husband found downstairs?'

'In all probability it's her sister Maria Cristina who was murdered.'

The woman allowed herself to lean back against the settee, her head resting backwards while she blew smoke into the air. For a few minutes she did not speak. From time to time, the tip of the cigarette glowed as she inhaled and the cool room filled with the combined smell of burning tobacco and the cooking sfrizzoli in the kitchen.

She had pretty, tanned legs. There was a long scar beneath the left knee. Signora Boatti was not wearing shoes; beside her feet were the two flat pieces of cloth that served as slippers on the marble floor.

Trotti had opened a packet of grissini and nibbled at one of the sticks. In this part of the city, there was little noise from the street. Somewhere, over towards Borgo Genovese, an imprecise church bell chimed.

She leant forward to tap cigarette ash into the ashtray. 'I grew up very rich. Rich and not very pretty, but fascinated in languages. I was a good pupil at the liceo classico and I was always top of the class. All the best prizes – but never a boyfriend.' She raised her shoulders, 'I didn't mind too much. I never really liked it when I had to dance with a boy and his hands would start wandering. It's not that I found it revolting or anything. It's just that it all seemed so silly. Then at seventeen I fell in love. A teacher of Greek at the liceo and I thought he was God. But he wasn't God. He was a married man from Ferrara.'

'Ferrara,' Trotti repeated.

She smiled to herself. 'There was nothing between us – nothing. Once in class his hand touched my cheek – by accident. And another time – it was at the end of the lesson, and I invented some silly question about Aristophanes or something – we were alone in the classroom and I touched his hand. He didn't stop me. His name was Mario Siccardi and I liked to imagine he was unhappy with his wife. There was nothing between us, nothing – but it took me more than ten years to get over him.'

'And that's when you met Giorgio?'

Her cigarette was stubbed out in the ashtray. 'Giorgio is eight years younger than me. When we met, I was already teaching at the university. I wasn't a virgin any more – but I wasn't a liberated woman, either. A feminist of course, but I can't say I was liberated. Not interested in men.' She sipped her whiskey, 'Or rather, I thought I wasn't interested in men. Then one day . . .' Trotti heard her laugh to herself. 'One day I overheard one of the Oriental library staff referring to me as the spinster. Spinster?' She shook her head, 'I was thirty-one years old and I knew I wasn't very pretty. But a spinster? Never being married, never having children. That evening, I can remember so clearly, I went home – I had a little flat at the back of the town hall – and I looked at myself in the mirror. I stood naked and I looked at my hips and at my breasts that were beginning to sag.'

'And?'

'What do you think?' She looked at Trotti and her smile revealed the brightness of her teeth. 'I wept.'

Downstairs there was the sound of a car engine.

'A few weeks later, I met Giorgio – he was on my Cantonese beginners' course and within the year we were married. It took me another four years – and a couple of miscarriages – before I managed to have my first child. Giorgio still can't speak a word of Cantonese. And Rosanna . . .' She stopped.

'And Rosanna?'

'You are quite sure she's alive, hommissario?'

'We don't know where she is – but there is no reason to think she's dead.'

'I've always been jealous of Rosanna. Very jealous.'

'Rosanna never had children.'

'That didn't stop me from being jealous.'

'Why?' Trotti raised his shoulders in surprised amusement. 'Rosanna is a lot older than you. Scarcely a rival, I would've thought.'

'She was Giorgio's friend – a friend of the family. That's how we got this flat. Rosanna was – is a lovely woman, I'm sure. She's kind and she's generous.'

'Why jealous, signora?'

'Why?' She laughed. She made a dismissive move with her hand.

'What could a young woman like you be jealous about?'

'A woman has her intuition – there are little things that she sees – that she understands.'

'What things?'

She was lighting another cigarette. Her hand trembled slightly. 'You see . . .'

'Yes?'

She raised her glance to look at him, 'There are times when I have thought that Giorgio preferred Rosanna to me. Between them there has always been something – a kind of intimacy.' She shook her head, 'Giorgio says she's like a mother to him – but it's more than that. I don't know what it is between them – but for me, it is quite palpable.'

Trotti could hear Boatti coming up the stairs.

'I'm very jealous. This unattractive, middle-aged woman sitting in front of you, chain-smoking, is capable of tremendous jealousy.

Blind jealousy, hommissario Trotti. I love my husband very much. Very much. To you he may not appear the most wonderful man in the world, but you don't know him. For me he is the most wonderful man. I love him. Like the stupidest woman in a foto-romanzo, I love my man, heart and soul.' An apologetic smile, 'I think there are times I could have killed your Rosanna Belloni. The blind stupid jealousy of a woman who loves her man – and who refuses having to share him with any other human being. Giorgio is mine . . . and mine alone.'

COST OF LIVING

'When I was a student at the university here, I never smoked Nazionali.' Boatti appeared more relaxed than earlier. He was no longer sweating. The round face smiled comfortably. 'They cost too much.'

'I didn't know you smoked.'

(The television was on, but the sound was down. Lilli Gruber mouthed in silence the telegiornale on RAIDUE. Pictures of the Middle East, more 'Ndrangheta murders in Calabria, the stock market dropping in Milan, Maradona back from a holiday in Argentina, Antibo running the ten thousand metres.)

'I don't,' Giorgio Boatti said. 'And I wish my wife didn't. I managed to get her to stop during the two pregnancies.'

Signora Boatti was in the kitchen, tidying the plates into the dishwasher. 'Amor, dammi quel fazzolettino,' she quietly sang to herself.

'But once the little girls were born, she started again worse than ever. Now she's back down to a packet and a half a day.'

'Nazionali?'

'Why Nazionali?' Boatti laughed, 'Marlboro. It's people like you who can still get hold of Nazionali.'

'I gave up smoking years ago.'

'That's why you eat so many sweets, commissario?'

'In the last ten years, I've smoked three cigarettes.' As if to prove his point, Trotti took a sweet from his pocket and popped it into his mouth. 'I need the sugar.'

'My wife seems to think you're very nice.'

'So much for feminine intuition. She doesn't work with me. Nor does she want to write a book on police procedure.'

'Back in the early Seventies, there were Alfa and Sax and Calipso that we students used to smoke. Straw and dung, but they were cheaper than Nazionali and they gave you a decent nicotine level in the blood.'

Trotti nodded.

'Then the government put filterless Nazionali – along with bread and coffee and all the other prime necessities – on to the cost of living index.' Boatti grinned. 'And to keep the inflation figures down, they kept the cost of Nazionali down at a time when prices were soaring. Nearly fifteen years now that Nazionali have cost less than three hundred lire a packet – scarcely the cost of a phone call. And so, of course, Nazionali've virtually disappeared from circulation. Too cheap. You never see them in the tobacconist's. Nearest thing is Esportazione. And Esportazione cost fourteen hundred lire.'

'It's only people with friends in the state tobacco monopoly or people who work for the Customs who can now get hold of Nazionali.' Trotti poured himself some more water. He felt sleepy, 'Thank goodness I can get by on sweets.'

'Your sweets have made you bitter, commissario.'

'I've lived in this country too long to be bitter.' Trotti added, 'I'm sorry about the book, Boatti.'

'Cynical, then.'

'If you're not cynical, you can't keep your head above the water. Not in Italy – not where there is a political or vested interest behind every action. Even behind the price of cigarettes.' Trotti paused, 'What're you going to do about the book?'

'Book?'

'If Rosanna's alive, there doesn't seem to be any point in your police procedure book. Must be a bit of a disappointment.'

'I'll be happy enough just to see Rosanna alive and well.' A disarming smile, 'And there's nothing to stop me writing a book about a policeman – a successful commissario coming to the end of a long and fruitful career.'

'You haven't received a card or anything from her, Boatti?'

'A book about a man and about a provincial city.'

'Rosanna hasn't contacted you?'

The smile vanished, 'I told you that she rarely wrote to me when she was on holiday.'

'But she'd phone?'

'No.'

'Then why would she write to Signora Isella?'

'They're friends.' Boatti looked at Trotti, 'You still think she wanted to build herself an alibi?'

'The postcard – and the post date – they could be construed as evidence of her not being in the city at the time of her sister's death. Very useful.'

'You honestly seem to believe that Rosanna is capable of murdering her sister?' Boatti shook his head, 'You really are too cynical – or perhaps you just don't know her well enough.'

'You yourself said that she hated Maria Cristina.'

'Not to the point of smashing her sister's head.'

'Being cynical – that's the price I pay for my job. Always assume the worst in people – until it's proved to the contrary.' Trotti snorted, 'And it rarely is.'

'Thanks for the compliment.'

Trotti bowed his head.

'You knew Rosanna, commissario.'

'I'm not sure you can ever know anybody. Other people are a cipher, an iceberg, and you can only see the tip. The rest is assumption. We're alone, Boatti – all of us. You don't seem to understand that. But then you're young.'

'Because I'm younger than you, you think I haven't suffered?'

'We are born alone, Boatti, we die alone – and we go through life thinking – hoping that we can make ties. Solid ties. But even the most solid of ties are transitory. Only separation is for good.'

'Your job makes you so jaded? It really is time you retired.'

'Retire to do what?' Trotti shook his head, 'Write a book?'

'You've never made solid ties in your life?'

Trotti laughed, 'I thought I knew my wife, Boatti. We lived together for more than twenty years. A beautiful wife, a beautiful daughter – I honestly believed we were all happy together.' He clicked the sweet against his teeth, 'My wife now lives in America. Happy? Perhaps she's happy now, but now I realise she was never happy with me.'

'You must've realised that at the time.'

'I chose to believe what suited me.' Again Trotti rattled the sweet against the back of his teeth. 'A book about a policeman? Not very interesting, I should think.'

Boatti gestured to the bookcase. 'I always have several projects. And the case isn't yet closed.'

'Not for you, perhaps, Boatti. For me it's closed.'

Boatti glanced sideways at Trotti, raising an eyebrow.

'Loyalty, friendship – I think I've done my bit for Rosanna Belloni. I thought she was dead – and I was misled. Perhaps even deliberately . . . I don't know. I do know, though, that I've put enough people's backs up. Not least the questore's. It's time I took my holiday. That's what everybody's been telling me – and that's what I feel like doing.' Trotti yawned and only belatedly put a hand in front of his mouth. 'Would you mind if I lay down for a few minutes on the couch? It's hot.'

'Of course not.'

'Your wife is an excellent cook.'

'If you wish, you can go into the girls' bedroom. It's cool there.'

'I shouldn't have drunk the Grignolino. Red wine always puts me to sleep.' As an afterthought, Trotti added, 'I still don't understand the card.'

'The postcard, commissario?'

'Normally Rosanna doesn't write.' Trotti shrugged, 'If she doesn't write to you, I imagine she's not likely to write to anybody else. Not even to Signora Isella. There's something artificial about the card.'

'Rosanna's a bit of a poet, you know.'

'If Rosanna wanted to wax poetical about the beauty of the Po delta, she'd've written a letter. But her card . . .' Again he yawned, 'It's like something copied from a TCI touring guide.' Trotti shook his head. 'A five-minute catnap. This heat . . .'

'Commissario, Rosanna would never have murdered her sister.'

'So you tell me.'

'I know her well.'

'If she's alive she'll turn up. Sooner or later. All the sooner if Maria Cristina's death gets into the national press. And when she turns up . . .'

'Yes?'

'You can be sure Rosanna'll have an alibi. She'll have rock solid proof she was somewhere else at the time of her sister's death.'

TRIADS

A brief siesta and then a shower.

At half past four, Trotti left San Teodoro. Boatti, who wanted to go to the editorial offices of the *Provincia padana*, agreed to accompany him as far as Corso Cavour.

'What are you going to do now, commissario?'

Trotti smiled. He unwrapped a rhubarb sweet and put it in his mouth before answering. 'Do?'

'Rosanna's alive and well and probably somewhere in the Po delta. As you said, sooner or later she's going to turn up.'

'I'm going to phone my daughter in Bologna to see how she is – she's expecting her baby any minute. Then I'm going to tidy up my desk in the Questura, say goodbye to my friends. This evening I'll go out for a meal, perhaps even a film. Long time since I've been to see a film. And tomorrow I'll have a little holiday. Time I got away from this city – that's what everybody's been telling me. I'll get my car out of the garage, put oil in the engine and check the tyres. And at six tomorrow morning, before the build-up of holiday-makers on the autostrada, I'll drive up to Gardesana.'

'Where?'

'My wife has a villa on Lake Garda. I need a rest – and I need to get away from this . . .' he glanced at Boatti, 'from this equatorial heat.'

'Isn't Gardesana where Lawrence used to live?'

'Lawrence who?'

'D. H. Lawrence – he was an English writer.'

'You must ask my wife. She knows everybody in the village.'

'She lives there?'

'My wife's in America – in Evanston, in Illinois.' A blank smile, 'She invents new kinds of saccharine for a big American chemical firm. She's very happy.'

Boatti fell silent. It was still hot and a humid haze had turned the sky to a leaden grey. They walked along the empty streets that smelt of wine, cork and the afternoon dust.

'Rosanna,' Trotti said, taking Boatti by the arm. 'Your wife said she helped you get the flat.'

'Rosanna's always very helpful.' He added, 'I've lived there now for over fifteen years. I moved in before I was married. And fortunately for us, Rosanna doesn't ask for a very hefty rent.'

'Why?'

'Why is she helpful? That's the way Rosanna is. You knew her, commissario, you must have seen how she feels the need to be useful. A genuinely kind person.'

'But she's been particularly kind to you.'

Boatti said nothing.

'Why's she so nice to you, Boatti?'

'I don't understand your question.' Boatti stopped walking. He had started to perspire again. They were outside the Città di Pechino, a small Chinese restaurant in Via Langobardi. The restaurant had not yet opened for the evening, but a couple of flat-faced Oriental men were carrying out dustbins from the neon-lit kitchen. A cassette-player wailed in strange, foreign music.

(It was generally believed in the Questura that il treno del sesso – the evening train from Genoa bringing African and Brazilian prostitutes to work the night and early morning in Voghera and along the Via Aurelia – was organised by Chinese triads, working out of the Città di Pechino and other restaurants in Lombardy.)

'You don't understand my question? Let's say Rosanna matters a lot to you.'

Boatti nodded.

'Yet when you thought she was dead, you didn't cry.'

'I didn't cry in front of you, commissario. You didn't see me cry.'

'You want to write a book. For her sake.'

'She is a friend. I thought she was dead.'

'That's all?'

'What're you getting at?' He pulled his arm away from Trotti's hand. 'I'm not sure I like your insinuations, commissario.'

'You knew Rosanna wasn't dead, Boatti.'

He replied hotly, 'You've no right to say that.'

'You invent a cock-and-bull story about wanting to write a book – but it's just a big hoax, a way of getting in on the enquiry.'

'Ridiculous.'

'A way of keeping an eye on me.'

'You think you're that important?'

'Only I was taken off the case.'

'What do you want from me, Trotti?'

'What did you want from me, Boatti?'

'What do you want?'

They stood looking at each other, in the cobbled street, while the Chinese, taking no notice of the two men, prepared for the evening's custom. Somewhere within the Città di Pechino a woman laughed.

'The truth.'

'I know no more than you, commissario.'

'You were lovers, weren't you?'

'I beg your pardon.'

'You and Rosanna Belloni – you were lovers, weren't you? You've been screwing her for fifteen years, haven't you, Boatti?'

The round face went pale.

'Old enough to be your mother and you screwed her.'

Boatti slapped him. One brisk, fast slap of Trotti's face. Then he turned and walked fast away.

ENVELOPE

The Questura was cool and almost empty.

Taking the lift, Trotti thought about the birth of Pioppi, with her round, squashed face and dark hair. Nearly thirty years ago. He remembered Agnese's pride. 'Our first child, Piero,' she had said.

First and only child.

Smiling at the recollection, Trotti stepped out of the lift at the third floor and went into his office. 'Time I phoned my daughter,' he said to himself as he opened the windows, letting the enclosed air escape into the mid-afternoon. Outside it was still hot, but the air over the city was getting cooler; on the roof, the pigeons had started to coo after the long intermezzo of the midday heat.

Trotti's eyes ached. For no apparent reason, the radiator started to vibrate with distant banging.

Trotti set the chill can of Chinotto on the table top.

There was an envelope on his desk: Repubblica Italiana, Polizia di Stato. 'Piero, I'll want this back if you're going on holiday.' Trotti frowned, trying to decipher the signature; it took him time to realise that the elided letters were Maiocchi's initials.

He opened the manilla envelope and took out the square photograph.

It was a polaroid, with the flat, washed colours of flash photography.

The couple sat at a table. Both were wearing T-shirts, with the white, superimposed letters, NY, on the left side of the chest. At first glance, Trotti recognised neither face.

The man was young, with a fresh, Mediterranean complexion. Like the woman sitting beside him, he was looking at something to the left of the photographer, out of the picture. Luca's left fist propped up his chin; his right arm rested on the woman's shoulder.

The bright light of the flashlight no doubt attenuated the woman's wrinkles. The face was slightly bloated. She had a double chin and the dyed hair was pulled back in an unkempt, unflattering bun.

It could have been Rosanna's face, but plumper, coarser. And younger. The make-up – lipstick, eyeliner and mascara – was thick and gave the impression of having been applied by an unpractised hand.

Heavy loops of gold hung from Maria Cristina Belloni's ears. Like Luca, she was smiling, but there was something tense about her features. The pupil of one eye was red. Her hands were propped against the edge of the table; the large fingers grasped a glass of amber liquid.

07 21 90.

It was a few seconds before Trotti realised it was the date – American style – that had been printed in pinprick letters in the bottom right-hand corner of the frame.

There was a message on the reverse side: a heart pierced by an arrow and the carefully handwritten words: 'Luca e Snoopy – per sempre.' The immature handwriting of a schoolgirl.

Trotti turned the cardboard around and was still staring at the photograph as he reached out for the telephone.

A young woman entered the office.

UNCLE

'Zio!'

Trotti looked up.

'Zio Piero.'

'Your uncle?'

The girl came into the room and Trotti, replacing the telephone in its cradle, stood up, smiling and frowning at the same time.

She smelt of fresh hay and youth; standing on tiptoe, she kissed him on both cheeks. 'You don't recognise me, zio?' She stepped back smiling and put her head to one side, 'Your own goddaughter?'

'Anna?'

She nodded.

'Anna Ermagni?'

She laughed as Trotti took her in his arms and squeezed her, 'Anna, I thought you'd gone back to Bari.' He moved backwards. 'I thought you'd all gone back to Bari.'

'You see how you care about me.'

'How long have you been back in the city for? But you're a big girl, Anna.' Trotti put his hands on her shoulders – she was wearing jeans and Enrico Coveri T-shirt – 'Let me look at my Anna. The fringe has gone – no, no, the last time I saw you you had a pony tail. But what are you doing here? Sit down, sit down, Anna.' He kissed the top of her head. 'And Papa? And Simonetta? And the little boy – what's his name? He must be nearly ten years old now.'

'You forget even that, Piero Trotti? You forget that my brother is called Piero?'

'A drink, Anna?'

She shook her head as she dropped into the modernistic armchair.

'I don't believe it? Is this the little girl that I found at the bus station? The little girl they kidnapped?'

'A long time ago, zio.' She revealed regular white teeth.

'Too, too long ago.'

'And zia Agnese? How is she?'

'My wife's in America.'

'And Pioppi?'

'I was about to phone her as you came in. She's married, you know, and now in Bologna. She's expecting a baby any minute.' He grinned, and his eyes no longer felt tired, 'You're looking at a man about to become a grandfather.'

'How exciting.' The beautiful eyes – the eyes of her late mother – looked at him and the soft skin – peachlike with a gentle, blonde down – wrinkled with pleasure. 'Pioppi was always so beautiful.'

'Beautiful.' Trotti shrugged, 'There were the hard times, too. For nearly a year she went without eating. We were very worried – but then she met Nando.'

'Nando is her husband?'

'They've been together now for four years. He's a lawyer. And you, Anna – why here? Your papa came to see me before you all went off to Bari.'

'I'm at the university. Starting in October.'

'How old are you? Eighteen?'

'I'm studying languages – English and French and Russian.' A broad smile, 'One day, after I've come back from London and New York, they're going to have to employ me as an interpreter. At FAO.'

Trotti placed his hands on the table. 'Here's a girl who knows her own mind.' He put his head back and laughed – telling himself it was the first time he had laughed happily in a long, long time.

'I thought you were on holiday but Pierangelo said you'd be here, zio.'

'Pierangelo?'

'Pisa.'

'Pierangelo? Do you know him?'

'Pisanelli, zio.'

'Pisanelli,' Trotti repeated dumbly. 'My Pisanelli?'

She nodded, 'Pierangelo.'

'Pisanelli's called Pierangelo?'

'My Pisanelli prefers to be called Pierangelo.'

'Your Pisanelli, Anna?'

'He didn't tell you?' Again the soft skin around the eyes wrinkled with pleasure. 'We've been engaged for a couple of weeks.'

'Oh, my God.'

'He wants to marry me.'

FLOWER

Jealousy?

'Zio, I knew that you were going to be happy for me.'

'You've grown into a woman.'

'Pierangelo is very special – Pierangelo understands women.'

'You, Anna, engaged to Pisa?'

'He told me about the death of Signorina Belloni. She was always so kind – so good with us children.'

Trotti shook his head, frowning, 'Pisa told me he had a girlfriend. He told me that I knew her. But little did I think it was my goddaughter.'

'Have you found out who killed her, zio?' Anna shivered.

Sitting behind his desk, Trotti leant forward and placed his hands on the back of hers. 'My little Anna, so serious, so quiet, with her fringe of black hair and her white schoolgirl socks, sitting in the bus station.' Trotti laughed, feeling his eyes tickling him. 'And now a grown woman. A beautiful woman.'

A big smile as she tilted her head coquettishly to one side, 'You find me pretty, zio Piero?'

'A flower. That's what Rosanna used to say – children are like flowers. And you are like a beautiful flower in blossom.' Slowly Trotti shook his head, 'I'm only sorry that I never did more for you.'

'You did enough, zio.'

Trotti looked around at the ugly little room, 'My job – the Questura, a poky little office – that's always been my job. My life. I've always put my job first – even before my wife and my daughter. And before all those people I should have loved more – and better.'

She shook her hair, black, lustrous and now worn short. 'You were always there – even if I didn't see you.'

Trotti looked at her.

'That's what Papa says about you, zio. A busy man, you like to give yourself work, you always like to feel you're doing something. Papa says that you were very stubborn and that you thought you could get by without the help of others. But Papa knows that when he needed you – really needed you – you were there.'

'Not quite true.' Trotti rubbed at his nose, ran a hand along his mouth, 'I haven't been much of a godfather for you. You deserved better than this surly old policeman.'

'Papa always speaks well of you – and if I haven't seen more of you, it's because I have a father and a mother and a little brother of my own. I've never needed you because there has always been enough love at home. But I've always known that you were there, to be counted on.'

Trotti said nothing.

'And now I know you're happy for me. Happy for me and Pierangelo.'

Jealousy? The slow movement in the pit of his belly? The cool touch of her soft young hands beneath his.

'And your little brother? How's he?'

'You know that Papa named Piero after you? After the death of Mama, he was very unhappy – and he says if you hadn't helped him, he'd've never married again.' The young woman sat back and folded her arms. She had an oval face, with red lips that smiled to reveal regular teeth.

'Tell me about your brother.'

'Signor Ermagni Piero is now nine years old. He doesn't like girls and he thinks that any man who gets married must be very stupid. Instead of a wife, he says that when he's earning money he's going to spend everything on his Lego collection.'

'Lego?'

'Building bricks. He has motors and cranes and he makes little cars. When he grows up he says he's going to be an engineer and an architect. And he says he's going to live in the Lego village in Denmark and he's going to design new toys and games.'

'A very decided young man, young Piero.' Trotti laughed.

'And his older sister's a very decided young woman – very decided and very lucky.'

Trotti looked at her, admiring her youth, her vigour and her happiness, and sensing a pinching feeling in his nostrils. The years that creep by, the nostalgia of the days that hurry past. 'Piero,' he said. 'Not a bad name.'

'At home everybody calls him Rino. He can be a little monster – but he's affectionate . . . when he want to be.'

Trotti picked up the telephone, and banged the button.

'Switchboard.'

'Can you put me through to this number, signorina . . .'

'Commissario Trotti?'

'Yes. Can you give me Bologna 232 34 23, please?'

'Commissario Trotti, there was a young lady looking for you.'

'My goddaughter is here with me now.'

'And Commissario Trotti.'

'Yes?'

'Commissario Maiocchi was here. He had something to give you.'

'I got his message – he left it on my desk. Thank you.'

'Commissario Maiocchi said he would be back. Something that he wants to talk to you about.'

'Thank you, signorina. Now if you could please get me 232 34 23 in Bologna . . .' Without waiting for a reply, he replaced the mouthpiece back in its dirty cradle. He smiled at Anna Ermagni, 'I just know that Pioppi's going to have a boy. I can feel it in my bones. And I just know that she's going to call him Piero.'

A wide grin, 'I'd like to have children. Lots and lots of children.'

'Not yet, Anna,' Trotti said, frowning again. 'Wait until you've got a job. You're still very young – you're not even twenty. Pioppi, you see, she's nearly thirty. Perhaps a bit late for a first child – but she spent a long time studying. And now she's got a good job.'

'Pierangelo says we're going to live in the country.'

'And FAO?' Trotti asked, worried. 'And your interpreting in Rome?'

'Don't worry, zio. Don't worry – I won't do anything foolish. Before I do any settling down, I've got to learn English and French. Although every time I look at Pierangelo, I go very weak.'

Trotti sighed, 'I know what you mean.' He added quickly, 'I want to speak to Pioppi. Haven't spoken to her for four days. She's expecting any day now. I only hope that blonde woman can get the line for me.'

As if on cue, the light on the telephone started to blink.

'Yes?'

'Commissario Trotti, your call to Bologna – you didn't tell me if it was a private call.'

'To my daughter – she's expecting a baby.'

'It's a private call, commissario?'

'Does that matter?'

'You know the new regulations, commissario. You know that the questore now asks us to log all long-distance calls. He says there are too many private conversations and that they cost too much and that they jam up the switchboard.'

'Jam up the switchboard? It's nearly the Ferragosto, for goodness sake. There's virtually nobody around.'

'But it's a private call?'

'Private call? If I had my own phone like Maiocchi or Merenda or one of the others, I wouldn't even have to go through the switchboard.'

'Please try to understand.'

'Signorina, I'm about to be a grandfather – you please try to understand.'

'I'm only doing what I've been told, Signor Commissario.'

'Doing what you've been told,' Trotti snorted. Angrily he slammed down the receiver, 'Thanks a lot.'

BOLOGNA

The blonde woman must have relented because the ugly green phone began to ring. Hurriedly Trotti snatched up the receiver. 'Pioppi?'

'I beg your pardon?'

Trotti had raised his voice. It echoed off the empty walls, 'Nando?'

'Who's speaking?' A man's voice, the familiar accent of Bologna.

'Signor Trotti – I'd like to speak to my daughter. Is that you, Nando?'

'Nando's not here. Who's that speaking please?'

'Pioppi's father.'

'I'm sorry – I don't understand.'

'Signora Solaroli's father – Pioppi's father. Is she all right? How is she?'

'The policeman?'

'Where's Pioppi?' Trotti was almost shouting, 'Is she all right? Where's Nando?'

'I'm sorry – I'm Nando's brother. Nando's at the hospital.'

'How is she? I thought the child wasn't expected for another day or two.'

'She went into hospital last night.'

'Has she had the baby? Is it a boy?'

'We're still waiting – I don't know.'

'What d'you mean, you don't know? Is my Pioppi all right? Has something happened?'

'I think Nando said he was going to phone you.'

Trotti's knuckles were white around the receiver. He was frowning, concentrating, staring downwards at the slanting, yellow light on the floor of the office.

Anna Ermagni watched him, her beautiful eyes unblinking. She reached out and touched his wrist.

Somewhere a pigeon was cooing.

'Is my daughter well?'

'She had pains last night – at about two o'clock in the morning – and they sent an ambulance. There was some bleeding. But it seems it was a false alert. She's in the hospital. She has a private room and my brother is with her. Mama is with her.'

'There's nothing wrong?'

'Listen, I can give you the number, Signor Trotti. Ospedale Civico – Bologna 423 42 53.'

Trotti repeated, '423 42 53,' writing down the number with his left hand on a pad that Anna Ermagni pushed towards him. 'Thanks a lot. You say she's all right?'

'Last night Signora Solaroli was a bit tired – but she ate well. A false alarm.'

'Is there an extension?'

'It's a direct number.'

'Thanks,' said Trotti, and depressed the hook of the receiver. He immediately banged the white button.

He glanced at Anna who was smiling at him, her fingers crossed.

The receptionist came on to the line.

'Signorina, 423 42 53, please, in Bologna.'

'I hope this isn't a private call.'

'Perish the thought. Bologna 423 42 53.'

'A boy or a girl, commissario?'

'The sooner you give me the number, the sooner I can tell you.'

'Pioppi, is that you?'

'Papa.'

'Pioppi, are you all right?'

'Where are you phoning from, Papa?'

'The man at your house told me you were in hospital. I should've phoned earlier. Are you all right, Pioppi? I'm catching the next train to Bologna.'

'There's no need.'

'And the baby?'

'There's no baby – not yet?'

'The man said you'd started to bleed.'

'It's nothing.'

'It can't be nothing if you're in hospital. Why did you start to bleed? And when are you going to have your baby?'

'A false alarm. I lost some blood.'

'Why did you bleed?'

'The baby's due for the day after tomorrow.'

'Why didn't you phone me?'

'There's really nothing to worry about, Papa.'

'Of course I'm worried about you, Pioppi.'

'There's no need. You must rest. Are you phoning from the lake?'

'Where's Nando?'

'Nando's with me now.'

'I'm getting the train tonight, Pioppi.'

'That's absolutely stupid.'

'I'll be there by tomorrow morning.'

'Tomorrow morning the baby won't even be due.'

'Have you phoned your mother in America?'

'Mama has got better things to worry about.'

'Why are you so stubborn, Pioppi? Why won't you accept my help? I am your father – I want to be with you.'

'It is really not necessary.'

'And the little boy?'

'What little boy?'

'The baby – it's going to be a boy, I suppose.'

'Listen, Papa, there's no need for you to come down. I am all right. The baby's not yet due. I will ring you tomorrow. I will ring you at the villa on the lake. And in the meanwhile, have a holiday. Relax. I'm with Nando here. His mother and his sister are with me. I'm all right, I swear to you. Don't worry about me – and there's no need to bother Mama. Tell her I'm well. Just look after yourself, Papa. Ciao, amore.'

'But Pioppi . . .'

'I love you, Papa. Ciao.'

SNOOPY

'Pretty girl.'

'My goddaughter.'

The unlit pipe was in his mouth and Maiocchi raised his eyebrows in mild, amused surprise. 'You get around, Piero.' He was sitting on Trotti's desk.

'My goddaughter Anna Ermagni – whom I haven't seen in years.'

'Bit young for you, isn't she?'

'She's Pisanelli's girlfriend – his fiancée.'

Maiocchi laughed. Then he nodded to the envelope on the table, 'What d'you think?'

'The photo?'

'You recognise the woman, Trotti?'

'It's Maria Cristina Belloni.'

'You were at the autopsy?'

'I left halfway through – when an uncle identified the corpse.'

'As Maria Cristina?'

Trotti nodded.

'I wanted to go to Broni,' Maiocchi said. 'But I waited for you, hoping you could come. I hung around here until past one o'clock –

by which time I heard that the corpse was identified as the younger sister.'

'Maria Cristina,' Trotti nodded.

Maiocchi took the pipe from his mouth and thoughtfully tapped it against the palm of his hand. 'If it's the younger sister who's dead, what d'you think, Piero?'

'I don't think anything until I've seen Bottone's report of the autopsy.'

'You have an opinion. What d'you think?'

Trotti shrugged, 'What do I think?'

'Well?'

'Nothing, Maiocchi. I think nothing. Not now.'

'You're not helping me.'

'Think? I should've stopped thinking a long time ago. All I know is that my daughter is in hospital awaiting a baby any moment. All I know is that she's already had a slight haemorrhage.' Again he shrugged, 'What d'you want me to think?'

'Who killed her?'

'Nobody killed Rosanna.'

'Who killed her sister?' A prod of the pipe stem towards the polaroid, 'This wretched woman in the photo.'

'Listen,' Trotti tapped his chest. 'I thought it was Rosanna they killed. The face was smashed in – it was badly bruised and covered with dry blood. I thought it was Rosanna. Zani at the scene of the crime said it was Rosanna. Boatti said it was Rosanna. Everybody seemed to think it was Rosanna.' Trotti paused, 'Rosanna Belloni wasn't a close friend – but I knew her. And what I knew of her I liked. She was a kind, good person. For all I know, she still is. Some ten, twelve years ago she used to be the headmistress of that pretty young woman you just saw – of my goddaughter. I honestly thought Rosanna was dead – and I thought I could help.' Trotti sighed, 'Apparently she's not dead. That's good and I'm very pleased. Yet nobody seems to know where Rosanna Belloni is. Nobody knows who she's with or where she's gone. She sent a card from the Po Delta – but she hasn't been seen in her hotel for four days. She went off with a man in a four-wheel-drive Fiat, Ferrara registration.'

'You're looking for her?'

'I don't think I really care any more.'

'Piero, it doesn't make any sense.'

'I could've told you that.'

'Snoopy and Luca – the Snoopy woman was Rosanna's sister. From the photo you can see that the Snoopy/Beatrice woman is Maria Cristina.'

'She's dead now, lying in the morgue.'

'The phone call, Trotti, was on Tuesday morning . . . when we got called down to the river. But the Snoopy woman was already dead. You people found her on Monday night.'

'Giorgio Boatti – a neighbour – found her.'

'Dead people don't make phone calls.'

A dry laugh, 'I certainly don't get to make phone calls – perhaps the questore would like me dead. I have to go through the blonde woman on the desk.' Trotti looked up at Maiocchi. His face was pale.

'Somebody's trying to pull the wool over our eyes.'

'A lot of people are trying to pull the wool over our eyes.' Trotti took the packet of sweets from his pocket, 'Occupational hazard. It's something you get used to.'

'Luca's here,' Maiocchi said, putting the pipe into his mouth and biting on the stem. He looked like an earnest university professor, 'You'll speak to him, won't you?' He took a box of kitchen matches from his pocket.

Trotti unwrapped a sweet.

'Since you're here, I'd like you to see him, Piero.'

'I'm not free, Maiocchi.' Trotti put the sweet in his mouth, 'My goddaughter – I've promised to take her out for a meal this evening. Her and her fiancé Pisanelli.'

'Piero, I'd very much like you to talk to him.'

'I'm going to follow my daughter's advice. Tomorrow I'm going up to the lake. Perhaps, later, when the little boy's born, I'll drive down to Bologna. Pioppi doesn't want me there for the time being. Her husband's with her – and I'll get down later. Once the worst is over. She seems to think that I want to take charge of her life – but I simply want to help. I want the best for her.'

Maiocchi stood up. The young face was drawn. He gripped the unlit pipe between his regular teeth; he ran a hand through his hair. 'I am asking you for a favour – a favour between colleagues. A favour between friends.'

'Understand me, Maiocchi.'

'The whole Belloni affair stinks and I honestly thought you of all people, Piero, would want to get to the bottom of this thing before Merenda.'

'Merenda?' With an unexpected vehemence, Trotti shouted, 'For God's sake, don't talk to me about Merenda, will you? Merenda, Merenda, Merenda. I'm sick to my back teeth of hearing about Merenda.'

It was suddenly very quiet in the small office.

'You know where you can stuff your Merenda.'

GUSTAVO

The young man was waiting for them.

Maiocchi's office was clean and very neat. A map of the city on the wall above his desk, another of Lombardy, dotted with coloured pins. Grey filing cabinets along one wall. There was none of the bulging, beige dossiers that seemed to have invaded most of the Questura. A desklamp, a telephone (electronic keys and no need to go through the switchboard) a crucifix and a crystal ashtray that was free of the slightest trace of ash.

A potted dieffenbachia basked in the waning sunlight.

'This is a copy of the suicide letter we found down by the river.' Maiocchi gestured to an armchair and Trotti sat down.

'"Feelings are not to be thrown away, like a discarded toy . . ."' Trotti read out. 'Juvenile handwriting, clearly female. A couple of spelling mistakes.' He dropped the photocopy on to the dustless desk. 'Signed "Snoopy".'

'And this gentleman', Gustavo Maiocchi nodded to the young man, 'is Signor Luca Pontevico. I thought that he could help us – you and me, Commissario Trotti – with our enquiry.'

The young man was sitting opposite the two policemen. His handsome face was drawn. Dark hair that glinted in the warm yellow light, soft skin and the black shadow of a fast growing beard. Behind the thick lashes, the eyes were dark brown. The features were regular and the bushy eyebrows rose in an amused, ironic curve. Deep dimples in the cheeks. He was wearing a white T-shirt and faded jeans. The muscular arms were tanned and dark with hair, the hands strong, the nails clean. A small tattoo on the right forearm, a military motif. There was a packet of cigarettes tucked into the rolled cuff of his T-shirt sleeve.

The firm, young jaw moved slowly as he chewed on gum, his mouth open.

He wore American-style cowboy boots; he had crossed a leg over his thigh and Trotti could see the worn heel.

'Commissario Trotti is coordinating the investigation into the death of Beatrice . . .' Maiocchi spoke to the young man, 'The woman with whom you – by your own admission – had intimate relations.' Maiocchi paused, 'Snoopy – the woman who's been murdered.'

'She's really dead?' The dark, liquid eyes looked at Trotti.

'We don't yet have the autopsy report,' Trotti said. 'You would like to see the corpse?'

'Dead?'

'Murdered.' Maiocchi had pulled a penknife from his pocket and was cleaning the bowl of his pipe. The black ashes he tapped into the earth of the dieffenbachia.

'How can she be dead if she left her stuff down by the river?' Luca shook his head, 'That's not possible.'

'Perhaps somebody wanted us to think she was alive.'

'What on earth for?' The eyebrows arched.

'Perhaps you can tell me that, Signor Pontevico.'

'I can't tell you anything. I've already said everything. There's nothing else.' He paused, 'You think I killed her?'

Trotti said, 'You may well have a motive.'

'Motive? I scarcely knew the woman.'

'Well enough to get into bed with her.'

The pale face relaxed slightly; the hint of a smile of satisfaction, 'I never asked her to go to bed. It was all her idea. We'd scarcely been dancing – at the nightclub in Redavalle – we'd scarcely been dancing ten minutes when she had her hand in my trousers.'

'That's par for the course? A woman you hardly know – within a few minutes she starts making lewd advances?'

'It's not the first time it's happened to me.'

'Lucky man,' Maiocchi said.

'Hard work. Picking up women is a skill – it's something you learn. With experience, you can normally get what you want.'

'What you want?'

Luca shrugged with false modesty.

'And so you screwed her?' Trotti asked.

The corner of the lip turned upwards, 'That's what she wanted.' He took the packet from his sleeve and lit a cigarette with an American lighter. He did not remove the gum from his mouth. His eyes squinted as the smoke rose from the smouldering tip. 'Women need their sex, just as much as we do.'

'You must've realised she was a lot older than you?'

'Sure.'

'That didn't bother you?'

'Women are like cars – they need to be run in. You can get more mileage out of a thirty-five-year-old model than out of an eighteen-year-old. Like prototypes, young girls need a lot of tuning. And they're capricious. Difficult to keep to a steady cruising speed. The great thing about older women is they need their sex. And they're honest enough to admit they like it.' He shrugged the broad shoulders of his T-shirt, while the sensual lips parted in a brief sneer. 'I was doing her a favour. I didn't really desire her. Goodness sakes, I knew she was over forty-five. With tits like that, I knew she had a lot of mileage on the clock.'

'You found her pretty?'

'Pretty? I wasn't intending to marry her, was I? She wasn't pretty – and I don't know whether she could cook and sew.'

'You sound very professional,' Trotti said.

'Professional? I do a bit of car racing – rallies, that sort of thing. I've done several laps at Monza.' With finger and thumb, he removed the cigarette as he exhaled, 'Listen, she was OK. No Ornella Muti. But OK. Good company. Fun to be with. At first she seemed very lively.'

'Where was this?'

'At Redavalle – it was a Saturday at the end of July.'

Maiocchi glanced at a wall calendar, 'The twenty-first?'

'My parents had just gone off to the sea. They left on the eighteenth.'

'How old are you, Signor Pontevico?'

'Twenty-seven.'

'And your occupation.'

He shrugged, 'I help my father.'

'Doing what?'

'We raise chickens and export them, mainly to the Middle East.'

Trotti jotted something down on a piece of paper. 'You say that Signorina Belloni was lively.'

'It was like Beatrice – she called herself Beatrice – was on some kind of drugs. On uppers. Very nervous, and she kept whispering dirty things in my ear.'

Maiocchi had lit his pipe, 'What sort of things?'

Looking at Trotti, Luca said, 'And she insisted on paying for the drinks . . .'

'She had money?'

'That's the difference between young and old women. Young women are out for what they can get – one way or another, you have to pay. Nothing comes free.'

'Belloni had money?'

'A lot of money.' He whistled softly as he shook his head, 'She even wanted to give me some.'

'You accepted?'

'A Latin lover.' His left hand fiddled with a gold crucifix hanging at his neck. 'Signor Commissario, I'm a Latin Lover.' He raised his shoulders again, 'Perhaps you go fishing. Or you like soccer – or your friend likes to smoke a pipe. We all have our little hobby – and I'm a lover. Nothing wrong in that. You think women don't need sex? You think they don't like it?'

Trotti shrugged, 'Long time since I've been in the thick of things.'

'I'm not a gigolo, if that's what you think. I don't do it for money.'

'Why did you screw her?'

'Why not?'

'Why?'

'I told you, it's my hobby. More than a hobby, it's a job. You're a policeman – I'm a lover.' A satisfied shrug, 'To use your expression – a professional.'

'Not afraid of catching diseases?'

From the hip pocket of his jeans, he fished out a little plastic capsule. 'Tatù – I take my precautions, commissario. In your job, I imagine you sometimes have to wear a bullet-proof vest.' A grin, 'We professionals know the risks. And we come prepared.'

LIES

The jaw ceased to chew. It fell open, revealing the round ball of pink gum on the triangular tongue. 'You think I'm lying?'

'That's not what I said, Signor Pontevico.'

'I'm a liar?'

Trotti took another sweet from the packet of Charms, 'You're hiding something from us. Suppression of the truth.'

Luca resumed his chewing. He fiddled with the crucifix at his throat.

'You were her lover. You were this Snoopy woman's lover. She – or a friend of hers – phones 113 and says Snoopy's going to commit suicide. For love. Unrequited love for you.'

'Nothing to do with me.'

'That's what you say, Signor Pontevico. But the same woman is now dead – beaten to death. And it's my job – it's our job to find the culprit.' Trotti paused, rattled the sweet nervously against the back of his teeth. 'At this moment, you would seem to be our best suspect. Oh, I know, it's nearly Ferragosto. You, me, Commissario Maiocchi here – we'd all like to get away from the city. Get away from the dust and the heat and spend a few days at the sea. Or in the hills. Or on the lakes. But the point is – you must understand this – Maiocchi and I are professionals in our way. Perhaps you're not guilty. It's possible, it's even probable. You seem a nice sort of person. But try to understand our position. Professionally we need to put somebody away.' Trotti breathed in, shaking his head. 'Why not you? You might be innocent, of course. That's no major problem. If you're innocent or if there's not enough solid proof to justify your presence in prison, the judge can always let you go at the beginning of September. Innocent or guilty, the evidence available to us would appear to be against you.'

Maiocchi asked, 'Is it really against him, Trotti?'

'Christ's sake, Maiocchi, we can put him away. What've we got to lose?'

Luca stubbed out his cigarette. He was now nervously rubbing the crucifix between finger and thumb.

'What solid evidence do we have?'

Trotti turned to face the other policeman. A fat cloud rose from Maiocchi's pipe. 'Why don't you take up sweets. That thing smells atrocious.'

'What solid evidence do we have, Commissario Trotti?'

'What do you suggest, Maiocchi? I want to get out of this place. I'm not going to hang around here. I want to get down to Bologna, see my daughter, see my grandchild. And if this man is guilty, I don't want him to be going off to the Adriatic coast, enjoying himself with frustrated German hausfrau or with sex-starved rich old ladies. On his own admission, he's a lady's man. What if he's a murderer? You realise what'll happen if he gets up to something down in Rimini or wherever he's going? Another corpse and we'll get to carry the can, Maiocchi. Better for everybody if we put him away for a couple of weeks.'

Silence.

Maiocchi smoked his pipe, placidly watching Luca from behind the clouds of smoke. 'Perhaps he's telling the truth, Commissario Trotti.'

Trotti sucked his sweet.

Luca stared at his hand. He was sweating. 'Of course I'm telling the truth.'

After a while, Trotti got up and went to the window. In a conversational tone, he said, 'It was her money you were after, wasn't it?'

'Don't be absurd.'

'Then why did you kill her?'

'You must be mad.'

'I'm in a hurry, Signor Pontevico. Please tell us the truth. Tell us the truth – then perhaps we can let you hurry back to your tanned women in the nightclubs of Rimini.'

The young man sighed.

'You took her to Garlasco, didn't you?'

He folded his arms, a hand at the crucifix, 'Yes.'

'You ran her back to the Casa Patrizia?'

'Where?'

'You knew she lived there.'

'The private home? That building you can see from the railway?'

Trotti nodded, 'The Casa Patrizia.'

'That's where they keep the insane people. It's . . .'

'Yes?'

'It's a private lunatic asylum, isn't it?'

Trotti said, 'That's where you took her, isn't it? After you screwed her, that's where you took her?'

His face was very pale, 'I left her at the railway station.'

'Please don't lie.' Trotti turned to Maiocchi, 'You got an arrest form?' He smiled, 'This place is so tidy, I wonder where you can keep everything.' He leaned over and tapping Maiocchi on the arm, asked in a conversational tone, 'I forgot to ask you, Gustavo – how's the wife?'

'I think he's innocent, Commissario Trotti.'

'He's hiding something.'

Luca released the crucifix, 'I took her to the station at Garlasco. And that was the last time I saw her – until we met at the station a week later.'

'Station?'

'In the city. The central station. She kept phoning me – I don't know how she got my number in Rimini – it was becoming an embarrassment. And anyway, I had to come back to Broni. So I drove into town. And that's where we met.'

'She was on drugs?'

He raised the shoulders of his T-shirt. 'I suspected something. The first time we made love – she fell asleep. And in her sleep, she couldn't stop shivering. And then I saw her at the station, here at the city station. In the days I hadn't seen her, she'd got a lot thinner. And her breath smelt – you know how it is with people who aren't eating properly. She was nervous – more agitated than at Redavalle. I felt sorry for her but . . .'

'Yes?'

'I was embarrassed. There weren't many people about in the station – but she had a very strange behaviour. In public, like that.'

'What?'

'She pulled at my belt, she said she wanted to make love. She said she loved me. She called strange names – names of other men. It was quite scary. Without me, she said she would die.'

'What did you do?'

'It was embarrassing. There were people who knew me.'

'Very embarrassing.'

'I managed to get her out of the station entrance . . . There's a fountain, a water fountain, near the left-luggage office. I got her there and then I got angry. I told her that it wasn't possible – that everything was over. I told her I was engaged to another woman.'

'And?'

'She started screaming and shouting – and suddenly she collapsed. Christ, I was scared. I thought she was dead. I splashed her with some water and when she came to, she was like another person. A quiet little girl. She started to cry. She said she wanted to go home. She was scared, she said. She knew that she was going to die and that it was my fault because I didn't love her. Because I wouldn't protect her. That's what she said. But not hysterically. She spoke calmly. She kept blinking, like somebody who'd just woken from a long sleep.'

'Home to Garlasco?'

'I put her in the car and I ran her home.'

'Home where?'

'I can't remember the name of the street.' Again Luca Pontevico shrugged, 'I was surprised, I thought she lived in Milan. That's what she'd told me. I didn't know she had a place in the city.'

'San Teodoro?'

Luca shook his head and smiled, 'No – I know San Teodoro.'

Trotti asked, 'Via Mantova?'

'That's right.' He nodded vigorously, 'Via Mantova. I had to carry her up some steps. She lived on the first floor.'

'You took her to her place in Via Mantova – and then you screwed her. As good a way as any of spending the afternoon.'

'You have an unpleasant mind, commissario.'

'We professionals never miss an opportunity.'

Luca's hand resumed its autonomous fingering of the crucifix.

'You took her home, Signor Pontevico. Then what did you do?'

He hesitated.

'Well?'

'She was pale – she was trembling. I was frightened. And she was sweating.' He bit his lip.

'So you tiptoed out and left her to sweat it out?'

Luca said nothing. His eyes went from Trotti to Maiocchi.

'Well?'

He looked down at his hands, 'I called a friend. I went down to the car and I called a friend.'

'What friend?'

'A doctor.'

Maiocchi was frowning, 'Why did you hide that?'

'Hide what?'

'You never mentioned a doctor. Why did you hide that from us?'

Trotti sighed with repressed irritation. He turned to face his colleague while sadly shaking his head, 'Maiocchi, you're deliberately trying to be stupid?'

'Stupid?'

'He didn't give a shit one way or another about the girl. But can't you see she was blackmailing him? Tatù or no Tatù, she was playing at being pregnant. A trick as old as the hills. And that's why he needed a doctor. To see if she needed an abortion. A common enough risk in his profession.'

ABORTION

'I'm going home,' Trotti said.

'We need to see the autopsy report.' Maiocchi accompanied him along the corridor of the third floor. The blonde receptionist had disappeared.

'To find out whether the woman was pregnant?'

'You think she was blackmailing him, Trotti?'

It was past seven o'clock. The air was now a lot cooler. Trotti felt tired; his head was heavy from too much concentration. 'A cold shower – and then a meal with my two young lovers.' He glanced at the clock on the wall.

'You think Maria Cristina was blackmailing him? You don't really think she was pregnant?'

'It doesn't matter whether she was pregnant or not. For all I know, the Belloni woman had already been through the menopause. The autopsy's not going to tell you anything. The point is that he was scared. And he called for his doctor friend . . . There was something wrong with her and he was scared. Not for her, but for himself. What did he say the doctor's name was?'

'You think we should arrest Luca now?'

'What evidence have you got against him?' Trotti smiled to himself, 'You remember Gino?'

'The old blind receptionist?'

'Gino always used to say I was too hard on my men. He said that was why I'd lost Magagna.'

Maiocchi asked, 'You want me to arrest Luca?'

'And he said that I'd lose Pisanelli too.'

'You think Luca's guilty?'

'Do I think your young film star Luca murdered Rosanna's sister?' Trotti stopped before the open door of his office. 'It's possible – anything's possible. But you'd still have to explain all the song and dance about Snoopy and the letter addressed to him. If he really murdered her, why did he want to call attention to himself? And how did she get to San Teodoro?'

'I shouldn't arrest him now?'

'Get hold of the doctor.'

'Dottor Silvio Silvi.'

'Get the doctor first. Find out what happened. Perhaps the doctor can tell you how the body got from Via Mantova to San Teodoro. Hang on to Luca until you've spoken to his doctor. You'll probably find that he specialises in cheap abortions.' Trotti put a hand on the door handle. The other hand he placed on Maiocchi's shoulder, 'You, too, Maiocchi, ought to take a holiday, you know. Get away from here for a few days. Spend a bit of time with your wife. And with your children.'

The younger man shrugged, 'My wife doesn't want to spend any time with me. She's fed up with me, she's fed up with her policeman husband.'

'I don't believe that.'

'And now she's found somebody else.'

'It must be this building.' Trotti sighed before making a gesture towards the ugly walls of the corridor. 'Husbands and fathers – and this Questura makes us into monsters. Uncaring monsters.'

'This is my job. The Questura is my home.'

'Your job is your family, Maiocchi.'

Maiocchi smiled, 'I don't think you understand, Trotti.'

'I understand.'

'No,' Maiocchi said, shaking his head. 'Perhaps you've always been married to the job. But with me – with us – it's different. My wife doesn't like me. Sometimes I don't even think my children like me. So what else do you want me to do?' He tapped the ugly wall, 'The Questura – this job – it's all I've got. Let me hang on to it. Because there is nothing else.'

RALEIGH

In the air there was the perfume of honeysuckle blossom and the fumes of the buses.

Swallows perched, facing both backwards and forwards, on the light cables strung across the street. It would soon be eight o'clock and the air was now pleasantly cool. There was a slight hint of wind. As Trotti glanced up to the red tinged sky, he saw there was still no sign of rain.

Trotti stepped out of the Questura and went down the steps.

His head ached. He felt tired, but strangely cheerful. And now, he told himself, he would be taking a holiday. He wondered whether Eva was still in Via Milano waiting for him. He felt an unexpected pleasure at the thought she had cooked for him last night. Perhaps she had prepared something tonight – anyway, he would take her to the restaurant with Anna and Pisanelli. He turned north up Strada Nuova, enjoying the evening, enjoying the sense that the further he got away from the Questura, the freer he was of his problems. The trouble was, he knew, that he allowed his job to pervade his existence. Now, he told himself, he was going to relax. He looked forward to eating with the two young people. Perhaps in his way Pisanelli was the right person for Anna. 'Pierangelo?' Trotti smiled to himself and silently promised he would make an effort to be pleasant.

'Commissario Trotti?'

He turned.

The man was wheeling a bicycle – an English bicycle with high handlebars, a glinting bell, a leather saddle and with a white reflective strip on the rear mudguard. The yellow headlamp dimmed as the man halted beside Trotti.

'I am Signor Belloni. We met this morning.'

Trotti gave the man a smile. 'Of course. At the autopsy.'

'If you have a minute.' He propped the bike against the wall of the old pharmacy. (Several years earlier the wall had been covered with political graffiti. The graffiti had now been partly hidden by a new coat of ochre paint.) 'I would like to talk to you – about my niece. About my nieces. If you have a spare moment.'

'I'm afraid I really don't have any time. I'm going home – and tomorrow I'm going on holiday.'

The man was well dressed; he wore a cream-coloured suit, a blue shirt and a dark blue bow tie. His hair was white and very elegantly cut. Mid-seventies, Trotti thought, and wondered whether he, Piero Trotti, would be as well preserved in ten years' time.

In ten years' time, when the little Piero Solaroli would be ten years old. Quinta elementare.

'My niece always spoke well of you, Commissario Trotti.' He placed a hand on Trotti's sleeve. 'Please, just a moment.' The patrician face and the pale blue eyes were pleading. 'You would be doing me an immense favour.'

For a moment Trotti hesitated.

He thought of Pisanelli, he thought of Anna Ermagni. He had promised to take them for a meal. He thought of Eva. 'Just five minutes,' Trotti said, knowing well that he could stay with the retired banker as long as it was necessary to find out the truth. The hidden truth – that was why he had become a policeman. Not – as his wife always maintained – because he enjoyed bullying people or manipulating them or having a hold over them. He had become a policeman because he had always wanted to know the truth. Trotti was not an educated man but he liked to think that he understood human nature. The truth about people. Why they did what they did. As he looked at the older man, Trotti sensed that at last perhaps he was going to understand what had happened to Maria Cristina, what had led up to that final, fatal moment when she had been beaten to death at San Teodoro.

And perhaps he would find out what had become of Rosanna.

Rosanna Belloni, his friend.

Trotti asked, 'You care for a drink? We could go to the Bar Dante.'

The man smiled with satisfaction. 'Good man.' He took a key from the jacket pocket and locked the rear wheel of the black, Raleigh bicycle – the letters in imperial gold down the main frame. 'I'd rather we were alone.' He made a gesture towards the high walls of the university on the other side of Strada Nuova. The Italian flag hung limply, scarcely affected by the feeble breeze. 'And I loathe the smoke in bars.' Signor Belloni took the newspaper – Indro Montanelli's *Giornale* – from where it was clipped to the handlebars and put it in his jacket pocket. He slipped his arm through Trotti's and together they crossed the road and entered the high archway of the university.

He wore soft brown shoes.

Overhead, the swallows did not seem to notice that the street lights had come on, but continued to bicker passionately among themselves.

MAGNOLIA

The neon lights in the concierge's office were already switched on.

Trotti and Signor Belloni went past the engraved stones that had been embedded into the walls like stamps in an oversize collection. Through the small doorway and into the courtyard. Their footsteps echoed hollowly.

The Cloisters of Magnolia.

A couple of lovers were sitting beside the wall, enjoying the gentle air of the passing day. Despite the late hour, a man in overalls was sweeping the cobbled courtyard. The birch broom moved in regular, short strokes. The man was sweeping away the dust of another long day in the city. Another day without rain.

Trotti noticed the scent of the magnolia. 'It's a long time since I've been here.'

There was a bench.

Trotti looked quizzically at the older man.

Signor Belloni took the newspaper from his pocket and placed it on the stone bench. He then pulled at the creases of his trousers as he sat down. The pale eyes seemed amused, 'Commissario, a bank manager is not very dissimilar to a priest. In the course of time, many secrets are confided to a bank manager.' He smiled, 'A priest or perhaps a policeman . . . Like Rosanna, I never got round to marrying. But perhaps not for the same reasons as her. It must be a satisfaction to have your own family.'

Trotti was leaning forward, with his arms now on his thighs. He turned to look at the banker, 'Why did Rosanna never marry?'

The old man gave a bland smile.

'She was intelligent – she was at one time a very beautiful woman. And she loved children.'

'You didn't stay to the end of the autopsy, commissario?'

'Why don't you answer my question?'

'Why did Rosanna never marry?' The banker laughed and raised his pale hand. 'I will answer your question, I swear. But I'm a methodical sort of person. An old maid, I'm afraid.' He paused, then looking about him, said, 'This lovely perfume – is that the magnolias?'

Trotti nodded.

'Bit late for magnolias, isn't it?'

'Marcescent.'

'What?'

'Magnolia flowers can wither without dropping off – if the conditions are right.'

'Marcescent,' the man repeated admiringly. 'You're an educated man, commissario.'

'An ignorant policeman,' Trotti said. 'Ignorant – but not necessarily stupid.'

The two lovers had got up and were now walking away, hand in hand, towards Piazza Leonardo da Vinci and the scaffolded towers.

'Of course, it could be the girl's perfume,' Trotti remarked.

Smiling, the old man watched the young couple leave. 'I will tell you about Rosanna, Commissario Trotti. In a way, that's why I wanted to see you. But in my own time and in my own, old-maidish sort of way.'

He paused again. 'My brother was twenty-one years older than me – my mother gave birth to Giovanni when she was only nineteen. She was herself a very pretty girl. She started life working as a maid for my father's family in Monza. The Bellonis were rich – they sold knives – and so for her, marrying my father was a good catch.' Belloni smiled sadly, 'If he was alive today, Giovanni would be nearly a hundred. Ninety-five, to be precise. It doesn't seem so long ago.'

Trotti did not move. He sat with his elbows on his thighs, his hands hanging between his legs.

'After Giovanni my mother had several other children but they all died at birth or in the first few months. No prenatal clinics in those days. I think the doctors expected me to die, too. That was in 1916. I feel I've disappointed them. As you can see,' Signor Belloni tapped his thigh conclusively, 'As you can see, I'm still very much here.'

'Your brother was Rosanna's father?'

A frown. Signor Belloni continued, his hands beside him on the cool stone of the bench. 'Giovanni married when he was twenty-six. He married a woman who came from another rich family. An old family that had fallen upon hard times. During the Great War, at a time when a lot of people were building up fortunes – fortunes that are still around – how do you think Agnelli in Turin got to be rich? For all those northern industrialists, the Great War was a windfall – during the Great War my sister-in-law's people lost a lot of property, much of it in Udine and bombed by the Austrians. Consequently the marriage was a fairly good idea . . . at least for my sister-in-law. The Bellonis from Monza weren't exactly nouveaux riches – but their money was bluer than their blood. My sister-in-law was an aristocrat – and not much else. She had grown up in a sheltered environment. She had had private tutors until the family could no longer pay for her schooling. She could not cook, she could not sew. Yet Gabriella had one great virtue in Giovanni's eyes.' The old man paused.

'One virtue?'

'She worshipped the ground that my brother Giovanni walked on,' Belloni said and laughed. 'Goodness knows why. My brother Giovanni wasn't a very nice person, I'm afraid. He got out of fighting – Mama wasn't going to risk both her husband and her firstborn in the war. But in 1919 he came down with influenza – nothing very serious, but people seemed to think that afterwards he was a changed man.' Belloni tapped the side of his head, 'The influenza left its mark upon my brother.' He paused, 'She was a silly thing, Gabriella. It is funny how history repeats itself. My father married a young girl – and similarly my brother Giovanni married Gabriella when she was not yet nineteen. But there was very little similarity between Gabriella and my mother. My mother was hard. She came from peasant stock and believed that life was cruel. She honestly thought that it would have been a mistake to let us children think that we could expect anything from other people. A hard woman. Love was not the sort of thing my mother had time to indulge in. She was a good woman, but, you know, I can't once recall her ever kissing me with affection. She'd kiss me – but there was never any warmth. Not because Mama was cold, but . . .' He shrugged, 'I suppose because she felt she had to hold herself back. After all, how else can you cope with a succession of miscarriages and stillbirths other than by repressing your true feelings?' In the failing light, the pale eyes looked at Trotti, 'Nowadays, your modern psychologists would say a Prussian childhood like mine would inevitably end in homosexuality.'

The perfume of the magnolias seemed to grow stronger.

'Perhaps it was the lack of affection that drove my brother to do what he did. Being older than me, it was harder for him. By the time Mama got round to having me she had no doubt softened a bit. Or perhaps she was surprised that at last one of the children did not end up lifeless and wrapped up in a white cloth.' He looked at Trotti, 'Life can be very hard for a woman – much harder than it ever is for us.' He paused for a moment, waiting perhaps for Trotti's reaction. 'It was about the time that Giovanni's first child . . .'

'Rosanna?' Trotti asked.

'It was about the time Rosanna was born – it must have been in 1930. Father died and Giovanni took over the family business. Our father never had any time for the Fascists or Mussolini. In his way, I think father was a poet. A poet and a dreamer. He ran the family business well, but without enthusiasm. He loved to read poetry and I have memories of him shutting himself away in the library and me not being allowed to go anywhere near the old oak door. I can still remember the smell of Papa's library. He loved Dante – and he loved the Germans, Schiller and Goethe. Papa hated the war – he always said that he had been against Italian intervention in 1915. I scarcely knew him – in those days, there wasn't the kind of intimacy between parents and children of the bourgeoisie that there was among the other classes. I loved Papa dearly – but from a great distance. So he went off to war, leaving his wife, his two sons and the factory – he didn't want to go, he loathed the interventionists, he loathed D'Annunzio, he loathed the Irredentists. Papa was already over forty, but he felt it was his duty. To his country and to his class. He was with the Alpini and it was at Tremalzo in Trento that he lost his health. He was at the front – where frostbite was as much an enemy as the Austrians. I can remember him coming back. I was only three years old. So handsome, so very handsome in his lieutenant's uniform. He took me in his arms . . .'

Trotti waited.

'When Papa died, I was still a young boy – and anyway, I had no desire to go into the knife business. There was Giovanni and he was a good business man – like most people from the Brianza. Business is in our blood. Other Italians say we Brianzoli are mean. I don't think we're mean – it's just that we know how to drive a good bargain. By now, we Belloni were making swords and knives and bayonets for Mussolini's imperial army – and doing well. That's when Giovanni became a Fascist. Out of conviction or out of self interest, I never knew. More than anything, I think, it was out of a desire for recognition.'

From Strada Nuova there came the occasional sound of passing traffic – a bus, a taxi, the muffled whine of a Vespa.

'That's right,' Signor Belloni said, now counting on his fingers. 'Rosanna was born in 1930 and Maria Cristina was born in 1941.' He thoughtfully bit the tip of his tongue, 'I think that at first my brother got into Fascist politics because he liked wielding the power and being recognised. He didn't really believe in any of it. He enjoyed the posturing. He liked the uniform – the tunic and the black shirt that hid his pot belly. And he probably enjoyed the attention he got from all the women. Fascist or not, he certainly did everything in his power to keep me from being conscripted. I was class of '16 – and without Giovanni I could have been sent to Spain or Greece. Or Russia.' He added, 'I lost friends in Russia. I sometimes wonder if it wouldn't have been a lot simpler if I had died along with them.'

Trotti said, 'My older brother died in the hills in 1945. He was murdered.'

'I was lucky. I got a job with an international bank. I was in Rome in '43 and I managed to move south. I have always been able to speak English – I spent a year at school in London – and so I soon found a job with the Americans. But from what I gather, at a time when I was making a lot of contacts in the south – contacts with people who were soon going to run the new Italy – my brother went berserk. I genuinely believe he went mad. Italy had changed sides and he felt betrayed personally. So once the puppet Republic was set up in Salò, he was determined to get his own back on all those people who had suddenly turned on him when the king removed Mussolini from power.'

'Where was he?'

'From what people tell me, he was worse than the Germans. A wild beast, thirsting for the blood of his enemies. You know what the Brianzoli are like. Slow to anger, but once their blood is up, there is no going back. And so . . .'

'Yes?'

'They murdered him. They murdered Giovanni. In the January of 1945, my brother was gunned down as he was leaving a brothel in Milan.' Signor Belloni looked at Trotti, an unamused smile on his face, 'A year later, my sister-in-law, Gabriella married again. To a young and charming Partisan leader from the south. She was forty years old and he was just twenty-nine.'

APRILIA

'He was from the south and in the last nine months of the war he had formed his own group of Partisans. In a way, you can understand Gabriella falling for him. He had those fine dark features that you sometimes find in the south. Beautiful skin. And he was fairly tall. It was only much later that I discovered that he had deserted from the Fascist army not for any noble, political reasons but because he had murdered a man – over a game of cards. And many men of his Partisan group were little better than ruffians.'

In the deepening blue sky overhead, clouds had turned from pink to an angry red.

'I'd like to think that Gabriella did what she did out of a desire to keep the knife factory in the family. Perhaps she thought that by marrying a powerful anti-Fascist she could get the Bellonis back into an odour of sanctity. In point of fact, after the war, the factory was confiscated by the young Republic . . . this was of course after the iniquitous referendum on the monarchy. Most of the remaining wealth her new husband managed to squander fairly effectively. On clothes, on women, on horses. At a time when only a few could afford a bicycle, he used to run around in a shining Lancia Aprilia. He had his crowd of friends. Some were old Partisans but most were criminals from the south who had been exiled to Milan. I'm afraid Vitaliano was not a very savoury person.'

'Not a wise marriage for your sister-in-law.'

'Fortunately for the family, my brother Giovanni had invested much of his wealth in bricks and mortar. And having now qualified as a lawyer – I was working for an American oil company in Milan – I was able to protect some of the possessions from Vitaliano's depredations. With time, he got more and more demanding. In the early Fifties – he didn't have a job – Vitaliano started to have a serious drinking problem. Once he was drunk, Vitaliano could become very violent. He was violent with his wife – and he was violent with the children. He came from Foggia and he had been married – his first wife died before the war. The two children – nice children, younger than Rosanna but older than Maria Cristina – came to live with Gabriella and her girls. They got on well – perhaps a fear of Vitaliano united them all. There was very little that I could do. For many people, Vitaliano was still a hero of the anti-Fascist war – and we Bellonis were dyed-in-the-wool Fascists. That was my brother's legacy. I knew Gabriella was unhappy but, as you can remember,' Belloni said, tapping the newspaper spread out on the bench, 'there was no divorce in those days. Italy was still a staunchly Catholic country – and married women had to put up with their lot in silence.'

Trotti said, 'You sound like a feminist.'

He smiled, 'I admire women – I admire them for their self-sacrifice. Perhaps that's why I never married.'

Trotti raised an eyebrow, 'Why not?'

'To be a man you have to be hard. Hard, reliable and intransigent. That's what women require of a man – and I don't think that was the sort of person I have ever wanted to be.'

'You have to be hard, reliable and intransigent to be a banker manager.'

He laughed, 'I nearly married – a long time ago, commissario. And in a different city. The young lady went off and got engaged to an English officer with a long nose and a swagger stick. And so in time, I invested my affection elsewhere.' He paused, 'That is no doubt why I am so fond of Rosanna.'

'You think she's alive?'

'Commissario, I wouldn't be wasting your time if I didn't feel what I've got to tell you was useful.'

'Why are you telling me all this?'

He held up his hand, 'I saw you this morning at the hospital. I wanted to talk to you – but you hurried away with your two friends. You see, I can remember Rosanna mentioning you to me.'

'Me?'

'I believe you took her out for a meal on several occasions.'

Trotti laughed, slightly embarrassed, 'She told you that?'

'She liked you a lot. You were kind. She said that you were lonely, that your wife had left you.'

'Rosanna and I met once or twice – but there was nothing in it. Friends – I like to think we were friends.'

'You believe in friendship between a man and a woman, Commissario Trotti?'

'Signor Belloni, I met your niece at the time of the Aldo Moro affair. I met her for professional reasons. She loved her job. It didn't take much insight to realise that she loved her job as headmistress because she loved the children. A couple of years later I bumped into her in town – in the underground market, of all places. She was – she still is, I hope – a charming woman. I was living alone, my wife was already in America.' Trotti shrugged, 'I invited her out for a meal. We met on several occasions after that. But you must understand, I was a married man. I still am.'

'Do you see your wife?'

'My wife is now in Illinois – in Chicago.'

'You see her?'

'The last time I saw Agnese was when Pioppi, my daughter, got married.'

'You could always have divorced your wife, commissario.'

'Never.'

'Why not? Times have changed. Divorce is no longer a cause of shame.'

Trotti unwrapped a sweet and put it in his mouth, 'What interest could Rosanna have in an irascible policeman?'

'She has always spoken well of you.'

'If Rosanna had spent fifty years not being married, it wasn't likely that she was going to give up her freedom to marry a divorced policeman. And, anyway, Signor Belloni, to be quite frank, I don't think that's what she wanted. Rosanna liked children because she liked people – but I don't think she was interested in men. At least, not in this man. Not physically. Kind, good – even very affectionate. But she always gave me the impression of being – of not wanting any physical commitment.' Trotti paused, looked at the banker, 'As far as I was concerned, at least.'

'I understand.'

'With her, I always felt that I was a big, clumsy male. She was very delicate. When there was physical contact – I don't know, my hand accidentally touching hers – she would draw back. Like a frightened animal.'

Signor Belloni said something.

'I beg your pardon.'

'He tried to rape her.'

'Who?'

'Vitaliano – her step-father. He attempted raping her. I don't think it happened more than a couple of times, but it was enough.'

'What?'

'It was much later that I found out. Believe me, commissario, if I had known at the time, I would have killed him. A monster and I would've killed him with these hands. I who abhor all forms of violence, I would have murdered him – and without the slightest compunction. It would have been better for us all. Rosanna and I were almost like brother and sister. I am fourteen years older than her but we grew up together in the same house.'

'Her step-father raped her?'

'Rosanna never revealed her secret.'

'When?'

'When did he try to deflower her? After the war – it was in '47 or '48. Rosanna was already an adult – and this was before he had started drinking seriously. But if she kept her secret, I think it was in order to protect her mother. Rosanna felt that her mother had married that man to protect the family fortune and . . .'

'He got her pregnant?'

'No,' the old man said softly. 'There was never any physical penetration.'

'Rosanna never had any children?'

It was now almost dark and Trotti had difficulty in seeing the older man's face. He repeated the question, 'Rosanna never had a child by her step-father?'

'You ask strange questions.'

'And the photo I saw?'

'What photo, commissario?'

'At San Teodoro.' Trotti's mouth was dry; he swallowed the sweet, 'At San Teodoro. In her place. The photo of a little girl that Rosanna was holding in her arms? A little girl that looked a bit like her. A pretty little girl. A photo taken in a town hall.'

'No, Trotti.' Signor Belloni placed his hand on Trotti's leg. 'For several years Rosanna liked to look after the baby.'

'Whose baby?'

'It wasn't a girl – it was a boy. It was Maria Cristina's little boy.'

'Maria Cristina's?'

'Vitaliano managed to get Maria Cristina – he managed to get his other step-daughter pregnant. She was only nine when he started abusing her.' A shrug and the glint of his teeth in the dark, 'Not really surprising, is it, that Maria Cristina's always been so fragile?'

AUTOPSY

'He knows?' Trotti asked after a long silence.

'Who?'

'Boatti – Giorgio Boatti.'

Belloni took his time before answering. 'Giorgio phoned me this afternoon. He said that he had been with you – and he told me that you believe he's involved in Maria Cristina's death.'

'I think he's trying to protect Rosanna Belloni.'

'He seems to believe you think he's guilty.'

'Is he, Signor Belloni?' Trotti stood up. He started walking backwards and forwards in front of the bench, with his hands in his pockets. The last shreds of red light were leaving the sky. Mosquitoes had returned to the city from the fields. 'I've never understood why he was so interested in Rosanna's death.'

'Giorgio has always loved Rosanna.'

Trotti stopped walking, 'How long's Boatti known Rosanna for?'

'For ever.'

'What?'

'Maria Cristina was fourteen years old when Vitaliano got her pregnant. Today things would have been different. Today a fourteen-year-old girl would have got an abortion and that would have been the end of that – if there can ever be an end to the damage caused by sexual abuse.'

'She gave birth to the child in the photo?'

Belloni nodded.

'Why?'

'There was no choice.'

'No choice?' Trotti made a dismissive gesture. 'You had friends. I imagine you're a Freemason.'

'Freemason?'

'You could've done something. A Freemason doctor friend in the hospital, a quick operation.'

'Perhaps, but Maria Cristina was nearly four months into her pregnancy by the time she told the truth to Rosanna.' The old man added, 'And you forget that it wasn't my decision to take.'

'And so Maria Cristina gave birth to an illegitimate child? The child of her step-father.'

'He killed himself. Vitaliano got drunk – this was before Giorgio was born.'

'Giorgio?'

'What did you think, Trotti?'

Trotti sat down heavily on the bench, 'Boatti is Maria Cristina's son?'

A cold laugh, 'That's why you saw him in Rosanna's photograph.'

'He murdered his mother?'

The man laughed disparagingly, 'Your can't believe that.'

'Giorgio Boatti is Maria Cristina's son,' Trotti muttered softly under his breath.

He spoke in a matter-of-fact voice, 'Fortunately for everyone, Vitaliano was killed before we even knew Maria Cristina was pregnant. He got drunk and he killed himself. In a fog near Casalpusterlengo – he went straight into a lorry.' Belloni crossed his arms and began to rock gently on the bench. 'Not a great loss. Other than for the Lancia Aprilia that would be worth a fortune now.'

'I suppose Boatti – the adoptive father – is a Freemason?'

'Giacomino Boatti was an old college friend of mine. We studied at Ghislieri together.'

'He adopted Boatti and gave him his name?'

'His wife was infertile – and they both had desperately wanted a child. They had tried for years unsuccessfully. Mino was a good man – Trotti, you can't imagine how good Mino was. He was a Republican – Garibaldi's party. Mino was perhaps the only honest politician I have ever met. Mino Boatti accepted the little baby boy with open arms. With Loredana, Mino gave the little Giorgio a happy home. And in the end, Giorgio went to Ghislieri too.'

'And Rosanna?'

'The shame killed Rosanna's mother. Perhaps Gabriella had suspected something all along, even before, when Vitaliano had abused Rosanna. Gabriella didn't die for another twenty years – but it was the scandal that killed her. She spent the last fifteen years of her life in bed, with Rosanna looking after her.'

Trotti did not speak for a while. He sat with his hands hanging between his legs. Then he asked, 'Why the photo of Giorgio Boatti with Rosanna?'

'In the early years, Rosanna saw a lot of Giorgio. In a way Giorgio was the child Rosanna never had, the child she would've liked to have. In the Fifties the idea of an unmarried woman bringing a child up by herself was out of the question. Of course, Rosanna could've got married – but you can understand her being frightened of men. The whole scandal had to be hidden. For the sake of appearances.'

'For the sake of the child's welfare.'

'Precisely. Maria Cristina was sent off to Switzerland for the last four months of her pregnancy. I was in Lugano with Rosanna for the birth. Then Giacomo Boatti and his wife came to take the little boy. They brought him back here.'

'And Maria Cristina? How on earth did she react to losing her boy?'

'The next few years Maria Cristina lived in Milan.'

'She saw the child?'

'Maria Cristina went to school in Milan. She even got her diploma in accountancy.' The old man shook his head, 'I never once heard her mention her child. Never – it was as if nothing had happened, as if she had never been raped, as if she had never carried the baby in her belly. It wasn't until about five years later, when she was nearly twenty, that she started having her depressions. Her terrible black depressions when she needed to be calmed by a doctor . . .'

'By Doctor Roberti?'

'I see you've done your homework, Trotti.' A dry chuckle in the darkness. 'Roberti came later – in the early Sixties.'

'I thought Roberti specialised in venereal diseases.'

The old man shrugged, 'Maria Cristina would have her depression after a period of phrenetic sexual activity. She would disappear and later we'd discover she was in Genova living with a sailor. Or living in Turin with another woman. Maria Cristina had several turbulent lesbian affairs. And when we came looking for her, she resented Rosanna's concern. She saw it as interference.' Again the humourless laugh, 'The two sisters reacted differently to their terrible experience at the hands of their step-father. Rosanna was frightened of sex. Maria Cristina actively sought it. She sought reassurance and affection and she thought she could get that by sharing her body.' He paused, 'Maria Cristina died as she had lived – craving affection. And never finding it.'

'How did Giorgio Boatti see his relationship with Rosanna?'

'An aunt. He called her aunt. He was told that Rosanna was one of Signora Boatti's cousins. You see, Rosanna was also his godmother.'

'I accused him of having an affair with her.'

'That's what he told me.' Belloni had placed his hands on the bench. 'You really believed that?'

'I wanted to see how he'd react.'

'Either you're incredibly spiteful . . .'

'Or?'

'Or amazingly thoughtless, Trotti.'

A brief smile, 'I couldn't understand his attitude. Understand me, Signor Belloni. I'm a policeman, I've a job to do. Boatti didn't appear upset or particularly emotional the night he found the body. When I went to see him, I found him strangely detached. It's not every day you discover a corpse – and I've seen how people can react before sudden death. Within a few hours Boatti was on to me, telling me he wanted to write a book about police procedure.' Trotti shrugged, 'I didn't believe him because I couldn't understand his motive.'

'He loved her,' Belloni said simply. 'Giorgio has always loved Rosanna.'

'When did he discover that Maria Cristina was his mother?'

'I'm not sure he ever has. In life, people tend to believe what they want to believe. I don't think Giorgio has ever suspected that he was an adopted child.'

Trotti raised his head. He faced the banker. 'Did Giorgio Boatti genuinely believe it was Rosanna's corpse? If he knew Rosanna well, he should have realised it wasn't her.'

'I thought it was Rosanna's corpse.' Abruptly Belloni stood up and he started folding the newspaper. 'Maria Cristina had lost a lot of weight since coming out of the Casa Patrizia. The face was badly bashed in. You know, this morning in the morgue, I had to look very carefully. Don't forget that when Giorgio saw the body lying on the floor at San Teodoro, the face was covered in blood. There was no reason for him to think it was anybody else. For all he knew, Maria Cristina was at the Casa Patrizia. And . . .'

'Yes?'

'Giorgio was never very close to Maria Cristina – she wasn't somebody he saw frequently. But then, nobody saw much of her once she went into the Casa Patrizia. Before, when she was in the city, she used to work with me. I can't have seen her more than three times in the last five years.' A grimace, 'Four times, counting this morning.' A repressed shudder, 'It's getting late. I've told what I believe you needed to know. I think we can go.'

Trotti stood up, 'Why did Boatti suddenly change his attitude towards me? On the night I went to see him, he was stand-offish. He was supercilious.'

'That's the way he is – perhaps it's something he inherited from Vitaliano, his father.' The old man slipped his arm through Trotti's.

'The next day Boatti bought me lunch. He was all smiles and flattery.'

'He's a journalist, Trotti.'

Accompanied by the echo of their footfalls, they walked out of the courtyard, out of the university and into Strada Nuova.

'You honestly think he killed her?' Belloni asked.

'I've no idea who killed her,' Trotti said simply.

'Boatti has always loved Rosanna.'

'It's not Rosanna who's dead.'

'Who killed Maria Cristina?'

'No idea.'

'Commissario Trotti has no idea?'

'I don't know and I don't really think I care.' Trotti peered at the dial of his watch.

'You cared before.'

'I cared when I thought it was Rosanna who was dead. And now, Signor Belloni, I will catch a taxi home. And then I'm going out for my meal.'

'I hope I've been of use to you, commissario. For Rosanna's sake, I felt that I had to talk to you.' They headed towards the chained Raleigh bicycle.

'You've been very helpful.'

'There is one other thing.'

Trotti stopped and looked at the older man, 'One other thing?'

'Something you ought to know.'

'Well?'

'Understand, Trotti, that Maria Cristina never liked me. Like her sister, I was one of the people who'd come looking for her. And that she couldn't forgive – when she was living one of her adolescent love stories and we insisted on bringing her back to the city. She's always hated me, in the same way she hated Rosanna. She always felt that we were against her.'

'And?'

'She came to see me two weeks ago.'

'Where, Signor Belloni?'

'Maria Cristina came to the Banco San Giovanni – you know, I still go in in the mornings. She said she wanted money, she said that she didn't have enough pocket money, and that she needed more. Especially as she was now on holiday.'

'You gave it to her?'

'I asked her what happened to her allowance – to her very generous allowance that was paid to her at Garlasco.'

'And she said?'

'I got the impression she wanted to talk. I got the impression that if there hadn't been the old rancour, then she might have talked. There was something in her eyes – she was agitated, and I could see that she wasn't taking her tranquillisers. I could see she was losing weight – she looked younger, better than in the Casa Patrizia. And

I got the impression that it was fear I could read in her eyes. Fear of something – and that she needed money as a kind of protection.'

'You gave her the money?'

A dry laugh, 'The money in the bank is hers. Rosanna and I have tried to protect her – and the money – but ultimately she can spend it as and when she pleases. It belongs to her. In Garlasco she has her allowance – but all the rest is hers. All hers.'

'A lot?'

'I paid out to her ten million lire from her life savings.'

Via Milano

The windscreen was brown with dead mosquitoes and other insects.

Trotti sat in the back of the taxi. He was tired, he felt dirty and wanted to get out of his sticky clothes.

Water in the lungs.

He closed his eyes.

(In 1978 he had been to the school. It was in the Scuola Elementare Gerolamo Cardano that he had first met Rosanna Belloni. Trotti remembered wondering how old she was; in her mid-forties, he had decided. The grey hair made her appear older, but she still had the living softness that disappears as a woman goes through the change. A few years older, perhaps, than Agnese.

He had asked her about the disappearance of Anne Ermagni.

'You don't think it's a maniac who's taken Anna, Signora Direttrice?'

'I don't understand.'

'A maniac, a child molester. You don't think that Anna Ermagni has been kidnapped by a sex maniac?'

'I know of only one case of child rape,' Rosanna had said rather coldly. 'And that was a couple of years ago.' She had spoken in a dull, flat tone. Trotti had felt that he was annoying her.

'In this school?'

'On the other side of the river, in Borgo Genovese. A twelve-year-old girl was made pregnant. She was mentally deficient.'

'Raped?'

'Every evening. By her two brothers.')

When Trotti opened his eyes again, the taxi was already in Via Milano, going by the newly enlarged Fiat showrooms.

It was nine o'clock when Trotti reached his house. He got out of the car, paid the driver. The taxi did a three-point turn and drove back into the city.

Trotti was crossing the road when another car drew up alongside him.

'Bit late, commissario?'

'I got held up, Pisanelli. What've you done to your hair?'

For once Pisanelli was not in a police car but in his own, battered Citroën Deux Chevaux. For a reason that Pisanelli had never made clear, it had a Cremona registration plate. Pisanelli pulled the car off the road into the forecourt of the pizzeria.

'My hair? What's wrong with my hair?' He was not wearing his shabby suede jacket but a white shirt and tie. He also wore a garishly checked jacket. He had put some sort of cream in the long hair at the side of his head and combed it backwards over his ears. The hair formed an irregular fringe at the back of his neck. He got out of the Citroën, slamming the tin door. It refused to close. He kicked it shut with his heel. Pisanelli was grinning, his hands in his pockets. 'Anna's been waiting for you for over half an hour. She has to be back home before eleven.'

'What have you put in your hair? It smells – you smell like a whorehouse.'

'Always a kind word, commissario.'

Trotti took Pisanelli by the arm and they crossed the road. 'You've heard about the autopsy?'

'On the Belloni woman?' A satisfied grin. 'I haven't been back to the Questura.'

'I didn't appreciate the way you vanished at San Teodoro.'

'A man needs his rest and recreation.'

'You'll have plenty of time for rest and recreation when I've retired, Pisanelli.'

'I'm on holiday, commissario.'

'What?'

'I've managed to change my timetable with Giordano – and so I'm going to take ten days off. With Anna.'

'But I need you, Pisanelli.'

'You're going on holiday too, aren't you?'

'Why didn't you tell me you wanted to get away?'

'Wouldn't have made any difference.'

Trotti clicked his tongue while fumbling for the house key in his pocket. 'Maria Cristina was not battered to death. She was drowned. There was water in her lungs.'

The garden gate was open.

'Let Merenda get on with the enquiry. Learn to relax, commissario.'

'Maiocchi's holding the Luca man.'

'Why?'

Trotti went up the stairs. No lights came from the house.

'Why don't you just take a holiday, commissario? Rosanna'll turn up. Get away, go and see your daughter. Enjoy yourself.'

For nearly twenty years Trotti had lived in the detached building, above the garage. When Pioppi was growing up, the house had seemed very small; now it seemed empty.

'Maria Cristina was pumped full of addictive substances. Goodness knows what they were giving her at the Casa Patrizia. Carnecine was supposed to tell me what she was taking. He's left no message. We'll have to get back to him.'

'You, commissario, you'll have to get back to him – I'm on holiday.'

'Probably get the Casa Patrizia closed down – strange that Finanza hasn't already put Carnecine out of a job. The man's a charlatan. Christ, I'd like to know why he was feeding her with all those chemicals.'

There was an outside staircase, an iron banister and potted plants, geranium and cyclamen, to each concrete step. With the drought, the plants needed frequent watering. A couple of pots had been overturned. Eva, Trotti thought irritably, taking his keys from his pocket.

The door was not locked.

Surprised by his own reflexes, Trotti flattened himself against the wall. He pulled Pisanelli with him. Pisanelli almost fell.

'Visitors,' Trotti whispered harshly.

In the feeble light the wood of the door jamb showed signs of splintering.

'I hope you've got a gun, Pisa.'

VISITOR

It was stupid to risk your life at sixty-two, when you were about to become a grandfather for the first time and when you had not been back to the training school in Padua for fifteen years and when you were unfit and out of training and when the effort of going up a single flight of stairs put you out of breath for half an hour. When you were just three years from retirement and from the house in the hills.

But this house in Via Milano was Trotti's house. This is where I live, Trotti told himself. He had no choice. A territorial imperative. Consequently he was very relieved when he saw Pisanelli draw a gun from the holster in the small of his back.

In the flickering light from the street lamps along Via Milano, Pisanelli's face appeared haggard. He clasped the light Beretta in his right hand; his left hand gave support to the clenched right fist.

There were no lights on in the house.

'Do you ever get that feeling of déjà vu, Pisa?'

'Déjà vu comprà?' Pisanelli crouched down. 'Ready when you are, commissario.'

With an outstretched arm, Trotti pushed the front door inwards. It creaked unpleasantly. Trotti stopped, waited. Then he pushed some more.

The door came open.

Pisanelli put out his head and glanced along the hallway. Then bent double, close to the right wall, he moved indoors.

Silence.

'Behind you.' Trotti had a walking stick in his hand – he was scarcely aware of picking it up from the umbrella rack. He went along the hall, following Pisanelli, moving slowly, the smell of Pisanelli's haircream in his nostrils, his shoulders against the wall and trying to remember what the English instructor in Padua had tried to teach him. About surprise, about keeping the eyes adapted to the dark, about not presenting a target.

'Open the door and at the same time turn the light on,' Pisanelli whispered. 'Make sure you shade your eyes.'

Trotti found the switch.

'Now.'

Trotti turned on the switch and threw the door open, standing out of the doorway, allowing the hall light to flood into the bedroom.

Beside him Pisanelli waited a fraction of a second then moved.

Pioppi's old bedroom appeared empty.

Pisanelli butted hard against the inner wall and in a fast arc swung his arms upward, the gun outstretched.

'Shit.'

The myopic teddy-bear stared down from where he was perched on the top of the wardrobe. The glass eyes were dusty.

Pisanelli was sweating. He ran the back of his hand along his forehead. The two policemen went back into the hall.

Lavatory and bathroom were empty.

Carefully Trotti opened the bedroom door.

The bedside lamp had at some time fallen but was alight, casting an intimate pink glow across the lower part of the room.

Pisanelli still held the Beretta with both hands. He tried to grin. His face remained pale. 'A tornado.' He let out a sigh of relief and allowed himself to relax.

Drawers had been pulled out and emptied of their contents. Agnese's clothes lay scattered everywhere. Trotti noticed the stole he had bought her more than thirty years earlier. It had been ripped apart. Spilt coffee, cigarette burns in the carpet, curtains pulled down.

'Looks as if your visitors have left, commissario.' Pisanelli dropped his hands to his sides. 'After enjoying themselves.'

'Eva,' Trotti said simply.

'Your house guest?' Pisanelli laughed.

'Uruguayan prostitute.'

'You choose your friends carefully, commissario.'

'I never said you were my friend, Pisanelli.'

The mattress in the bedroom had been dragged from the bed and sliced with a knife. The pillows had been gutted and small feathers danced into the air as Trotti moved round the bed. He bent over and picked up the cracked frame of a photograph.

Agnese, Trotti and Pioppi at the Villa Ondina on Lake Garda, a happy nuclear family smiling into the camera. The summer of 1967. (Wurlitzer juke box, Bobby Solo, Fausto Leali.)

'I met her a few months ago.' Trotti shook his head as he looked down at the spilled sheets, feathers and clothes. The telephone had been ripped from its socket. 'She said she came to Italy because she had been offered a job when she was in Uruguay. She thought she'd be teaching in an aerobics centre in Milan – and that she could send money back to her little boy.'

'Some aerobics.'

They went into the kitchen.

Plates and utensils were scattered over the floor. The sink tap was running. The kitchen smelt of vinegar.

Incongruously, the clock continued its ticking, untouched and faithful on the top of the refrigerator.

'Place is empty,' Pisanelli said. 'Whoever they were, they've left.'

Trotti stepped on a broken plate as he went towards the sink. He closed the running tap. 'I wonder how they found her – poor cow.'

'She used the phone.'

Trotti suddenly felt very tired. He put down the walking stick and slumped on to a kitchen chair.

'Why Uruguayan, commissario?'

'The Sicilians have moved on. On and up into narcotraffic, narcodollars, high finance. The Uruguayans have taken over much of the prostitution in Milan. In Genova it's the Chinese and the Nigerians – new Mafias moving in where the Sicilian Mafia is no longer around.'

'You met her in Milan?'

Trotti was breathing heavily, still out of breath, 'What a mess.'

'I didn't know you went to Milan for your pleasure, commissario.'

'Think what you want, Pisanelli.'

'You thought you could help her? You thought you could save a whore?'

Trotti shook his head. He was still holding the photograph of the

Villa Ondina. He stood up and placed it on the refrigerator, beside the clock.

Pisanelli was amused, 'Commissario Trotti goes to Milan and uses the services of exotic prostitutes.'

Trotti had got his breath back and was leaning against the sink. 'Eva wanted to go back to South America and she thought I could help her.'

'Good screw?'

'Pisanelli, a man's not thirty years old for ever . . .'

'What are you going to do now, commissario?'

'Nothing – at least not now. A meal with you and Anna – and then tomorrow, I'll have to change all the locks. If Eva had really wanted to go back to South America . . .' Trotti fell silent.

A figure appeared in the door.

Pisanelli instinctively raised the small, ineffectual gun.

'Don't shoot me.'

'Don't tempt me.'

The southern face smiled in condescension. The dark eyes did not leave Trotti's. 'Commissario Trotti, Polizia di Stato?' The man was tall, with a swarthy skin, and was wearing a black beret and a leather jacket.

HELICOPTER

The helicopter banked and looking through the dark dome of perspex, Trotti saw the lights strung out along the Adriatic coast. Over the clatter of the motor, the pilot shouted, 'Comacchio.' He gestured with his thumb downwards.

The helicopter banked again, dropped height and soon the pilot was bringing it down. On the ground there were headlamps that lit up a stretch of dyke. The pilot spoke into his microphone while Trotti found himself gripping the aluminium bars of his seat, concentrating his attention on the bank of glowing gauges. The aircraft seemed to sway sideways, hanging beneath its rotor in the empty night. It projected a beam of white light down towards the land.

They touched down and somebody opened the door beside Trotti, inviting him to step out on to the ladder. The white letters CARABINIERI stood out on the dark fuselage. Overhead, the vast rotor was losing speed, its whine gradually becoming less acute. Instinctively Trotti bent down. The air pulled at his hair.

'Colonello Spadano is waiting for you.'

'Colonello?' Trotti said.

The wash of the rotor blades tried to blow away his clothes. Trotti walked along the dyke accompanied by a carabiniere in a track suit.

Several official cars had been parked on the dyke. Small searchlights had been set up and they pointed downwards. Incandescent beams shone on to the murky tea-coloured waters of the canal. Men were sitting in two cars; several whiplash aerials rising into the sky. The sound of distorted voices over metallic radios.

Trotti found himself admiring the organisation of the carabinieri. A purposefulness and efficiency he had never known in the state police. A purposefulness that was impressive and slightly frightening.

There was a mobile crane, partly in the shadow. A man within the cabin was manipulating the controls. Opposite him, on the other side of the canal, a carabiniere was giving directions into a walkie-talkie.

'Good to see you, Trotti.'

'Ah, thank goodness.'

Physically Spadano was small. He was not wearing uniform but evening dress, a starched white shirt and a red bow tie that now hung loose at the open collar. He had put on a pair of wellington boots over the dress trousers. The oblique light of the lamps was caught in his grey eyes. The hair was cut very short and brushed backwards; it was turning white at the temples. 'I'm glad you're here.'

'I was about to go for a meal when your man appeared. Thanks for the ride.'

'Part of the Carabiniere service.' A tight smile, 'I hear you've been quarrelling with your girlfriend in Via Milano.'

Trotti gestured to the canal, 'What's happened, Spadano?'

Spadano glanced at the river and frowned, as if he were surprised by the question. He then raised his shoulders, 'You must forgive the clothes. I was having supper in Venice when they informed me of the car. I came straight over.'

'By helicopter?'

Spadano took a packet of Toscani from his dinner jacket and lit a stubby cigar. A pungent cloud of smoke. 'One of the advantages of rank. Believe me, Trotti, I've been in enough helicopters to last me a lifetime.'

'I thought you were in Sardinia fighting bandits.'

'I am in Calabria fighting bandits.'

'Then what are you doing in Venice? What are you doing here in the Comacchio?'

Behind the foul-smelling cigar, Colonello Spadano grinned with pride, 'A married man is allowed to spend time with his family.'

There was a shout on the far bank and people began to move down the wet grass and mud to the edge of the canal. For a moment the radios seem to fall quiet; the chain hanging from the crane went taut. Drops of water danced in the air and fell in a rhythmic cascade.

Like frogs, two divers broke through the surface of the dirty water and clambered on to the bank, helped by the carabinieri, actors in the circles of bright light.

Trotti laughed softly, 'You're married, Spadano?'

The man with the walkie-talkie gestured with his free hand and the motor on the crane began to move. Within his cabin, the crane driver released the long handbrake.

The chain was run upwards slowly.

A bump, like the back of a big fish, broke through the surface of the water. The bump grew larger and larger until Trotti could recognise the rear of a car.

For a moment the chain ceased to mount, even though the crane engine continued its whining.

'I thought this might interest you, Piero Trotti.'

Turning on the axis of the chain, the entire car drew clear of the water. Water poured from the open windows, from beneath the bonnet, from under the glistening wheels and cascaded back into the canal.

Both front doors were open, giving the car the appearance of a small fish with enormous gills.

A four-wheel-drive Fiat Panda. A brown Fiat Panda.

The car that Rosanna had disappeared in.

MARRIAGE

'I can remember your words, Spadano. "One thing's certain – I'm not going to find a wife in the Sopramonte. Just sheep, wind and rain – and foul-smelling Sardinian peasants and murderers."'

'You don't seem very excited about discovering the Panda.'

'The insignia and the pips of the Carabinieri tattooed into your flesh.' A small laugh, 'When does a captain – sorry, when does a colonel of Carabinieri find the time to get married?'

'If you really want something in life, you work for it.'

'How long have you been married, Spadano?'

Spadano had to wipe the satisfied grin from his face, 'Eighteen months now.'

'Pity your wife hasn't got you out of smoking those things.' Trotti held out his hand. 'Congratulations – even if it does mean you've put on five kilos.' Then as the two men shook hands, simultaneously they both seemed to change minds and they hugged each other. 'Good to see you again, Spadano. And thanks.'

'Good to see you, Piero. Good to see you haven't changed – as prickly and irascible as ever. Don't tell me you've given up your boiled sweets.'

The two men laughed as they walked along the dyke. They got into a civilian car and sat in the dark. Spadano smelt of Toscani cigars and sweet eau de cologne.

'In Venice for an Interpol convention. In the last three years, it's only the second time I've been north. And for my wife it was time to get away for a break. Even if Venice is full of tourists.'

'Why Calabria?'

'Working on kidnappings in the Sila.'

'Can't be worse than staying on in our provincial backwater.'

Spadano shook his head, 'In 1968, there were two cases of kidnapping in Italy. In 1985 there were 265. It's all Mafia. Or rather the Calabrian 'Ndrangheta, but much of the actual work is done by Sardinians. That's my job. Trying to locate the Sardinian kidnappers.' Although Spadano had lived in the north for most of his life, he had not lost his accent. Palermo. 'And trying to release their victims.'

'You're home in the south, Spadano. You should be happy.'

'You always choose to forget the Carabinieri were a creation of Savoy. A pure product of the north.' Spadano paused. A muscular body and a thick neck. Hair that showed no sign of thinning. For a man of sixty, Spadano had aged well. 'You know, Piero Trotti, I've always maintained you're jealous of us.'

'Carabinieri or Polizia di Stato – it's the same thing. If we'd had the choice when we were young, this isn't the career we'd have chosen. I imagine that like me you joined up because it was a job – and there was not much choice for a young man from the countryside with ambition but little schooling . . . This is why you fetched me down here to the Comacchio?'

Colonello Spadano said, 'You don't sound terribly excited at finding your Panda car. Or even grateful.'

'Time I thought about retiring, Spadano.'

'Retirement? You'd be bored stiff. You like to moan – but without your job, you'd have nothing to do.' The tip of the cigar glinted as he inhaled, 'I saw there was a search out for a Fiat Panda. Your people put out a general alert.'

'Why contact me? Merenda's running this enquiry.'

'Merenda's not a friend of mine.'

'The prickly, irascible Piero Trotti is a friend?'

'I still have a lot of contacts in the city.'

'Including your wife?'

'Including my wife. I have you to thank for that.'

'I believe you're blushing, Spadano.'

'It's too dark. You can't see.'

'Signora Bianchini?'

'Signora Spadano. And how's your wife, Piero?' Light from one of the cars lit up the windscreen and, for a moment, the two men could see each other's face. Spadano could not hide his pride.

'My wife's in America.'

'And your daughter?'

'In Bologna, expecting a baby any day.'

'My congratulations. Perhaps being a grandfather will make you a little less irascible.'

'Being married to the lovely Signora Bianchini has made you fat.' Trotti switched on the yellow light inside the car. He gestured to the anthracite telephone installed between the two seats, 'Does that thing work?'

'You know what I do, Piero? You know what I do?' Spadano tapped his belly, 'You know why I've put on weight? A lot of the time, I'm sitting in a helicopter going backwards and forwards over the mountains, while over a loudspeaker we announce the hour and the date.'

'To entertain the squirrels?'

'There are wolves up there in the Sila.' Spadano tapped the ash of the cigar out of the window. 'Four-legged and two-legged.'

'Why the loudspeaker?'

'If and when a kidnap victim is released or manages to escape, if he can recall the time that he heard us going over, we can get a grid reference. Which enables us to move in on the hiding place.'

'You're successful?'

'Not very.'

Both men laughed.

'We work a lot with the Americans now. They believe the ransom money is chanelled into drugs. So we have the DEA and a lot of efficient American equipment – and I do a lot of sitting around talking pidgin English. And I drink a lot of American beer.'

'Your helicopter pilots don't complain about the Toscani?'

'Why were you looking for a Panda – a four-wheel-drive Fiat?' He pointed to beyond the windscreen. The car had now been landed on to the dyke. Rivulets of muddy water still trickled down the bank into the canal. 'Why aren't you over there, looking to see if there's a corpse in the boot?'

'A woman, Spadano. A friend – a woman I used to know.'

'What about her?'

'I thought – the Questura thought she'd been murdered. In fact it was a question of mistaken identity. It was her sister – a mentally fragile and unbalanced woman who was murdered.'

'And your lady friend?'

'She's disappeared.'

'In a four-wheel-drive Panda?'

'I think she was with a man.'

'The car looks as if it's empty.'

'Maybe she's drowned. Perhaps she's lying at the bottom of the canal.'

'You don't sound convinced, Piero.'

'Or perhaps I just don't care, Colonello Spadano.'

SAN TEODORO

Thursday, 9 August

Pisanelli whispered, 'I thought you were going to see your daughter in Bologna.'

'I thought you were going on holiday. What happened to all that grease in your hair, Pisa?'

'It's called gel, commissario.'

It was dark and pleasantly chill within the San Teodoro church. Trotti followed Pisanelli, both men walking silently. Mid-morning and a priest was taking mass. Old women muttered their responses and the air was heavy with the smell of dust and incense.

'Over here, commissario.'

At the back of the church, a woman in black sat near the font. She was caught in a circle of pale light projected from a round window high in the wall. Her waxy face was old and wrinkled, so too was her dress, and her dark stockings had been allowed to drift down to her ankles. She was wearing tartan slippers and in the gnarled white fingers she held a rosary. A black cardigan over her shoulders.

Beneath the woman's white hair that had been tinted and given thin, permanent waves, the hard face reminded Trotti of the old peasant women he had known in the hills when he was a child.

'Signora,' Pisanelli whispered gently, leaning over her. He was wearing his suede jacket and he spoke in a hushed, persuasive voice. 'Here is my colleague. He would like to speak to you.'

She did not look at Trotti, 'Why?' She sat by herself. A walking stick was attached to her chair. Her eyes remained on the officiating priest.

'Perhaps you can help him.'

'Why does he need my help?' She spoke in the city dialect, thick, harsh and asthmatic.

'Signora Belloni who was so cruelly murdered. My friend must find the killer.'

The woman crossed herself. She then kissed her index finger.

'He must find the killer before he strikes again, before he strikes another woman. Commissario Trotti's afraid the man may be a sex maniac.'

She turned her head and shoulders to look at Trotti, her wrinkled mouth open. She wore a little gold chain round her neck.

'And since you live opposite the entrance to Signorina Belloni's house, signora . . .'

The rosary disappeared into a pocket of the black dress. The woman got up slowly, putting her weight on the stick. Pisanelli helped her and they turned towards the west door. As she went past, but without stopping, she dropped a coin into the alms box. 'The widow's mite,' she said without smiling, as if she were repaying a debt.

(The parish church of San Teodoro was Romanesque in its architecture; on the north wall there were frescos depicting the city as it had been at the beginning of the sixteenth century, long before the many civic towers had been destroyed or allowed to fall down.)

Trotti pushed the wooden door open and they went out into the glaring heat and sunlight of the deserted city. Taking the church steps one at a time and moving sideways, like a decrepit, three-legged crab, the old woman made her way to the ground-floor flat opposite the brick wall of the church. From somewhere about her person, she produced a large iron key.

'Please enter, signori.'

Trotti and Pisanelli entered the dark room. It was cool, damp and smelt of boiled vegetables.

'You may sit down.' There was an old-fashioned cooker and she lit a gas ring, heating a blackened saucepan. 'You see,' a gesture towards the window, 'I can see everything that goes on.' She coughed, pulling at the cardigan on her shoulders.

'That's very good,' Pisanelli said encouragingly.

A bed, a pile of *Famiglia Cristiana* and on the wall a series of framed diplomas, a few artificial flowers, an almanac and an old photograph of Pope John XXIII.

'Tell the commissario what you saw last weekend, signora.'

For the first time the old woman looked at Trotti. 'I know you, don't I?' Her eyes approached his face and she peered at him carefully.

'It's possible, signora.'

She asked, wheezing asthmatically, 'You go to church?'

'Not as often as I would like to.'

'There is a lot of sin in this world.'

Trotti nodded, 'So my colleague here informs me.'

'The young people of today do a lot of things which are wrong.'

The two policemen acquiesced.

'I saw that girl.' The old woman, leaning against the back of a chair, gestured with her free hand towards the gate on the far side of the road.

'Signorina Roberti?'

'I suppose you'd like something to drink. My nephew was once in the police force.' Without waiting for an answer, she made her way, now resting her weight on the table, to a sideboard. She opened the cupboard and took out a bottle. 'He now works in Libya. Grappa, signori?'

Within the bottle, partially immersed in the colourless grappa, sat the wooden silhouette of an old man with a hat, stick and a dog at his feet. She poured a few drops of grappa into two grimy glasses. Pisanelli took one. The other he gave to Trotti.

(At the end of the war, an old peasant in Acquanera used to sell contraband grappa from a rubber inner tube, patched and repatched, that he wore slung over one shoulder. Villagers used to buy the colourless liquid, but it was rumoured that the peasant distilled the liquor from human faeces. Many years later, Trotti had asked Maserati in Scientifica if it was possible to make alcohol from human excrement. Maserati had laughed.)

'You know Signorina Roberti, signora?' Trotti asked, without touching his drink.

'A silly little girl. A child. She lives in the same building as the headmistress.'

'Signorina Belloni.'

'The headmistress doesn't come to our church very much – Don Lionello says she goes to Pietro in San Ciel d'Oro. She doesn't interfere in other people's business. She is an educated woman, but she is not proud.' Almost against her will, the old woman added, 'She always has a smile for the people she meets.'

'Did you see Signorina Belloni last week?'

'Sometimes the headmistress – your Signorina Belloni – some-times she brings me a little something. I have my husband's war pension but . . .' She raised her work-worn hands. At the same time she coughed.

'Have you seen Signorina Belloni?'

'I saw the girl.' Scarcely lifting her feet she went back to the cooker and threw leaves on to the boiling water. The air was filled with the pleasant smell of basil.

'When was this?'

'She has a boyfriend now. He comes when the parents are not there. I know the father.'

'Dr Roberti.'

'Dr Roberti. Once he came to see me about my lungs.' She tapped her flat chest. 'The doctor is a good man. Respiratory problems are not his speciality, you know. He is a dermatologist.' She added in a conspiratorial tone, 'He's from Turin.'

'I didn't know that,' Trotti said.

'I don't think he knows about the goings on of his daughter.' The old woman turned to face them, both gnarled hands on the table. The rosary had reappeared between the waxy fingers, 'I'm sure that if he did, he'd do something about it. I know that today there's no religion, no morals. Like the Americans.'

'Americans?'

'The Thursday witnesses,' she said with disapproval.

'You mean Jehovah's Witnesses,' Pisanelli said, smiling.

'Call them what you want – when they come to my door, I send them away. I don't want to talk with them. I am Catholic. I'm not interested in their American religion.'

'What do the Witnesses do, signora?'

'They come at all times of the day – even weekends. To get rid of them, I accept the magazines that they give me. But you don't think I read that heresy, do you? Don Lionello says it's heresy.'

'You throw the magazines away?'

'For the lavatory. I don't throw anything away. Money doesn't grow on trees.' She coughed. The small eyes were bright, 'I use their magazines in the lavatory.'

Pisanelli and Trotti looked at each other. Trotti then asked, 'Signorina Belloni – the headmistress – has she ever given you a magazine of the Jehovah's Witnesses?'

'The people – they're young people. They come to the door and they give me their magazines. But I don't read them.'

'Have you ever given a magazine to Signorina Belloni?'

'Of course not. Those magazines are heretical. Don Lionello says that I mustn't read them.'

'Of course, of course.'

'More grappa?' She lifted the bottle with its wooden man.

Trotti shook his head, 'To get back to the girl . . . You saw Signorina Roberti last week?'

'The doctor's daughter?'

'Signorina Roberti – her name is Signorina Roberti.'

'Roberti? I don't know if that is a Turin name. I went with my husband once to Turin.'

'When did you see Signorina Roberti?'

'I know she is the doctor's daughter. I know she's supposed to be studying at the university. But you know what the students are like. You know what the girls are like. Today everything's so easy. That's why there are no morals, signori. There's no hardship.'

Both Trotti and Pisanelli nodded their agreement.

'When I was a girl there was hardship. We didn't have any time for all this pleasure. I went out to work when I was thirteen. It didn't do me any harm. Nowadays there's all this sex. We never knew that.' Little bubbles of saliva had formed at the corners of her thin lips. She ran a hand across the old, waxy face. 'We were Catholic.'

'When did you see her?'

'With a man. And he wasn't her boyfriend. I know her boyfriend, I've seen him and I know that he's tall. But this man was shorter. A complete stranger. And with all these diseases they talk about on the television.' She raised her hand towards a television set on a stand at the foot of the narrow bed. The screen was concealed behind a curtain in floral pattern. 'There are no morals now. And too much sex.'

'When was this, signora?'

'Ever since divorce. We had a referendum. That's when it all started. Free love. No wonder there are so many diseases. Don Lionello says . . .'

'When did you see Signorina Roberti?'

The widow gave Trotti a long, appraising glance before answering, 'I can't always sleep, you know. The doctor at San Matteo says mine is a very difficult case. He gives me pills – but I can't always sleep. I have only one lung,' here she put a hand to the chest of her shiny black dress, 'I lost the other one, working at the SNIA Viscosa. They operated on me for over six hours. In 1981. I went to Lourdes but sometimes I can't sleep at night. I lie in bed and I cough. I cough and I think about my poor husband, God rest his soul.' She crossed herself, again kissing the index finger. 'That's why I saw her. Last Sunday morning – I knew I was not going to sleep and that I would be tired for mass. Don Lionello says that God is forgiving and that if I can't sleep, it doesn't matter if I miss mass. Don Lionello says I must look after my health.'

'You saw Signorina Roberti on Sunday morning?'

'The silly child with a different man. You think I don't know what they were going to do?' She shook her head, moving her shoulders at the same time, 'When I think that she is the good doctor's daughter.'

'Who did you see Signorina Roberti with?'

'A man. She must have been very drunk – which doesn't surprise me, because all the young people drink today. She drinks, she smokes. And I saw her coming home late, hanging on to him. A man, a small man.'

'What time?'

'Half past three – I heard the church bells. Half past three and the little idiot – no better than a cheap prostitute, she comes tottering home on the arm of her new lover.'

'Did you recognise the man?'

The eyes twinkled with venom, 'I never saw him leave.'

With venom and jealousy.

LAURA

They stepped out of the damp flat and it was suddenly very hot and windless in the Piazza San Teodoro. Pisanelli slipped on a pair of sunglasses.

'You didn't sleep at home, commissario?'

'I slept in Ferrara – at the Carabinieri barracks.'

Pisanelli whistled.

'The carabinieri found the Fiat Panda that Rosanna left her hotel in. It had been driven or pushed into a canal.'

'She drowned?' Pisanelli glanced unhappily at Trotti as they crossed the square. Coming in the opposite direction was a prelate in black cassock and partially hidden beneath a broad, black hat. He was sweating profusely as he talked into a portable telephone. Trotti heard the word 'confession'. Deep in conversation the priest took no notice of the two policemen. He scurried up the steps and into the church.

'Rosanna Belloni was drowned?' Pisanelli asked again.

'Nothing in the car.' Trotti shook his head, 'A hired car with Ferrara plates – and no prints. Not after more than a couple of days in the water.'

'And her luggage at the Pensione Belvedere?'

Trotti shook his head, 'According to the Carabinieri, there were just clothes. When she left, Rosanna must've taken the rest of her baggage.'

They went through the small doorway cut into the wooden gate and found themselves in the same, neglected courtyard. Up the stairs, following the walls and their grimy paint.

'When are you going off with Anna, Pisa?'

'I've decided to stay in town,' Tenente Pisanelli said simply, removing the sunglasses.

'Then you can accompany me. I need to see Carnecine at Garlasco.'

'Commissario, you're almost in a good mood. Eat one of your cherry sweets.'

'It has of course occurred to me, Pisanelli, that Rosanna Belloni is not guilty of her sister's murder.'

They came to a door. There was an oval name plate in burnished brass, 'Dott. Roberti'. Pisanelli rang the bell. He said, 'If she's got any sense, Laura Roberti's gone off to the Langhe – or gone to find her Gian Maria.'

'In Ferrara.'

'Ferrara. Like your Panda? A coincidence, commissario?' Pisanelli rang the bell again, this time more insistently. For a moment there was no sound. After a couple of minutes, a light came on behind the opaque glass. The door was opened.

Within the large apartment, all the shutters had been drawn.

She yawned. Laura Roberti appeared slimmer than before, dressed in a nightgown. Her black hair needed combing. She wore no make-up. There was sleep at the corner of her eyes which she now rubbed with a small fist. The tanned feet were naked, showing the neat line where she normally wore her espadrilles.

'Good morning.' An apologetic smile that reminded Trotti of other women. She ran her hand through her hair which fell back on to her face in a straight line. Although she had clearly just got out of bed, her face was surprisingly fresh. She pushed several strands away from her eyes and looked at Trotti. 'Excuse the mess.' There was eucalyptus on her breath, because she had just cleaned her teeth. 'I was sleeping.' She added, 'You'd better come in.'

The air was cooled artificially; Trotti noticed the quiet hum of air conditioning. Cool but not damp like the old widow's flat.

They followed her down the hallway to her self-contained bedsitting room.

The small television in one corner silently showed the flickering movement of a mid-morning Japanese cartoon. Trotti glanced at the kitchen range, the dishwasher, refrigerator, cooker and the overhead air aspirator. A couple of dirty plates in the sink.

The small bed was unmade.

Clothes and shoes were still scattered across the floor. Trotti recognised the same Vuitton suitcases that Agnese had bought before she left Italy for the last time – from which clothes tumbled on to the wooden floor.

'Still haven't tidied away your luggage, signorina?'

Laura Roberti ran a hand across her eyelids, 'Studying until late last night.' She shrugged, 'Would you gentlemen care for some coffee?' Without waiting for a reply she went to the cooker and taking an espresso machine, unscrewed it and filled it with water and coffee.

Trotti sat on the edge of the bed.

Pisanelli went to the window, opened it and undid the shutter. The light flooded into the room. He closed the window again.

'Signorina Roberti,' Trotti said, as the young girl handed him a cup of steaming coffee – with brown froth, as he liked it, 'I must ask you a few questions.' He deflected his glance away from the delicate breasts visible beneath the nightdress as Laura Roberti bent over.

She looked up and smiled.

'I'm afraid that the last time I was here you lied to me.' He paused. 'I think you know more about Signorina Belloni's death than you choose to admit.'

'Sugar, commissario?'

LUIGI LAVAZZA

The coffee was excellent and very hot.

'Saicaf?' Trotti asked, running his tongue along his lips.

'Lavazza – what else do you expect from a Turin girl?'

Looking at her, Trotti found it difficult to believe Laura Roberti capable of lying. A soft, delicate face and a small fragile body that was crying out for protection.

Her voice was calm, devoid of intonation, 'What makes you think I lied to you?'

'You said you were in Santo Stefano last week, signorina. I don't think you left the city. I think you were here at the time of the murder. And I believe that you know a lot more than you've already told me.'

'I know nothing about Rosanna's murder.' The features did not change but the delicate face turned pale.

'No, Signorina Roberti, it was not Rosanna who was murdered. It was her sister – the sister who lived at Garlasco. Maria Cristina Belloni.'

Her mouth fell slightly open. Laura Roberti closed it and put a hand to the chest of her nightdress. 'Maria Cristina?'

An act, Trotti told himself. The girl is lying.

'Then where's Rosanna, commissario?'

'I wish I knew.' He looked at her. He was sitting on the unmade bed, 'Last night I watched her car being fished out of a canal in the Po Delta.'

'She drowned?'

'The car was empty.'

The young woman bit her lip. 'I hope Rosanna is alive.'

'You've heard from her?'

She raised her eyebrows in surprise, 'Me?'

'What kind of relationship did you have with Rosanna Belloni?'

'I've already told you. Signorina Belloni was very kind to me. Occasionally she'd talk to me – like an aunt or a godmother. A kind person.'

'You've no idea where she is?'

'Why d'you think I should know?'

'Why did you lie to us, signorina?' Trotti gestured with his thumb towards Pisanelli who was standing by the window.

'Lie, commissario?'

'You weren't in Santo Stefano. That was an invention. You told us you'd driven back, that you were tired.'

'Commissario . . .'

Trotti held up his hand. 'You'd better give me your parents' phone number.'

'Why?'

'Your father – I'll ask your father where you were last Saturday night.' Trotti shrugged. 'He can tell me if you were in Santo Stefano.'

'You're accusing me of killing the woman?'

'D'you have an alibi, signorina, for last weekend?'

'Why should I want to kill anybody?'

'I'm not saying you killed anybody. I'm asking you where you were.'

'With him.'

It was Pisanelli who spoke, pulling himself away from the window ledge, 'With who?'

'Gian Maria. I was with my fiancé.'

'Where?'

A slight sigh, 'You're right – I didn't tell you the truth.'

Pisanelli asked, 'Why not?'

She raised her shoulders, 'You must understand me. My parents wanted me to go with them to Santo Stefano. They always want me to stay with them.' A sound of irritation, 'What can I do there? I ask you, what am I supposed to do in the Langhe? Sit around in the fields, watching my dear father's grapes growing on the vines? Talk with Papa? He's never there – or if he is he spends his time with the peasants playing at the gentleman farmer and discussing the grapes and the harvest. Or you want me to talk with my mother? My mother? An ageing princess? What can I talk to her about? She hasn't got two ideas in her head to rub together. Other than her Stéphanie of Monaco and the Aga Khan, she's not interested in anything. *Oggi* and *Duemila*, that's all she ever reads. She's not interested in me – she never has been. I hate Santo Stefano. I hate the Langhe. I hate Piemonte.' There was an unexpected vehemence in her voice. 'And I hate my parents who in twenty years have given me everything – everything – Vuitton suitcases and Lacoste shirts, the best schools and holidays in Chamonix – everything except one moment – one tiny moment of genuine affection. Everything, commissario, except warmth.'

She fell silent, looking defiantly at the two men.

'Why did you lie, signorina?' Pisanelli had pulled up a chair and now he sat on the edge, leaning towards the young girl, his elbows on his knees. His shoes, Trotti noticed, were highly polished and spotless.

Her glance went from Trotti to Pisanelli and then back to Trotti. The young face was pale.

Trotti touched the back of her hand, 'Why?'

'I was afraid.'

'Afraid of what?'

She didn't answer.

'You thought you'd be accused of the murder?'

She moved her head to one side and raised her shoulders slightly. 'Well?'

The girl remained silent.

Trotti said, 'I think you'd better give us his phone number.'

'Who?'

'I'll need to speak to Gian Maria.'

There was a long silence.

'You will give me his number?'

She started to cry reluctant tears that pushed their way from out of the corner of her eyes, 'He doesn't love me.'

Trotti touched the back of her hand, 'Don't cry, Laura.'

'Gian Maria's not interested in me as a human being. But I can keep him warm in bed. And for his family and friends, I'm a pretty little ornament that he can show off.' She pushed a tear angrily away.

Pisanelli was almost laughing, 'The man you're going to marry, Signorina Roberti? The man you're going to marry as soon as you have your degree?'

Abruptly the slim young woman stood up. She looked at the two men coldly. 'Excuse me please.' Without another word she went out of the room, closing the door behind her.

'She's lying, commissario.'

'Why?'

'To protect somebody. She's trying to protect somebody – and I don't think it's herself.' Pisanelli shrugged. 'Unless of course she murdered the woman.'

With a single gulp, Trotti raised the cup to his lips and finished the coffee which had now grown cold. He winced, then popped a rhubarb sweet into his mouth.

'What's she doing?'

Trotti gestured to the telephone that lay on the floor, attached to the wall by a long red cable. 'You'd better listen in case she's trying to phone someone.'

'Gian Maria?'

Trotti tapped the narrow bed he was sitting on. 'I don't know where Signorina Roberti spent this night,' Trotti said, 'but it wasn't in this bed. Nobody's slept in this bed since the last time we were here. No room here for two people.'

Pisanelli laughed unpleasantly.

BED

Trotti knocked on the door and then without waiting entered the bedroom. It had been decorated in the same scarlet silks as the hall. Two armchairs, lots of cushions, a thick carpet. There was an old painting of Madonna, Child and plump angels on the wall. Because the blinds were closed to the morning light, the bedside lamp was on. The air was stuffy.

'Spying on me, commissario?'

She had got dressed and now was wearing jeans and her espadrilles. She sat in one of the armchairs. Her eyes were red from crying.

'Tenente Pisanelli and I must go, Signorina Roberti. I need to know what your plans are. You see, I'd be grateful if you didn't leave the city without informing me. And I'd be grateful if you'd give me your boyfriend's phone number.'

'So you think I killed the Belloni woman?'

'At my age,' Trotti said in a soft and reassuring voice, 'I've learnt that it's best not to think anything.'

She turned her head away. She started to cry.

Trotti approached her, aware that her small face was pretty, that her small body was fragile, 'I don't see why you felt you had to hide the truth, Laura.'

'Because I was here.'

'There's no crime in loving a man, signorina. And there's no harm in spending the night with him.' He made a gesture towards the church, 'And only an old bigot, a sour old font frog, would say it was wrong to go to bed with a man you loved without being married.'

'A font frog?' Laura Roberti smiled through her tears. Then as suddenly as it had appeared, the smile vanished, 'The trouble is I don't think I love him. Just as I don't think he loves me. We're just using one another. He wants my body – and I need warmth. Is that too much to ask for? I need to be loved. And even if the love isn't sincere, I can always pretend.'

'You didn't have to lie.'

She shrugged without looking at the two men. Pisanelli was leaning against the door. He sniffed, rubbed his nose. There was still gel in the lank hair that hung down over his collar.

'You were here with him on Saturday night?'

Laura did not reply.

'You heard sounds? Maria Cristina was most probably murdered some time Sunday morning. In Rosanna's flat. Did you hear anything?'

She shook her head.

'You must tell me the truth, Laura. You see, you've already lied. Don't make things worse for yourself.'

She sighed, 'I was at the Lido until eight – I'd spent all the day of Saturday with friends. He came to pick me up at the Lido. We got back here, we phoned for a pizza and then we watched television. I was very tired. I had sunbathed – and I had swum. We were in bed by ten o'clock.'

'Did you make love?' Pisanelli asked and Trotti turned to give him an irritated glance.

The eyes glinted behind the tears, 'That's none of your business.'

Trotti nodded towards the bed, 'It's here that you sleep, Laura?'

'This is my parents' bedroom, but it's the only double bed.' She shrugged.

'You shouldn't have lied to me, signorina.'

'I'm sorry.'

'How tall is Gian Maria?'

She frowned, 'Why do you ask?'

'Is he tall?'

She shrugged, 'Average height – perhaps a bit taller. Why do you want to know?'

'Do you know of any small man coming into this building?'

She put her hand to her cheek, 'Small men? I don't think so. Should I?'

Trotti gave her a reassuring smile and moved towards the door. The girl stood up. In the red light her face was drawn, 'I never really met Maria Cristina, although I think I saw her a few times. She was mad, wasn't she?'

'She was often on sedation.'

The girl accompanied them to the front door.

'If you leave the city, signorina, you must please contact me. And you understand, I'll need to speak to Gian Maria.'

Laura Roberti nodded docilely. She closed the door behind them and they heard the bolt being drawn.

'She's lying.'

Pisanelli shook his head, 'Not lying.'

'I don't believe her.'

'She's not lying – she's suppressing the truth.'

'What makes you say that?'

'Commissario, when does she sleep in that big bed?'

'When she has company?'

'But Gian Maria is in Ferrara. That's what she says and it's probably true. Yet from the stale air in that room, it is fairly obvious that a man has spent the night there.'

'A man? Who? You mean last night?'

Pisanelli chuckled, 'Her visitor got away while she was making you your Lavazza coffee. Or perhaps you didn't notice the hand-held dictating machine on the bedside table.'

MASERATI

'Ah, commissario.'

The two men turned. Trotti squinted against the light.

'I was looking for you,' Maserati said and gave a forced smile. It was rare that he was to be seen out of his white lab coat. 'Actually, I was about to go for an early lunch.'

'Bit early for an early lunch, isn't it?'

'I've got a headache. Been at the university all morning. I don't like working on spectrographic analysis.' He wore jeans and a loose jacket; the top three buttons of his shirt were undone. Since getting married, he had put on weight. There was the beginning of a double chin. Although casually dressed, Maserati somehow appeared ill at ease away from his laboratory. 'I hear you were at the autopsy of the Belloni woman, commissario.' He did not look at either Trotti or Pisanelli.

'I left half way through.'

'Getting squeamish?'

'I had more important things to do.'

'So you weren't there for the cause of death?'

Trotti frowned, 'Bottone has already submitted his report?'

Maserati shook his head, 'Nothing written – and I don't suppose there'll be anything for a couple of weeks. He's waiting for our lab analysis. Dr Bottone is already in America.'

'America?'

'On some forensic course. At Baltimore, I think. One of these American universities where they do courses in crime scene investigation.' A dry laugh, 'Great admirer of the Americans, our Dr Bottone. What the Americans say is gospel. That's why he places so much importance on crime scene investigation. He was absolutely furious he didn't get called down to San Teodoro. Bottone hasn't got much time for Dr Anselmi.' Maserati raised his shoulders, his eyes looking past Trotti, 'But then, Dr Bottone doesn't have much time for anybody other than Dr Bottone.'

They were standing, Trotti, Pisanelli and Maserati, in the

entrance of the Questura. Outside the sun shone on the near-deserted city. A couple of women who had primly tucked their skirts under their saddles cycled slowly along Strada Nuova.

Italia Felix.

Maserati touched Trotti's arm and said, 'You know the Belloni woman was drowned, don't you?'

'That's what I heard.'

'I'm not a chemist, of course. That's Antonioni's field – and more often than not, we have to send stuff to Milan, because we just haven't got the equipment. We can't even do X-ray diffraction, for heaven's sake. But there wasn't much problem on this. You see, commissario, the human lungs were never conceived to absorb water.'

'Water?'

'What do you think? Bottone may be arrogant but he knows his stuff. He was quite right to drain liquid from the lungs as well as taking blood samples. We've been able to analyse it. Antonioni did the diatom test at the Faculty of Pharmacy this morning,' Maserati smiled with professional satisfaction. 'It's not tap water – and most certainly not the local tap water which has a high content of sulphur.'

'You can identify the water in her lungs?'

'Traces of aquatic weed, that sort of thing.'

'Meaning?'

'Meaning that it has to be fresh water.' He thrust his hands deep into his pockets. 'Sea water has a higher osmotic pressure than blood and so it doesn't get drawn through the lungs into the bloodstream. Belloni's blood has been diluted with water – most probably with water from the river.'

'How do you know that, Maserati?'

'My professional opinion is that she was drowned in the Po. Or at least the water in her lungs comes from the river. Diatoms are algae that exist in both sea and fresh water. They get absorbed into the blood. That's why Dr Bottone sent us samples of body tissue. If the woman was already dead at the time of drowning, there wouldn't be diatoms in her body tissue. But there are.'

'Maria Cristina's corpse showed no sign of immersion. And there was blood on her head – and on the floor.'

'If you're strong enough,' Maserati gave Trotti a brief, nervous glance, 'you can murder somebody in a bowl of water.'

'And the blood?'

'You can't strike somebody while you're drowning him? Believe me, commissario, the woman was drowned. She was also hit with a blunt instrument prior to her death, but that was not the cause of death.'

'Then in your opinion, Maserati, Maria Cristina was drowned – possibly in a bowl of water – in her sister's flat at San Teodoro?'

'I don't know where she was killed. There don't seem to be traces of a struggle. But there is adrenalin in the blood, implying that the woman was scared, that she knew what was coming – the fight or flight syndrome. However, Antonioni and I are merely scientists. Unlike Dr Bottone, I have no pretensions of being a crime scene detective. All I can tell you is what I know to be scientifically verifiable.'

'What do you know?'

Slightly offended by Pisanelli's question, Maserati took a deep breath before answering. He looked at neither of the two men. 'Our spectrum analysis would suggest that the victim was drowned in water from somewhere upriver from here. Somewhere where there is less industrial pollution. But whether she was drowned in the Po or in the flat at San Teodoro, I don't know. As you say, commissario, the body shows no signs of immersion. That's your problem. You're the detective – I'm just a humble scientist.'

TASTE

'Humble, my eye.' Pisanelli slumped down into the ugly new armchair. He had removed his jacket. There were large patches of sweat under the sleeves of his denim shirt. The hair hung in greasy strands at the side of his head. 'You're going to arrest Boatti, commissario?'

Trotti leaned across the artificial teak of the desk and gestured with his hands clasped together, 'For screwing the little Roberti girl?'

'You don't think he's guilty of killing Rosanna's sister?'

'If what Maserati says is right, I don't see how a single person could have killed Maria Cristina – supposing of course that she was drowned in the apartment.'

'Why not, commissario? The murderer bashed her over the head. Then he stuck her head in a bowl of water.'

'A bowl of river water? A bit complicated, isn't it? Why not use tap water?' Trotti clicked his tongue in irritation, 'I don't really see how Boatti can be screwing and murdering at the same time. And anyway, there's no motive.'

'He lied, commissario. He told us he was in Vercelli – and his wife corroborated that. Instead he was here in the city on Saturday night. In bed with Laura Roberti. And if he was in the building the night of the murder, there's nothing to have stopped him going up to Rosanna's flat and killing Maria Cristina.'

'Nothing other than a motive.' Trotti sat back. He opened a drawer and placing his feet on the side of the wooden slat, pushed himself back in the armchair.

'Nothing other than a motive, commissario? Maria Cristina was Boatti's natural mother.'

'Assuming that he knew that.'

'He must have known Maria Cristina was his mother, surely?'

For a moment, Trotti remained silent. 'Why kill her now, after so many years?'

'Because she was in the city, no longer tucked away and out of sight at the Casa Patrizia. Because he was ashamed of her, because he hated her.'

Trotti shrugged his shoulders.

'Your mother's on drugs . . .'

'That's not what Maserati says.'

Pisanelli nodded, 'At the Casa Patrizia, they were feeding her with neuroleptics. Traces of chlorpromazine. Admittedly, she'd come off the stuff since being back in the city. But you heard what Maserati said about addiction, commissario. Carnecine and his doctors had wittingly or unwittingly transformed Maria Cristina into an addict – and she was unstable when she came off her antidepressants. You can understand how Boatti feels. The woman – his mother – screws around like an animal on heat. You wouldn't be ashamed of her? You wouldn't be afraid you've inherited her madness?'

Trotti raised a finger, 'If Boatti hit Maria Cristina with a blunt instrument, what's happened to the instrument? And anyway, how did Maria Cristina get into the flat?'

'The old woman saw two people but it *was* in the middle of the night – perhaps it was Maria Cristina who was drunk. Perhaps it was Boatti who supported her.' Pisanelli frowned, 'And . . .'

'Yes?'

'Perhaps he was supporting her because she was already dead.'

Trotti was silent. The dark, tired eyes looked at Pisanelli sitting in the armchair with his jacket over his knees.

'Why didn't you get her Gian Maria's phone number from Laura Roberti?'

'What?' Trotti's thoughts were elsewhere.

'You're not eating your sweets, commissario.'

Trotti laughed as his eyes focused on the younger man, 'Pisanelli, you must think I'm an addict, a sugar addict.'

'Why didn't you take her boyfriend's number?'

'Laura's boyfriend? Not much point.'

'Why not?'

'By the time I could get to him, she would've already contacted him and told him what to say.'

Pisanelli smiled indulgently. Like Maserati, he was beginning to age, but unlike Maserati, Pisanelli was not yet married. 'It's Boatti who's been screwing the Roberti girl.'

'That doesn't make Boatti a murderer.' Trotti added, 'You know, I think you're jealous, Pisanelli.'

A snort of laughter.

'You like the Roberti girl more than you care to admit.'

'She's pretty – if you care for that sort of thing. Pretty, wealthy and spoilt.' A dismissive gesture, 'Boatti spent last night in the Roberti flat. His wife's on holiday, so this morning he could lie in with Laura Roberti. He was there when we arrived – she took more than a couple of minutes to answer the door bell. And while we were chatting to the girl in her flat and you were flattering her over her Lavazza coffee, the fornicating bastard made his escape. He crept out of her place, back upstairs. But he forgot his little recording machine.'

A nod of agreement, 'Which would explain the Grignolino.'

'What Grignolino?'

'Not a common wine. Grignolino's from the area around Asti in Piemonte and it's not the sort of wine that you can find easily in the supermarket. Yet both Laura Roberti and Signora Boatti offered me Grignolino. Which probably means that it comes from Dr Roberti's vineyards.'

'You agree he's screwing her?'

'It doesn't really matter.' Trotti raised his shoulders. 'Boatti's wife suspects something. She didn't say as much – she just told me that she loved her husband. Frightened of losing him. She suspects him of having an affair and she hinted pretty heavily that it was with Rosanna. Why not? Rosanna was no spring chicken, but she was – she is certainly not unattractive.'

'You should know.'

'Signora Boatti suspects something – but why should she suspect the sweet, fresh little Laura Roberti? Especially when the Roberti girl's got her boyfriend.'

'Why give Boatti Grignolino?'

'Neighbourliness.'

'What on earth can that silly girl see in a fat ageing failed journalist like Boatti?'

'Good question.' Trotti took his feet from the drawer and the chair fell forward with a resonant bang. 'What can the pretty Anna Ermagni see in Tenente Pisanelli?' Trotti then laughed with genuine amusement.

Pisanelli was offended. 'I beg your pardon.'

'In this profession, one of the first lessons you must learn is that there is no accounting for taste, Pisa. Greed is far-seeing – but love is blind.'

CHARMS

'How do you explain the Jehovah's Witness stuff?'

Trotti's feet had returned to the side of the drawer. 'I don't think there's anything to explain. There's no particular reason to believe the *Watch Tower* was brought there by the murderer. The Witnesses do their proselytising throughout the city – throughout the country. The old widow has the magazines – so why should Rosanna have refused them?'

'And the drugs?'

'What drugs?'

'Perhaps the murderer was looking for money – that was a hypothesis of yours.'

'When I thought it was Rosanna who'd been killed. But it wasn't Rosanna, it was her sister. Money's not a motive.' Suddenly Trotti banged his forehead with the palm of his hand.

'Swallowed your sweet, commissario?'

'Yesterday, with Beltoni, I had a rendezvous for midday.' Again he banged his forehead, 'I need to see him.'

'Why?'

Trotti pulled the telephone towards him, 'The questore's keeping tabs on me – and if it's not Boatti, it may well be Beltoni who's relaying things back to him.'

'Why Boatti?'

Trotti was looking through the pages of a pocket notebook. 'This book stuff of Boatti's – I've never believed it. An excuse to be in on the enquiry – but why? What does Boatti want? He's after something – and it's not journalism.' Trotti was about to raise the receiver when there was a knock on the door.

Commissario Maiocchi entered the small office. He looked flustered and unhappy. His long hair was ruffled. He closed the door softly, approached the desk, and emptying his pockets he covered the plastic teak with several packets of Charms sweets. And two tins of Smith and Kendon barley sugar. 'Spoil yourself, Trotti.'

'My birthday?'

Maiocchi walked over to the radiator and leaned against it, 'I thought I'd give them a try. They seem to work for you, Piero Trotti. At least, sometimes. Trouble is they get stuck between your teeth and the taste stays in your mouth for hours.'

'An acquired taste – it takes time,' Pisanelli remarked.

Commissario Maiocchi ran a hand through his dark hair. Then he stuck the unlit pipe between his teeth. 'My wife has always said my breath stinks of tar, that my teeth are dirty and that if she'd known I was going to smoke a pipe for the rest of my days, she would never have married me.'

Trotti and Pisanelli laughed.

'It's not funny.'

'Do you blame her, Maiocchi?'

'I came to talk to you about Luca.'

Pisanelli grinned, 'You can talk about your marriage, if you wish. Commissario Trotti is an expert on marriage. And on women. Extremely objective, having gained the peace of the senses.'

'A phallocrat – me and all the other men in the wretched Questura.'

Seeing the smile die on Pisanelli's face, Trotti asked, 'What about your Luca, Maiocchi?'

'Off to the Adriatic.'

'It's you who should go to the Adriatic. You could do with the holiday. And perhaps an adventure with a Danish blonde or a German hausfrau'd help you get things into perspective. Get some iodine into your lungs. Give up that pipe. Start eating sweets.'

'What has everybody got against my pipe?' Maiocchi raised his shoulders in a movement of irritation, 'I like my pipe, for heaven's sake.'

'You will have to choose between your wife and your pipe,' Pisanelli said.

'If you love your wife, why do you spend all your time in this wretched Questura?'

'Where d'you want me to go, commissario?' Maiocchi turned and looked out of the window at the opposite wall of pebbledash. 'Here at least I'm useful. Here I'm doing something.'

'Go down to the Adriatic.'

'I'm already missing the kids.'

'Any news on the doctor.'

Pisanelli had been rubbing at the leather of his shoe with the sleeve of the suede jacket, 'What doctor?'

'You never listen, Pisanelli. When this man Luca met Snoopy . . .'

'Maria Cristina,' Pisanelli said, raising a finger. His shoes were spotless.

'When Luca met her at the railway station, she fell into a faint. He ran her down to Via Mantova and called up a doctor.'

'You never told me that.'

'Luca suspected she was pregnant.'

'If Maria Cristina was pregnant, Bottone would've noticed it at the autopsy.' A pause, 'Pregnant at fifty?'

'Pregnant or not pregnant, Luca couldn't know the truth. And perhaps he was frightened.'

'Dottor Silvio Silvi,' Maiocchi said, 'Luca's doctor friend is Silvio Silvi.'

'And where is he?'

'On holiday.'

'Of course.' Without concealing his irritation Trotti opened one of Maiocchi's packets of pineapple Charms.

'On holiday in Calabria.'

'We get the Carabinieri to pick him up?'

It was Maiocchi who grinned, 'You're not going on holiday after all, Trotti? You're not going up to the lake?'

'Don't worry about me, Maiocchi. Let's see if we can get hold of this doctor.'

There was a light tap at the door.

Trotti let out a sigh, 'The old woman says she saw two people – a rather drunk Laura Roberti and a man – entering the building at San Teodoro at three in the morning. We have good reason to believe that Boatti and Signorina Roberti were already inside the building. What we don't know is how Maria Cristina got from her place in Via Mantova to San Teodoro. Perhaps if we know that, we can find out who killed her.'

Again the light tap and Pisanelli ceased brushing at his shoes, got up and went to the door.

'The last person to see her in Via Mantova was Luca. And this doctor. Dr Silvi may just happen to know how she got to San Teodoro. Did Maria Cristina arrive in her sister's flat alive or dead?

If she was already dead, who carried her? Did the old woman mistake Maria Cristina for Laura?'

Maiocchi said, 'I'll see if I can trace this Silvi . . . if you're not going on holiday.'

'You should've traced him a long time ago, Maiocchi. Am I supposed to do everything?'

'You really could do with a holiday.'

'I'm going on holiday, don't worry about me. I'll be going down to Bologna – but not straight away.'

'News of your grandson, Piero?'

'Pisa?' Trotti looked up irritably and frowned, 'Why are you whispering like that?'

Pisanelli stepped back from the door and the person he was talking to, 'Agente Zani would like a few words with you, Commissario Trotti.'

'Zani?'

'It's about Rosanna Belloni.'

ZANI

Trotti picked up the packet on the tabletop, 'Where the hell d'you get your Nazionali from?'

Zani frowned, ill at ease in his uniform that was too small for the corpulent body. The red, sly face appeared redder and unhappier than Trotti remembered it. Agente Zani sat slumped forward at the table, one hand playing with the glass of Nastro Azzurro, the other holding a smouldering cigarette. The smell of the sweet, black tobacco irritated Trotti's nostrils. Zani stared at the beer in silence. He wanted to finish the contents of the glass but was waiting for Trotti to lift the long mozzarella sandwich to his mouth.

(In the Questura and down the three flights of stairs Zani had not uttered a word.)

'You've been drinking a lot, Zani.'

'Drinking a lot, smoking a lot and not getting much sleep.'

'You're sure you wouldn't like something to eat. A sandwich or something hot.'

He replied sullenly, 'I'm not hungry.'

'Perhaps you need a holiday.'

'A holiday? I need a new life.' A final gulp of beer and an oblique glance at Trotti, 'You're not looking so good yourself, commissario.'

His mouth full of sandwich, Trotti said, 'That's why I'm getting away from the city for a couple of weeks.'

'And Rosanna Belloni? You're going away? I thought she was a friend of yours.' He spoke with a slight Marche accent. Zani had worked for ten years in Macerata province.

'What exactly did you want to speak to me about?' Trotti did not hide his impatience. 'There are things I've got to do before I can get away.'

Trotti had hoped to get Zani to eat something. They were sitting at the back of the Tavola Calda da Pippo. It was a hundred metres up Strada Nuova from the Questura. In term time, the small, clean and efficient snack bar was a meeting place for students. Now a few customers were eating an early lunch of salad or pasta, taken from the buffet. A couple of girls with paper bonnets and in striped red and white dresses prodded at the steel dishes behind the glass counter. Stuffed artichokes, mauve squid, various varieties of pasta, several meat dishes, olive oil and basil.

Zani asked abruptly, 'You have a daughter, commissario?'

An unexpected tightening in the gut. 'She's in Bologna,' Trotti said in a neutral tone.

'You know what it means to be a father?' The small peasant eyes briefly searched his face. Trotti wondered if he was looking for sympathy.

'My daughter is married.'

'Married?'

'Pioppi's nearly thirty. She's expecting a child any day. That's why I'm hoping to get away. I want to go down to Bologna sometime over the next few days.'

Zani finished off the beer. 'It would have been better if we'd had a daughter.'

'Are you sure you wouldn't like something to eat, Zani? You need to get something into your stomach.'

'I'm not hungry.' Zani looked disconsolately at the glass in his hand, 'My son is a queer.'

Silence.

'A queer, commissario.'

Trotti searched for something to say, something to fill the sudden emptiness that seemed to separate the two men. Lamely he remarked, 'For nearly a year, I thought my little girl was going to die. She didn't want to eat.'

'Queer, gay – homosexual.' Zani tapped his left ear; the corner of his lip turned downwards. 'I need another beer.'

Trotti put out a restraining hand, 'No.'

He pushed Trotti's hand away. The small eyes looked carefully at Trotti. Zani pulled on the Nazionali. 'Commissario, the other day in San Teodoro . . .' He stopped.

'Yes?'

Another inhalation of the cigarette, 'You said that we were friends. You said that we had been friends for a long time.'

Trotti glanced around the dining room. It was almost midday and people were beginning to line up along the counter, their faces lit up by the brightness of the overhead lamps. 'I'm not sure that a policeman can have friends.'

'You're a friend of Rosanna Belloni.' He stubbed out his cigarette in the yellow ashtray advertising the *Provincia padana*. 'You were her friend – that's why you want to find her killer.'

'Not Rosanna.' Trotti shook his head, 'It was her sister who was killed.'

The sly smile of a cunning peasant, 'You didn't know that when you started your enquiry, did you?'

'It's Merenda's enquiry.'

Zani was about to say something. He opened his mouth and then, thinking better of it, took a fresh cigarette from the packet of Nazionali. The fingers of his right hand were yellow with nicotine. He turned in his seat to catch the attention of the waitress, a pretty young woman in uniform. 'Another beer,' he said curtly.

Trotti finished the sandwich.

Flour from the hard crust fell on to his hand and on to his clothes. He could taste the sharp olive oil and the softness of the mozzarella beneath his teeth. With food still in his mouth, he asked, 'Your son's sexual preferences still stop you from sleeping?' Trotti had slipped from 'lei' into the familiar 'tu' form. 'I imagine that's something you've known about for some time.'

'Commissario Merenda is in charge of Reparto Omicidi. I take orders from him,' Zani said, more an accusation than a statement.

Trotti frowned, not understanding.

'Commissario Trotti, both the questore and Commissario Merenda are convinced that my son Alberto is the murderer at San Teodoro.' The man sighed and took a photograph from the breast pocket of his rumpled tunic. 'What do you think this is?' he asked and, as he handed Trotti the photograph, a small tear ran from the corner of the small, bloodshot eye.

FLAG

Zani was slightly drunk.

'It's all her fault.' The small eyes were damp and he held his head to one side to avoid the smoke rising from the Nazionali in his mouth. 'I would have liked to be a good father but if he has turned out the way he has, it's his mother's fault.'

Trotti raised an eyebrow.

'It's obvious, isn't it? When she was pregnant, she thought it was going to be a girl.' A hand propped up his forehead, 'I don't blame her, I think she wanted to give her daughter the kind of happiness that she had never known when she was a young girl. But it wasn't a girl, it was a boy. My wife just couldn't accept that Alberto was a boy. It was her fault, it was my wife's fault. When Alberto was little, she dressed him in girls' clothes. He had long hair just like a little girl. She'd never let him go out and play with the other children. He had to stay indoors and she got me to make him a doll's house. Alberto was never allowed to have a gun or play at cowboys. He was her little doll, her little plaything.' A sigh, 'I suppose I should have done something, but you know, it's not easy.

And I had my job. Bringing up children – that's women's business and I didn't like to interfere. Now . . .'

(Zani's son worked in a bookshop in the city centre. The twenty-four-year-old Alberto Zani had been arrested on several occasions for disorderly or threatening behaviour. It was known in the Questura that Alberto, despite his aggressiveness, his air of virility and the many girls who accompanied him at various times on his motorcycle, had several homosexual lovers.)

Trotti looked at the photograph, 'Where did you get this from?'

'Her flat in San Teodoro.' He hesitated, then added, 'The night the journalist found the body – the night you turned up – I wasn't even on duty. But a friend in Operativa alerted me. Believe me, I got down there as quick as I could.'

Trotti frowned, looking at the old photograph, 'Not exactly incriminating evidence. It must be at least fifteen years old.'

'In the same frame with the other photos that you looked at.'

'Why did you take it?'

The small eyes avoided Trotti's, 'Signorina Belloni liked my son.'

'He was a pupil at her school?'

He nodded, 'She liked him – perhaps she felt sorry for him.'

'Why?'

'When he was little, Alberto was a good boy. Everybody said that. Everybody liked him. He was pretty.' Zani leaned forward and placed a damp hand on Trotti's, 'You can see, look. He's wearing his school uniform.'

A little boy – he had curling blond hair and socks down over his ankle boots – was waving the Italian flag on the end of a stick; rain had caused the red and green – varying shades of grey in the photograph – to run. The colours had dribbled on to his fist. There too was Rosanna Belloni; with a hand on the boy's shoulder, she stared at the camera.

Trotti turned the photograph over. Somebody had written in pencil, 4 November 1973.

'This photograph was taken a long time ago,' Trotti said.

'When Alberto was fifteen things began to change. He no longer liked his mother.'

'And you?'

Zani said simply, 'My son has always hated me.'

'Why?'

A cold laugh. The rising smoke continued to dance before his eyes, 'I'm not an educated person, commissario, and I don't have sophisticated tastes. I'm a policeman, unimaginative. Even honest, if that's possible. I could've just as well become a soldier. Or a criminal. I don't have many interests.' He looked at his hands, 'A couple of packets of cigarettes a week, the occasional drink. Totocalcio, a football game or a boxing match on TV – that's all I need.' His voice grew bitter, 'Whereas my wonderful son, he's better than us, always has been. He's going to become a famous writer. Or an actor. Or a clothes designer. He's always had wonderful friends, friends who're a lot better than his stupid dull father and his stupid, doting and indulgent mother.' The man banged at his chest, 'But his stupid father doesn't sell his arsehole away. His father is a man, a real man. Not a woman with a man's thing hanging between his legs.'

The round face had turned red.

'You think I didn't realise he was queer? When he was still only fifteen the phone would start ringing and there were these artists and painters and actors wanting to talk to Albert. Lisping and rolling their "r"s and using long words I'd never heard before.' A pause. 'At sixteen he ran away from home. We didn't see him for three months.'

'What's all this got to do with Rosanna?' Trotti wanted to get away from this man, get away from his suffering and his self-pity. He wanted to get to a phone and call Pioppi in Bologna.

(They would call the baby Piero.)

'When he came back to the city, Alberto stayed with her.'

'Her?'

'Rosanna Belloni. She gave him a bed and he slept there. She used to have a place in Via Mantova, near the old gymnasium. He stayed with her for over three months. And that's how he got his maturità. It was Rosanna who pushed him.' Zani was in the process of nervously lighting another cigarette. 'At the time I resented her interfering, but I realise now she did it out of kindness. Out of kindness because . . . because Rosanna is a kind woman.'

'That was a long time ago. Six or seven years ago. Your son must've sat his maturità at eighteen or nineteen.'

Zani inhaled; for a fraction of a second the eyes rested on Trotti's before being averted. The man folded his arms against the rumpled uniform shirt.

'He still sees her, you know.'

'They made love?' Trotti could feel a wrenching in his gut.

The small peasant eyes looked at Trotti, 'You liked Rosanna Belloni, didn't you?'

'I hardly knew her,' Trotti replied, aware of the defensive tone in his voice, aware that he did not have to answer.

'Should've married her, commissario.'

'I'm a married man.' Trotti wiped his hands on a paper serviette and brushed the flour from his trousers, 'Did your son and Rosanna make love?'

'That's what the questore believes.'

'How does he know about your son?'

'Alberto hangs around with a crowd of rich kids – young people who're a lot richer than him and who lead him on. A crowd that runs around on big motorcycles and who wear leather jackets. Alberto isn't rich – he works at the Libreria Ticinum, his father hasn't got money to bail him out when he gets arrested – I'm not a doctor or a lawyer. On a couple of occasions, the questore has wanted to speak to me. It was the questore who stopped Alberto from going to prison.'

'And the questore told you about Rosanna and Alberto?'

'At least she's a woman. She may be thirty-five years older than him, but if he's screwing her, it means that he's not with one of his queer friends.'

'The questore thought your son murdered Rosanna?'

'My son is innocent.' Zani snorted two brief clouds of tobacco smoke.

'Both the questore and Merenda now know it wasn't Rosanna who was murdered.'

There was a long silence. The restaurant had filled up with customers. A large woman eyed the empty seat beside Trotti before taking her tray to another table.

'About a year ago,' Zani said in a low voice, his eyes on the table, 'Alberto lost his temper. I don't think it was anything serious, Alberto is not someone to get violent.'

'He hit Rosanna?'

'You knew, commissario?'

'She accused him of being a homosexual and he grew violent?'

Zani looked glumly at Trotti. He nodded unhappily.

'And the questore now thinks your son murdered Maria Cristina for the same reason?'

FAX

'A coffee addict, commissario.'

Trotti turned, frowning against the light from Strada Nuova. The plastic cup was hot in his hand.

'This is for you, commissario.'

'What is it, Tocca?'

'A couple of faxes from Ferrara. From the Carabinieri.' Toccafondi was holding two sheets of printed paper in his large hand. 'Friends in high places, commissario?'

'In both high and low places. Carabinieri and Polizia.'

'Just arrived on the machine. I was bringing them up.' The policeman closed the door of Operativa behind him.

'Care to share a cappuccino, Tocca?' Trotti looked down at the cup of coffee he was carrying back to the office.

'A cup of sugar with a hint of coffee, you mean.' Agente Toccafondi slipped into dialect. He was very young and was one of the few men in the Questura that Trotti genuinely liked. 'Any news of your daughter?'

'Fax, Tocca?' Trotti frowned. 'Maybe one day I'll get to have my own fax machine. Or perhaps I'm just too old for all this modernity. What are they about? Why are the Carabinieri sending me faxes?'

(In dialect, everything sounded more real, more genuine.)

Toccafondi held the top sheet so that Trotti could look at it. A series of identity photographs. A man, left profile, right profile and full frontal. Beneath them, a larger photograph of the same head, but this time lolling against what appeared to be a white sheet. The mouth was open, the eyes closed in death and there was considerable swelling of cheeks and forehead.

'What on earth?' Trotti shook his head. He put the sandwich and coffee down on the floor. He took the fax from Toccafondi's hand. He read, 'Milovan Djencas, date of birth, 9 June, 1953 in Belgrade. First entry in Italy, 7 September, 1969. Residence permit N° TR 34237772. Criminal record, see entry.'

'Make any sense, commissario?' Toccafondi raised a thick eyebrow. 'A friend of yours?'

Trotti turned to the second faxsheet.

'Carabinieri, servizio coordinamento,' Trotti said, running his finger along the heading. He had to hold the handwritten fax at arm's length to get it into focus.

Toccafondi was smiling, his hands now in his pockets.

Trotti read aloud: 'Here's your corpse, Piero. The divers found him at two o'clock this morning. The body was carried towards the sea by the tide. Doesn't look very much like your Signorina Belloni, I'm afraid. Djencas is a Yugoslav national who has served several short sentences in this country for pimping, extortion, theft. The body is in the hospital morgue in Ferrara. Djencas hired the Fiat using American Express under the name of Giovanni Svevo, Via Addis Ababa, Trieste. The card was stolen, but for the moment there is no trace on Svevo. If I can be of help or if you require further information, don't hesitate to contact me in Venice. Good luck.'

The neat signature, 'Spadano', followed by a postscriptum: 'A boy or a girl? Let me know a.s.a.p.'

Mechanically, without removing his eyes from the fax, Trotti took a rhubarb sweet from his pocket and put it into his mouth.

Truth

'Signor Boatti would like to make a confession. He says he murdered Signorina Belloni.'

Trotti placed the now tepid cappuccino on the desk top. 'For over four days not a single lead.' With both hands he made an obscene gesture of frustration that referred to the present, bloated state of his testicles, 'All of a sudden everybody seems to know who killed Signorina Belloni.' He turned and looked at the journalist who was sitting in the armchair. Trotti grinned, 'You think you killed her?'

'I never said that,' Boatti needed a shave. His pale face looked unhealthy and his clothes were crumpled. He was wearing the same linen trousers and Saxone moccasins as on the night that Trotti first met him. He appeared older, as if it were only now that he was feeling the effects of the murder in San Teodoro. He ran a hand over his mouth.

'If you're trying to defend Rosanna Belloni, there is no point. Don't get yourself into further trouble. You've perjured yourself sufficiently, Boatti.'

Boatti said nothing.

'Do yourself and everybody else a favour. Tell us where Rosanna Belloni is.'

Pisanelli and Maiocchi were leaning against the radiator. Maiocchi was staring disconsolately at the pipe he held in his left hand. In his right hand he held the large box of kitchen matches. Pisanelli looked at Boatti, arms folded against his chest, a smile hovering at the corner of his lips. The suede jacket hung from the end of the radiator.

'You've always known Rosanna was alive.' Trotti said coldly, 'For a journalist, Boatti, you have a very cavalier attitude towards the truth.'

The eyes were tired, as if Giorgio Boatti had been crying.

'For once, do me a favour. Tell me the truth – the truth that you've deliberately hidden.'

'There are things more important than the truth.' Boatti's voice sounded high pitched and awkward.

A dismissive gesture. Trotti did not hide his irritation, 'You knew it was Maria Cristina, didn't you? From the start you knew it was her body, didn't you?'

An almost imperceptible nod.

'And you've always known where Rosanna is?'

Boatti was sweating; his temples were damp.

'You know where she is, don't you, Boatti?'

'How do you know that I didn't murder Maria Cristina?'

Trotti remarked mockingly, 'You haven't brought your little tape machine?' He moved round the desk, sat down and put his feet on the edge of the desk drawer. He glanced at his two colleagues.

Pisanelli said, 'He's left it with his girlfriend.'

'Gentlemen, Signor Boatti has come to the Questura of his own accord to tell us the truth.' Trotti picked up the coffee.

'Are we going to arrest Signor Boatti?' Pisanelli asked Trotti. Maiocchi continued to stare at his pipe.

'You want to arrest him for screwing the Roberti girl? You think that adultery is a criminal offence, Tenente Pisanelli? We put him away because he's been cheating on his wife, climbing into bed with the pretty little Turin girl in the downstairs flat.'

A deep blush worked its way across Boatti's damp face. 'I didn't come here to be insulted.'

Trotti gave a brief laugh. 'Why did you come?'

'There are things I can tell you now that I couldn't tell you before.'

Trotti got up and walked towards the two officers. 'You know what Zani told me, gentlemen?' He did not look at Boatti. 'He told me that his son Alberto was an old pupil of Rosanna's and he'd kept in contact with her since leaving the school more than ten years ago . . .'

'The homosexual that works in the Libreria Ticinum – with an earring and motorcycle boots? With a pretty little face? That's Zani's son?' Maiocchi said.

'Alberto Zani,' Trotti nodded. 'About a year ago – he'd been seeing her fairly regularly – for some reason he got angry with Rosanna, lost his temper and attacked her.' Trotti gestured towards the door, 'Rosanna must've unwittingly made a disparaging remark about the boy's sexuality. He attacked her – and Signor Boatti here fortunately happened to be going past the flat. He heard Rosanna shouting and went into the flat. He stopped Zani from strangling Rosanna and then he called the Carabinieri. Understandably, in everybody's interest, the matter was hushed up.' Trotti turned back to Boatti, 'Why didn't you tell me about the Zani boy?'

'Commissario Merenda knew.'

Bending towards the journalist, Trotti tapped his chest, 'I'm not Merenda. Why didn't you tell me, Boatti?'

Boatti didn't reply.

'You didn't tell me because you knew it wasn't Rosanna Belloni who'd been killed.'

A shrug.

'You knew that. You knew it was not Rosanna and that there was no reason for Zani to attack Maria Cristina. No motive – and, anyway, Zani wouldn't have been able to get into the house at San Teodoro without a key. You knew that.'

'Maria Cristina could've let him in. He wouldn't have been her first lover.'

'When everybody else thought Rosanna was dead, you knew the truth. You knew it was Maria Cristina. Commissario Merenda didn't know that. And neither did the questore. Fairly reasonable they should think it was Zani who had gone back to the scene of the crime. And that this time he'd really killed Rosanna.' Trotti took another sip of tepid coffee. 'A low profile,' Trotti said. 'Of course the questore didn't want me on the San Teodoro case. That's why he told me to keep quiet. He knew the culprit, or at least, so he thought. Trouble was the questore's culprit just happened to be the son of one of his oldest and most reliable policemen.'

'Agente Zani.' Maiocchi said, without taking his eyes from his pipe.

'The questore wanted the whole affair hushed up – to be swept under the carpet.' Trotti made a wry smile, 'That's why he wanted me out of the city. He virtually ordered me to take a holiday on Lake Garda.' He snorted, 'Low profile.'

Trotti was at a loss for words.

'That's what I said.'

'Greece?' Trotti repeated incredulously.

'They left yesterday.'

'They? Then Rosanna Belloni is not alone?'

'Of course not.' Boatti smiled blandly and glanced at the other two policemen leaning against the radiator, 'People tend to be accompanied when they go on their honeymoon.'

'I don't believe this.' Trotti shook his head. 'You're telling me – you're telling us that Rosanna Belloni is in Greece on her honeymoon?'

'She is nearly sixty years old, commissario. You don't think she's entitled to happiness at her age?'

'And her sister? Maria Cristina dead – murdered. Maria Cristina's not entitled to anything?'

'It's a lot better for everyone the way things are. Rosanna's always suffered – can't you understand?' A gesture of repressed exasperation, 'She suffered as a young woman, trying to protect her little sister. Rosanna's always tried to protect Maria Cristina – and what good's it done her? For all Rosanna's care and sacrifice, for all Rosanna's love, how has the sister ended up? A stupid, promiscuous woman battered to death by the last in a very long list of lovers.'

'You didn't murder her?'

Boatti ignored the question.

'Why's Rosanna Belloni in Greece?' There was still disbelief in his voice, 'Why's she on her honeymoon?'

'Because at last – at long last Rosanna Belloni has decided to take her life into her own hands. She's decided that she wants to live with a man.'

'What man?'

'The man she's always loved.'

'Who?'

Boatti shrugged, failing to understand Trotti's incomprehension, 'Achille Taleri. Her schoolteacher from Ventimiglia, of course.'

'Then you knew, Boatti?'

'I knew what?'

'You knew where Rosanna was. All along, you've known where she was and what she was doing. And you knew who she was with.'

'Of course I knew.'

'And you lied?'

Boatti looked at Trotti coolly.

'You lied?'

'Rosanna needed my help.'

'And effectively you screwed up my enquiry.'

'Not at all – I told you about Rosanna, I told you about the schoolteacher.'

'You lied, Boatti.'

'Rosanna needed protection.'

'Impeding the course of justice.'

'I don't give a shit for the course of justice, for the course of your justice.'

'And so you invent your own?'

'Rosanna is a good person, she has always made sacrifices for others. For her mother, for her mad sister – mad and very promiscuous sister. And now after a long, long time, she finally decides to get married. To get married to the man she's loved for more than fifteen years . . .'

'The man who screwed Maria Cristina?'

'Errare humanum est.'

Trotti frowned, 'She's married the man she once discovered in bed with her sister?'

'Rosanna is entitled to her happiness.'

'He betrayed her.'

'An adventure isn't necessarily a betrayal.' Again Boatti ran a hand across his mouth, 'It took Rosanna several years to convince herself – and when, in the end, she decided that she was no longer a young woman, it was me' – he tapped his chest, 'it was me who got her to see that marriage was the right thing.'

Pisanelli leant forward, his arms folded, 'As a faithful husband, you recommended the charms of monogamy?'

Boatti kept his eyes on Trotti, 'I was the only person who knew.

Not even her sister in Milan knew that Rosanna was on her honeymoon.'

'All this time you've been protecting her?'

'As soon as I discovered the body, I phoned Achille . . .'

'Her husband?'

'But they weren't at the hotel. They'd gone for a trip into the delta.'

'This Achille Taleri is her husband?'

'Achille and Rosanna are getting married in September.'

Trotti winced, 'The honeymoon before the marriage?'

'Afraid that she'll get pregnant, Commissario Trotti?'

Pisanelli tapped Boatti on the shoulder, 'Why did you phone the bridegroom?'

'I needed to tell Achille about Maria Cristina's death and I wanted him to get Rosanna out of the country.' He did not turn to look at Pisanelli but kept his eyes on Trotti.

'To Greece?'

Boatti nodded, 'I didn't want her coming back here, I didn't want her to be bothered with her sister's death. Really, Trotti, Maria Cristina's death is of no great loss to anybody.'

'It's a great loss to Maria Cristina.'

'She's better off dead.'

'You're joking, I suppose.'

'When Maria Cristina was a little girl, she was molested by her step-father. That was a long time ago. I believe that, after forty years, Rosanna is entitled to a little happiness of her own. Don't you?'

'So you lied?'

'Of course I lied.' Again the bland smile. 'I lied to you, Trotti, and I don't give a damn. I wasn't lying for myself. Rosanna was like a mother to me. More than a mother. My own parents had me late in life and my genetic mother never had very good health. It was Rosanna who would look after me. You accused me of making love with Rosanna.' He shook his head in disgust, 'You think a man makes love with his mother? You must be sick, Trotti.'

'Didn't Alberto Zani try to make love to her?'

'Alberto Zani is mad – he needs treatment.'

'You could've told me she was at Comacchio.'

'And you would've brought her back here? You would've got her to give up her honeymoon – something she'd waited almost half a century for? That's what you want? After she'd spent nearly five years making up her mind to take the plunge? Give everything up to come back here and worry about a sister who never merited all the affection Rosanna gave her. And perhaps destroy for ever Rosanna's chance of happiness.'

'Her happiness is so important to you, Boatti?'

'Yes, it is.'

'And so when you discovered Maria Cristina's body, you sent Rosanna off to Greece?'

'They didn't get back to the hotel until yesterday morning. And even then it took Achille a lot of persuading to get her to leave. She's always loved the delta and she was glad to be there with him. She didn't want to leave. She didn't want to go to Greece. She loves her walking holidays. Only Achille, like me, realised he had to get her out of the country. Away from the newspapers, away from the television.' A pause, 'In his way, Achille is a good man.'

'I hope so,' Pisanelli said.

'A bit limited, perhaps. A southerner. I believe they're going to be happy together.'

Trotti's coffee was now cold. He finished it in one gulp, then wiped his lips with the back of his hand. 'And the Fiat Panda?'

'What Fiat Panda, Trotti?'

'The proprietor of the hotel said that Rosanna'd gone off with a man in a Fiat.'

'He really told you that?' The round, damp face broke into a bright grin.

'You were with Pisanelli and me when we got through to the hotel on the phone.'

'Neither Rosanna nor Achille have a car.'

'The Panda was rented.'

'I can assure you, Trotti, there never was any car, Fiat or otherwise.' He raised his shoulders, 'A case of mistaken identity. Possibly Rosanna was given a lift by someone – there are a lot of 4 × 4s in the delta. Or perhaps the proprietor in the hotel is trying to confuse you.'

'Like you.'

Boatti lowered his head, as if recognising a compliment, 'In a manner of speaking.'

'Why would the proprietor lie?'

'Most probably he didn't lie. Most probably it was a lift – or a taxi.'

'Rosanna was still in the delta when I phoned? When we got through to the hotel?'

'Achille and Rosanna left yesterday afternoon.'

Trotti nodded thoughtfully, 'That's why you were worried?'

'Worried, commissario?'

'You knew she would return to the Pensione Belvedere and so when Pisanelli located her, you were afraid?'

'Trotti, I don't feel guilty in the slightest for what I've done.'

Pisanelli grinned, 'You'll be needing a lawyer.'

Boatti raised an eyebrow, 'For being too friendly with Signorina Roberti?'

'For withholding evidence, for lying, for prevaricating. And, Boatti, for being a squalid little shit.'

'You frighten me, Tenente Pisanelli.'

'With good reason.'

Trotti gestured Pisanelli to be silent. Looking carefully at the journalist, Trotti asked, 'When you went off to pick up your car, you phoned, didn't you? You phoned the hotel. You wanted to be sure she'd left.'

'Like a mother to me. In a way, perhaps I love Rosanna Belloni more than I love my own mother. I owe her a lot – more than I can ever repay. I haven't done many good things in my life . . .'

Pisanelli was going to say something but Trotti directed an angry glance at him.

'Protecting her was right – was very right. Achille agrees with me.' Boatti ran a hand along his damp forehead, 'If you want to arrest me, really, Trotti, I don't mind at all. A small price to pay to protect her happiness.'

'That's what you say.'

'When she comes back in a couple of weeks, she'll have to learn the truth. But now – now I want her to enjoy – to enjoy to the full – what little happiness life can give her.'

FUNCTIONARY

'You murdered Maria Cristina?'

Boatti ignored the question.

'Did you murder her?'

'Why murder the poor cow? I wasn't one of her lovers, was I? I never got into bed and climbed over her, put my thing where a thousand other men had put theirs.' He shrugged, 'Maria Cristina'd never done me any harm.'

'Other than ruining Rosanna Belloni's life?'

Boatti nodded.

'And by your own admission, you wanted to protect Rosanna.'

'If I was going to kill Maria Cristina, I wouldn't do it just as Rosanna at last decided to go on holiday with her fiancé.'

Pisanelli moved away from the radiator and sat on the edge of the desk, 'You admit you were in the San Teodoro building on Saturday night?'

For a moment there was silence. Then Boatti sat back in the armchair and crossed his legs. He bit his lips.

Trotti offered him a sweet from the tin of English barley sugar. 'Well?'

A shrug.

Trotti looked at the tin of sweets in his hand but did not take one. 'You were with the Roberti girl, weren't you? You weren't with your wife in Vercelli visiting relatives.'

'My wife . . .' Boatti sighed and nervously pulled at his wedding ring, 'My wife knows nothing.'

'But she was in the flat?'

'Yes.'

'And the story about Vercelli – she went along with it to protect you?'

'We're happy together – and we have two lovely little girls.' He paused. 'This may sound strange to you, Trotti, but my wife understands.'

It was Pisanelli who spoke, 'Understands what?'

'A man . . . she knows that a man can have desires, desires that don't mean anything, desires that can have no tomorrow, no future. My wife knows that. I don't say that she's happy . . .'

'You don't say.'

Trotti lost his temper, 'Pisanelli, for God's sake, shut up.'

'This man's a shit, commissario.'

'Not your problem Pisanelli.'

'He's got a wife and two daughters – what's he doing screwing a young student, young enough to be his daughter?'

It was Trotti who smiled, 'Pisanelli, I'd've thought you'd learnt by now,' he took a sweet from the tin and placed it in his mouth, 'that we're not here to pass judgement. Our job is to execute the orders that we receive, the directives we receive. We are functionaries of the state and . . .'

'All this time he's been playing with us, commissario. A shit.'

'Moderate your language.'

'A cock and bull story about wanting to write a book.'

Boatti swung an outstretched hand round and pointed at Pisanelli, 'Don't worry about my book, Tenente Pisanelli – it's going to be written. And I can assure you that I will tell the truth, all the truth about your very unprofessional behaviour.'

'You're threatening me?'

'No more than you're threatening me, Tenente Pisanelli.'

Trotti held up his hand, 'Silence.'

'It stands to reason, commissario, he murdered her. How else did the murderer get into the building and into Rosanna Belloni's flat?' Pisanelli looked at Trotti, gesturing towards Boatti with his thumb, 'He has the key and he murdered the woman. He's a maniac and . . .'

'A maniac?'

Pisanelli swung round on Boatti, 'Of course you're a maniac, a frustrated sex maniac. You don't care who you hurt or damage or kill just as long as you can gratify your lust.'

'And so I went into the flat and struck Maria Cristina Belloni over the head?'

'She was going to tell your wife. She was blackmailing you. Maria Cristina was blackmailing you.' Pisanelli glanced at Trotti, glanced at Maiocchi. He slid off the desk and moved round to stand in front of Boatti. 'She was going to tell your wife and . . .'

Boatti rose in the armchair, 'You're a pain in the backside, Tenente Pisanelli.'

'You're a maniac.'

'I bashed the poor cow's head in?' Boatti slumped back into the seat, 'A maniac?' The anger had vanished.

There was a long, awkward silence in Trotti's office.

'I bashed her head in? That's what you really think, commissario?'

Trotti shook his head, 'Nobody bashed Maria Cristina's head in, Boatti. She was drowned. There was water in her lungs.'

Boatti's bloodshot eyes were now focused on Trotti, 'And the bruises?' His lips trembled.

'The beating round the head was not the cause of death according to Dr Bottone. Maria Cristina was drowned in water – in river water.'

'Here? Here in the city?'

Again Trotti shook his head, 'Scientifica says that the water can't've come from the river here because it wasn't sufficiently polluted. According to Maserati, if the water in Maria Cristina's lungs came from the Po, it must've come from somewhere upriver.'

'Like Garlasco?'

'Bad luck.' Pisanelli shook his head in mock suffering, 'Garlasco isn't on the river, Boatti.'

A feverish grin, 'Perhaps not. But the Casa Patrizia is.'

'What?'

'The Po runs past the grounds of the Casa Patrizia. Beyond the plane trees.'

'Marry her, Pisa?'

It was late afternoon and the air still hot. Trotti sat in the back seat and shivered. He did not listen to the conversation between Pisanelli and Maiocchi. He felt slightly depressed. Perhaps he had been eating too many sweets.

Maiocchi sat in the front seat. He clenched the pipe between his teeth and let the air through the open window pull at his thick hair. Pisanelli could not hide his excitement. He was laughing and talking loudly, like an adolescent.

'Marry her, Pisa? She's half your age.'

Pisanelli shrugged his shoulders, 'A man should always marry a woman half his age plus seven years.'

The building stood at the top of a small hill. A discreet house, built at the beginning of the nineteenth century, in an amalgam of Austrian and Italianate styles, with a broad, red brick façade that dominated the surrounding flat countryside which ran down to the line of plane trees, standing like sentinels along the bank of the Po.

Another day without rain; not a cloud in the sky.

'She's in love with me – says she wants to have my children.' Pisanelli turned left and entered a long drive. There was an unlit neon sign announcing the Casa Patrizia. The drive was lined with chestnut trees. Old people sat or stood in the shade, taking no notice of the passing car. It was past five o'clock and the afternoon was beginning to lose its heat.

Again Trotti shivered; he was sweating.

Pisanelli parked in front of the building. The three men got out of the car. Trotti went up the flight of stairs and through the glass doorway that Maiocchi held open for him.

Trotti felt apprehensive, a tightness in the belly.

The familiar smell of floor polish, medication and muted suffering.

The same small, pretty, unsophisticated face behind the reception desk with too much make-up under the eyes. The girl stood up.

She wore a white blouse and blue cotton skirt. There was no brassière. She smiled, revealing uneven teeth and dark gums, 'Commissario Trotti?'

'I wish to speak to Dottor Silvi.'

The dark eyes went from Trotti to Pisanelli and Maiocchi. 'If you could . . .' She picked up the telephone.

Trotti caught her hand. 'Where is Dottor Silvi? I wish to speak to him. Immediately.'

Her face turned pale, 'The Direttore will know where you can find whomever you're looking for.' She looked down at Trotti's hand gripping her wrist and frowned unhappily.

'Where is Silvi?'

She looked up.

'Dottor Silvi – where is he?'

She caught her breath; the small breasts rose and fell, 'In the south.'

'Where?'

'I believe Doctor Silvi's on holiday. I believe he's returned to Calabria.' She nodded unhappily, her eyes on Trotti's hand, 'He won't be back with us for another couple of weeks.'

Trotti turned and looked at Maiocchi and Pisanelli.

Pisanelli grinned, running a hand through his long, lank hair, 'Boatti would've made a good detective, the fornicating bastard.'

DYED HAIR

At first Trotti did not recognise Carnecine.

The director of the Casa Patrizia had dyed the grey out of his hair. He looked healthier, fitter. He had been sitting in a stuffed leather armchair. 'Ah, please come in.' He now stood up, a forced smile on the narrow face, and held out his hand.

Trotti ignored the outstretched hand, 'Silvi told you, didn't he?'

'I'm sorry.'

'You were looking for Belloni and you didn't know where she was. You were worried.'

'Worried?' Carnecine's smile slowly changed into a frown. 'Gentlemen, please be seated. You would like something to drink, perhaps.' He gestured to where his name had been placed in sculpted wooden letters on the desktop. 'Please come in and sit down. A vermouth?'

'I'm talking about Maria Cristina Belloni, Carnecine.'

'Now how can I be of help? I'm not sure I understand what you're talking about.'

'Maria Cristina Belloni – the same Maria Cristina Belloni that you murdered last Saturday night in San Teodoro.'

A bland smile, 'You're joking, I presume.'

'Silvi told you where she was.'

'Dr Silvi? Dr Silvi's on holiday, I'm afraid.' He turned to look at Maiocchi and Pisanelli, shaking his head in embarrassed amusement, 'A joke? You're sure you wouldn't like something to drink?' Carnecine was wearing a clean white shirt with epaulettes. His dyed hair was very short and very black. 'Please sit down, sit down.' Carnecine lowered himself into the leather chair and placed his ungainly hands on the desk. Trotti noticed that the nails had been recently manicured.

'For several years you've been getting money out of her.'

Carnecine shook his head, 'I feel there must be some misunderstanding.'

'Out of Maria Cristina Belloni – through drugs. And perhaps through sexual manipulation. You've been appropriating her money. The golden goose. The golden goose who's too drugged to react.'

'You're making a lot of allegations, commissario.'

'Then the golden goose broke loose. All of a sudden you were scared. You were scared, weren't you, Carnecine?'

There was a long silence. As if looking for support, Carnecine glanced at Pisanelli and Maiocchi; then at the two photographs on the wall, one of the Pope, the other of Mother Teresa of Calcutta. 'Am I right in thinking you're accusing me of murdering Signorina Belloni?' An apologetic smile flittered across the small face. He did not appear particularly worried.

'Of drowning her, Carnecine – of drowning Maria Cristina in

river water.' Trotti made a vague gesture to the distant row of plane trees beyond the window.

'Maria Cristina Belloni? Our patient?' He raised his shoulders, 'I didn't even know she was dead.'

'She's dead, believe me. Battered severely in the head and then drowned.'

Carnecine lowered his head, 'How upsetting. I was led to believe it was her sister who died. How very upsetting.'

'You had no choice, Carnecine. You had to kill her.'

'I don't understand you.'

'Better dead than alive. She'd started telling people how you've been skimming her fortune. She already had an allowance, transferred from the Banco San Giovanni. But you wanted more.'

'Really?' Carnecine nodded his head briskly, 'You believe I murdered my patient?'

'We know you murdered her.'

'You're joking, of course.' The eyes were intelligent and dark. 'Until a few seconds ago, I didn't even know she was dead.'

'Strange – given that you killed her with your own hands. Premeditated murder. Drowning her in a few litres of river water.'

'The Finanza was here several months ago. We came to an agreement.' Another nod, 'I'm sure that the forces of order can reproach me with nothing.'

'I know nothing about the Finanza. Murder, Carnecine. We're talking about premeditated murder. You killed Maria Cristina Belloni, holding her head under water.'

'Why?'

'Why did you drown her? So that when the corpse was washed up, it would be assumed she'd committed suicide. That she'd drowned in the river and not in her sister's flat in the city. That she had thrown herself into the Po beneath the covered bridge. Suicide out of her frustrated love for Luca.'

'I don't know any Luca. Really, commissario, as much as I respect you, I can't help feeling . . .' He laughed.

'But you didn't realise that it would be possible to identify the water. You used water from the river where it is relatively unpolluted.'

'Luca? I know no Luca.'

'Luca needed a doctor and he called his friend Silvi. There was no way that Luca should've known Maria Cristina was a patient at the Casa Patrizia. Luca told your Dottor Silvi about his adventure with her. And Silvi told you. You knew about the whole affair. Because of Silvi, you knew where Maria Cristina was hiding – and you now had a way of murdering her with impunity.'

'I'd kill one of my patients? Seems a very strange way of running a home for people who need above all love and attention. People who as often as not meet with very little affection in their own homes.'

'Very strange indeed, Carnecine.'

'A wealthy client – why on earth should I want to kill Signorina Belloni?'

'Because you were scared.'

Carnecine raised a dark eyebrow, 'Of what?'

'You couldn't control her. She was running out of control, out of your control. You couldn't keep Maria Cristina quiet, you couldn't get to her with your tranquillisers. Perhaps even she contacted you – wanting her money back. Threatening you. But you didn't know where she was. You couldn't get your hands on her to silence her. You didn't know where she was until Luca unwittingly told Silvi.'

Again Carnecine glanced at the other two men. He smiled and nodded his head. 'Most interesting theory.'

'Maria Cristina left here at the end of July,' Trotti tapped the desk. 'She had gone to stay with her sister – she went away every year for the Ferragosto. You thought she would stick to the drugs you were giving her – neuroleptics, the drugs you've been feeding her with over the years. At San Teodoro she should've been under her sister's control. Only this time her sister couldn't really be very bothered with Maria Cristina. Rosanna Belloni's mind was occupied elsewhere. For once Maria Cristina was left to herself – for the first time in five years. And left to herself in her place in Via Mantova, Maria Cristina gradually stopped taking your stuff.' Trotti snorted, 'She started feeling better. The mist started to clear from her head. What was it you and Silvi were giving her? Massive doses of valium? Or something stronger like chlorpromazine? fluphenazine? She came off your poisons. Probably she compensated with marijuana and alcohol. And uppers. And once she started feeling human again, she understandably started looking for help. Help because she wanted her money back. For the first time in five years she was able to understand what was happening to her, what you'd been doing to her. And she started talking. With Luca. And with others. Talking about how she was being robbed by the director of a home for the mentally unstable.'

Carnecine nodded his head repeatedly, like a plastic puppy at the rear window of a car, while the deep-set eyes remained on Trotti, assessing him. Then he glanced at the other two men. 'Some gin, perhaps, signori?'

Trotti briskly took the armchair, sitting down close to the desk, his face close to Carnecine's.

Pisanelli remained standing. Maiocchi was leaning against the wall by the window.

A sigh, 'Not always very easy to run a home for . . .'

'For what, Signor Direttore?'

'You know, commissario, that here in Italy, there is no such thing as a mental asylum.'

Trotti banged his hand down on the desk. The lamp, a yellowed edition of *La Repubblica* and the wooden name block jumped. 'I can do without your pious cant, Signor Direttore. I'm not interested,' Trotti had raised his voice, 'I've seen too many corpses. I loathe murder.'

'You make allegations . . .'

Anger. 'I loathe murder and I loathe murderers.'

'Accusing me of murder, commissario?' There was astonishment in his voice.

'You murdered her because once she got her mind back and she could think straight, you were no longer safe.'

'Commissario . . .'

Trotti leaned forward and grabbed Carnecine by the collar. The movement was rapid and Carnecine's face sagged, 'Be careful,' Trotti said. His jaws clamped together. Then he released his grip and Carnecine slumped back.

Carnecine adjusted his shirt. He grinned, both amused and frightened, 'Signor Commissario, I can't help thinking it's you who should be careful.'

The anger was cold but it was still anger. Anger with the evil man in front of him. Not sex, but money. With a brushing movement, Trotti cleared the desk of everything. Of the telephone, of the outdated *Repubblica*, of the wooden name block. They fell to the floor; the telephone clattered noisily against the side wall of the desk, still supported by its flex.

GIN

'You're mad.'

Trotti leaned forward. With an outstretched index finger, he prodded hard against the man's chest. 'Why didn't you throw the body in the river, Carnecine? I want to know why you left her corpse in the flat in San Teodoro. Wasn't the idea to drop her body downstream?'

Maiocchi had moved away from the window and placed a restraining hand on Trotti's shoulder, 'How could he remove it during the day, commissario? By the time he'd killed Belloni, it was probably daylight. This man left the body there, waiting for night to fall.' A gesture of his hand. 'Unfortunately for him, Boatti had a key to the flat. Boatti went down to Rosanna Belloni's flat later in the day and found the corpse. And Boatti phoned 113, calling in the police.'

Trotti turned, 'That was Monday night, Maiocchi – but the body was there for two days – Sunday and Monday. Why so long?'

'Rigor mortis.'

There was a cupboard in the desk. Carnecine opened it and took out a bottle of London gin and a grimy glass. Carnecine gave Maiocchi an ingratiating smile.

'He could have cut it up,' Pisanelli remarked cheerfully.

Carnecine poured himself a drink. The hand shook almost imperceptibly. Carnecine's pink tongue licked the edge of his glass.

'Then why the phone call about the woman jumping in the river?' Trotti was looking up at Maiocchi. 'We'd already found the body. There was no point.'

'Probably all prearranged – and then he,' Maiocchi gestured towards the director, 'couldn't reach the woman. When precisely were alerted didn't matter. The corpse could be found in the river at any time. What was necessary was that the corpse should be identified as Luca's lover. With the help of his woman, Carnecine wanted Maria Cristina to be seen as a suicide.'

'What woman?'

'The female accomplice. The pretty little thing at reception, perhaps. She made the two phone calls, not realising that the body had been discovered.'

'You must be mad.' Carnecine took another swallow of gin. 'You must be mad, all of you.' The Adam's apple jumped in the wiry throat.

Pisanelli had not spoken. He came forward, slid casually on to the desk, sniffed at the bottle of gin, gave a nod of approval and drank from the neck. He wiped his lips with the back of his hand and jerked his thumb in the direction of Carnecine, 'It was all premeditated, commissario. He needed to get rid of Maria Cristina – you heard what Silvi said on the phone. Silvi found her in Via Mantova when Luca called him in. Silvi informed our good friend here who came looking for her.'

Somewhere a train hooted, one of the slow commuter trains along a rural branch line.

'Maria Cristina recognised Silvi when he came to help Luca out. So she moved out of her place in Via Mantova and moved into her sister's flat. She thought she'd be safer in San Teodoro.' Again Pisanelli took a swig of gin. 'Out of the frying pan.'

'The front gate to the place in San Teodoro was locked as was Rosanna's flat.' Trotti shook his head, 'How did Carnecine get in, Pisa?'

Carnecine asked, 'Did Dr Silvi tell you this?'

Trotti shook his head, 'I don't see how he got in. Or rather, how they got in. If we accept the account of our font frog – the little old lady in San Teodoro – Carnecine was accompanied by a woman.'

'Dr Silvi told you this?'

Pisanelli lowered the bottle back on to the desk. He turned and looked at Carnecine. His finger caressed the director's cheek, 'With a bit of persuasion, I'm sure that Signor Carnecine would like to tell the truth.' He placed a hand on Carnecine's head.

'The old woman in San Teodoro must've confused Carnecine's lady friend for the Roberti girl. And the man she took to be

Roberti's new boyfriend was undoubtedly Signor Carnecine here.'

Trotti rubbed his chin, 'But how did he get into the building? Maria Cristina had cleared out of Via Mantova because she was scared. Not very likely that she'd let anybody in if she was scared for her life.'

'Jehovah's Witnesses,' Maiocchi said.

'But not at three o'clock in the morning, for heaven's sake.'

'The first time.'

'What do you mean, Maiocchi? What first time?'

'Carnecine had a female accomplice. Perhaps that's how she got into the flat, posing as a Jehovah's Witness. Once inside, she got hold of the key – or made a copy.'

'And then Carnecine returned in the middle of the night?'

'Premeditated. He knew he was going to drown her – and then throw her into the Po. But she was difficult, and he had to use considerable force before he succeeded in killing her.'

Pisanelli said, 'Signor Carnecine wants to help us. Of that I'm quite sure.'

'Perhaps he left it too late, perhaps it was already dawn. For some reason, they didn't move the body out of the flat on Sunday morning. And then they had to wait.'

'Wait?'

'Because of the rigor mortis. But they had time to tidy up Rosanna's flat. Afraid of leaving fingerprints, no doubt, in case anything else went wrong. And it did. Boatti turned up.'

Pisanelli raised his voice, 'I think you ought to tell us, Signor Carnecine. Don't you?'

Carnecine drew back his shoulders. He had started to sweat and he was no longer smiling. 'We live in a backward country. A backward country which nonetheless has all the pretensions of the West and of advanced western thinking. Italy. Yet we have no mental asylums. Asylums need a lot of money if they're to be run efficiently – a lot of money.'

Pisanelli hit him with the back of his hand. The blow was not hard, but the movement was swift and unexpected.

The small dark eyes opened in surprise.

'I think you really should tell us everything that you know.'

'It is not always easy . . .'

Pisanelli was drawing his arm back menacingly when the door was opened suddenly.

Commissario Gabbiani stood there, looking more like a successful journalist than a policeman, 'I think Tenente Pisanelli can leave Sirno Carnecine alone.' He smiled while shaking his head, 'There are easier ways of getting to the truth.'

BMW

'About time – it's going to rain.'

'How did you know I was in Garlasco?'

'I guessed, Trotti.'

'You know Carnecine?'

'Yes.'

'And you knew that Carnecine murdered Belloni?'

'Yes.'

'You knew he killed her?'

'I can put two and two together.'

'You didn't tell me, Gabbiani.'

'When I saw you, Trotti, I didn't know it was the younger sister who was murdered.' Gabbiani laughed. 'You know, you really do need a rest.' A brief, mocking glance at Trotti. Both irritation and affection, 'I hope you are going to take a holiday now. Drive down to Bologna and see your daughter.' He tapped the telephone between the two leather seats, 'Has she had her baby?'

The large BMW was almost silent on the country road; just the gentle hum of the wheels along the tarmac. Pisanelli and Maiocchi were following in the Lancia. Mosquitoes battered into the windscreen.

Clouds were building up in the south west, from the Mediterranean beyond the hills; less than an hour and then rain should at last return to the parched plain.

'I'm supposed to be on holiday.' Gabbiani was wearing green

corduroys and a check shirt without a tie. His face looked clean, as if he had just shaved. 'You know, you should do the same. Now you've found the murderer, why stay on in the city?'

Trotti caught sight of himself in the car mirror. His face looked back solemnly at him – thin face, narrow nose and thin creases running down his cheeks. 'You knew all along what was happening at the Casa Patrizia? You knew that Carnecine needed money to keep his home running? And you didn't tell me that?'

'There's no reason to be pissed off with me, Trotti. I told you that if you needed information, you could come to me. Remember?' Gabbiani took his hand from the steering wheel and held up a finger, 'I told you it was just possible that I knew what you needed.'

'You knew about the Casa Patrizia?'

'Of course.'

'And you said nothing?'

Gabbiani laughed, 'The Finanza were in there earlier this year. The Carabinieri and the Nucleo Anti Sofisticazione have been called in twice in the last two years.'

'The Carabinieri?'

'Concerning complaints of impropriety. A woman complaining that her mother was being kept chained to her bed.'

'I never heard that.'

'That's not my fault, Trotti. You work in the city; what seems to be happening in the province seems to concern you less and less.'

'Anti Sofisticazione never informed me.'

'Perhaps you could be a bit more diplomatic in your dealings with the Carabinieri.' Gabbiani shrugged, 'I'm supposed to be running Narcotici. Unlike you, Trotti, I can't afford to have enemies.'

'Narcotici have been keeping tabs on Carnecine?'

'What do you think?'

'Carnecine's been dealing in drugs?'

'No longer.' Gabbiani shook his head.

'There've been drugs?'

'Several years ago some students were getting their hands on pharmaceutical preparations. At the time, we suspected somebody inside the Casa Patrizia. Not Carnecine – it would've been too dangerous for him. It could've been one of the doctors . . .'

'Silvi?'

'I don't know anybody of that name. It could've been an orderly.'

'Then why surveillance on Carnecine?'

'I never said surveillance.' He glanced at Trotti sitting beside him; then his eyes returned to the road. 'There are a thousand places like the Casa Patrizia throughout the country. The cities and the provinces just haven't got enough money for the number of beds required. And with the disappearance of asylums, it's got a lot worse. Which means there are a lot of people for the private sector to cater for. Private homes for the mentally feeble – but also for the old. A booming industry. For every well-run home, there are a couple that are in the business for the money. And even if there is legislation, it's hard for Health or the Carabinieri to keep a tight control. There's just not the manpower to go round – and anyway, with political support, a man like Carnecine can always be sure that he's going to get forty-eight hours' warning when there's to be an inspection.' He snorted, 'I imagine that for the last few years, Carnecine's been a Socialist.'

'Why Narcotici, Gabbiani?'

'Not drugs, I tell you.' He took his hands from the steering wheel in mock exasperation. 'Carnecine can get money elsewhere. For years he's been able to get money from old people. You know, with somebody whose brain is befuddled, who's old and waiting to die, a personable young man – he can make himself a fortune. A good bedside manner and an understanding smile. It's not very difficult to persuade an eighty-year-old woman who's not completely compos mentis to change her will, to make a donation.'

'Why didn't you tell me this?'

Gabbiani let out a sigh in muted irritation, 'Why should I have made a connection between the older sister . . . ?'

'Rosanna Belloni.'

'Why should I have made a connection between her and the Casa Patrizia? I thought it was Rosanna who'd been murdered. I didn't know it was the mad sister.'

'When did you find out it wasn't Rosanna who was dead but her sister?'

'When?' Gabbiani repeated in exasperation, 'I just found out – at four o'clock. Your friend Boatti called me – and that's why I came looking for you.'

'You know Boatti?'

'In a manner of speaking.'

'What does that mean? Boatti's a friend of yours?'

'He's been to see me on several occasions – said he wanted to write a book about police procedure.'

'You believed him?'

'Of course I believed him – I've seen a couple of chapters. Not bad – but what he really wanted, he said, was a murder enquiry.'

Seeing Trotti silent, Gabbiani resumed, 'And now I've got something to show you.'

'Show me, Gabbiani?'

'Why do you think I came looking for you when I could be up in the hills with my family?' Gabbiani's dark hair had kept the lustre of youth. The wide mouth broke into a humourless smile, 'The questore's right, Trotti. In your way, you do indulge in the cult of the personality – you do believe that you can get by on your own. And I really do believe that you don't care whose feet you tread on to get what you want. As the questore would say, with your eyes on the goal, you don't see the obstacles. You're obsessive, Trotti. Obsessive and your obsession can make you dangerous.'

'You flatter me.'

'Twice as many years as me in the police force, Trotti – but at times, you behave like a spoilt child. A spoilt, neurotic kid. You believe in friendship. That's OK, all well and good. We all believe in friendship. But in your mind, that gives you the right to barge ahead. For you, your friendship with Rosanna Belloni is more important than any professional consideration. No compunction at all, Trotti – you really have no compunction about barging in on Beltoni – on Beltoni whom I've been slowly building up. My Beltoni, Trotti – my informer, and you just don't give a shit.'

A long and very awkward silence. The inside of the car was air-conditioned. Yet both men were sweating. Both men were trying to hold back their anger and frustration.

'Why, Trotti? You didn't need Beltoni. What was the idea in your hauling in my informer? My informer?'

'I've been working with Beltoni for over ten years – long before you ever came to the city.'

'In public, in front of a crowd of whores and transvestites? Did you really need to do that? Did you really need to screw all our work up? Put a spanner in years of hard work? Or was it just a show you were putting on for Boatti's sake? For Boatti, the novelist. Something exciting that he could put into his book? His book about the supercop, Commissario Piero Trotti.'

Trotti did not reply.

'Well?'

'Beltoni owes me several favours.' Trotti rubbed his chin, now staring through the tinted glass at the approaching city skyline, the dome of the cathedral and the scaffolded towers, almost imperceptible against the darkening sky. Rain.

'I'm an old man, Gabbiani – an old policeman.'

'So what?'

'So what? A woman I once cared about was killed. No clues, nothing. Beltoni's been a contact for years – perhaps you don't know that.'

'And so you brawl with him in the city?'

Trotti caught his breath 'I don't trust Boatti. I don't trust him and I didn't trust his motives, his story about wanting to write a book.' Trotti shrugged, 'I couldn't help feeling he'd been sicked on to me – he was there to report back. I was most probably wrong – but I felt he was the questore's man.'

'That entitles you to screw up all our work?'

'Come on, Gabbiani – are you telling me there are people who don't know Beltoni's an informer? You really trying to tell me that?'

'You're dangerous, Trotti.'

'Dangerous perhaps.' Trotti laughed caustically, 'But at least I try to be honest. In my own way, I try to be honest.'

It suddenly seemed to get very chill inside the German car.

'And I'm not, Piero Trotti?'

'I thought that Maria Cristina was involved in Rosanna's murder – and I was looking for information off the street.'

'I'm not honest like you?'

'Information that perhaps Beltoni could give me.'

'Answer my question.'

Trotti remained silent.

Gabbiani pointed a finger at Trotti, 'Is that what you're trying tell me? I'm bent?'

Silence.

'I'm bent, Trotti?'

'Not for me to say, Gabbiani.'

'What the hell does that mean?'

'You have your conscience and I have mine.'

'You accuse me of not living up to your high standards of probity? Piero Trotti's high deontological standards of probity?'

Trotti did not reply.

'Is that it? Drug money – I'm living off drug money?'

'The last time you gave me a lift, it was in a little Innocenti.'

'Because I drive a BMW car, I'm on the take? Is that it, Trotti?'

'And a luxurious villa at Pietragavina?' Like venom that had a mind of its own, that Trotti could not hold back.

'Luxurious villa at Pietragavina,' Gabbiani repeated.

'Not the sort of thing that could come out of my policeman's salary.' Resentment. Old bitterness.

Gabbiani took a packet of Nazionali cigarettes from the dashboard. 'You don't have a villa on one of the lakes, Trotti?' The grey eyes now squinted behind the long, dark eyelashes as he lit the cigarette. Smoke rose from the dashboard lighter. The hand shook slightly.

'You're head of Narcotici. You do your job as you think best – and I try to do mine. We may not share the same values. I'm sorry about Beltoni – I'm sorry. Next time, I'll keep you informed. I'll send you a request in triplicate, Gabbiani. I'm sorry. As I said, I was making an enquiry into the death of a friend.'

'You don't have a villa, Trotti? On Garda, you've got a villa, haven't you?'

'It belongs to my wife.'

'And you're the only policeman to have a wealthy wife?'

PEACE OF THE SENSES

Boatti and Commissario Merenda were standing together beneath the same black umbrella.

Boatti was speaking into his voice recorder.

Finally the rain had started to fall, thick drops that fell on to the dusty earth and into the slowly moving waters of the river.

An ugly place, the edge of the city where the old houses gradually fell away and where the surfaced road became a cart track, running parallel to the river – a no-man's-land, inhabited by a thin phalanx of plane trees. One or two farmhouses beyond the high-water mark, mostly uninhabited. Beyond them, the allotments, then the textile factory, its smokeless chimneys and the satellite apartment blocks, squalid beneath the rain.

Trotti and Gabbiani got out of the car.

Toccafondi caught sight of them and hurried over, carrying an umbrella. Despite the warm evening air, he was wearing his uniform leather jacket and gloves. He grinned nervously, touching his beret.

'What is it?' Trotti gestured to where police lines had been put up. A small crowd had gathered, but there was no artificial light other than a police car with its main beam. It was hard to make out the dark, stumpy object that had been cordoned off.

The object cast a long shadow over the ground.

'Looks like a professional job. Badly mutilated, very badly mutilated. And then burnt with petrol.' Grinning bravely, Toccafondi closed his eyes, 'They cut most of his fingers off. Not a very pretty sight . . . I couldn't help . . .' He swallowed hard, then the smile returned to his young face.

'Who is it?' Trotti frowned and moved forward.

The arms and legs must have been tied together behind the back.

'Classic Mafia killing,' Gabbiani remarked calmly. 'You choke to death as your leg muscles can no longer resist the tension.' He snorted, 'And then they burnt him. Probably cut his tongue out, as well. Organised crime doesn't like informers. I think he's got a lot to thank you for, Piero.'

Beltoni.

Trotti stepped away from Gabbiani's umbrella; he ducked under the police rail and moved towards the black hump.

Surprisingly, the flames had left much of the face intact. Everything else was carbonised – black like a burnt tyre – but the face was untouched, cheek against the ground. The long hair had been singed, and the empty mouth lolled open against the dusty earth that was now forming rivulets of rainwater.

Trotti crouched down in the headbeams. The rain was now falling heavily, running down his face, seeping through his clothes.

Piero Trotti looked at what had once been the body of Beltoni, addict, drug dealer and police informer. Thirty-five years earlier, a mother's baby, and now dead.

No more hunger or thirst, no more desires, greed or pride. The true peace of the senses. Tortured, strangled and burnt to little more than a cinder lying in the dust beside the river Po.

'Too many deaths, too many deaths,' Trotti repeated to himself.

Somewhere towards the city, there was a distant whine of a siren.

He stood up.

Boatti, Merenda, Maiocchi, Pisanelli, Toccafondi and Gabbiani were there. They stood in silence, beneath the rain, looking at him.

'Gabbiani, for God's sake, give me one of your Nazionali.' Trotti ran a hand over his wet face, 'Fast.'

GLOSSARY

Carabinieri	Police force that is part of the Army and comes under the control of both the Ministry of Defence and the Home Office
Buon Costume	Vice squad
Finanza	Police force under the control of the Treasury. Deals with financial crime, tax evasion, customs etc
Nucleo Anti-sofisticazione	Part of the Carabinieri which deals with matters concerning food adulteration
Polizia di Stato	(ex-Pubblica Sicurezza) Police force under the control of the Ministry of the Interior
Procuratore della Repubblica	Public prosecutor
Questura	Headquarters of the Polizia di Stato
Questore	Officer at the head of the Questura
Reparto Omicidi	Murder squad
Vigili del Fuoco	Fire brigade
Vigili Urbani	City police, with limited power, concerned largely with traffic and other municipal matters